While hiking in Montana, the author came across a decaying mound of cast-off artifacts at the base of the Rocky Mountains. He surmised that the discarded items were part of the hopes and dreams that early settlers had for their new life in the Oregon Territory. He wondered what must have gone through their minds when they were forced to relinquish these precious treasures, and how much that loss altered their future.

The author's experience in Montana and the memory of his Grandfather's dog, Bones, ultimately led to the story of Billy Bones.

THE HILL COUNTRY

1. The lodge
2. Arthur Elk's hut
3. Omar Mountain Goat's cave
4. The store
5. Maurice Rabbit's dugout
6. The Vulture Brothers' hut
7. Lucinda Vulture's hut
8. Deputy Eagle's office
9. Calhoun Coyote's chicken farm
10. Sandy Antelope dugout
11. Mary Mc Mink's house
12. The Old Meetinghouse
13. The hotel
14. City Hall
15. Thaddeus Turtle's cottage
16. Elmer Prairie Dog's store
17. Sheriff Lone Wolf's office
18. The boardinghouse
19. The New Meetinghouse
20. The barracks
21. Rodney Wild Deer's lean-to
22. Rodney Deer's hideout
23. Olen Buck's lean-to
24. Victor Running Deer's lean-to
25. Nosey Coon's tree house
26. Needles Porcupine's hollow
27. Billy Bones' cottage
28. Justin Beaver's house
29. George P. Beaver's castle
30. Cornelius Van Mink's house
31. Gloria Meadowlark's farm
32. Percival Gander's shop
33. The Peccary Brother's shed
34. Milton Brown Bear's cave
35. Farmer Jason Crow's farm
36. Winston Wise Owl's tree house
37. Hester Groundhog's tree house

BILLY BONES

Book Two

IN THE SHADOW OF THE LYNX

RON OAKS

Acon Ring Publishing

https://www.aconring.com/

ISBN 978-1-7323499-6-4 Hardcover
ISBN 978-1-7323499-7-1 Paperback
ISBN 978-1-7323499-8-8 eBook

FIRST EDITION

Credits
Cover Painting by Howard Garrett
Illustrations by Ron Oaks

Edited by Anne Ostroff, Louise Carlson, and Laura Oaks
Cover and Interior Design by Delaney-Designs.com
Photography by Sandy Rothberg

To Jan and Laura

Table of Contents

PART TWO: UNTIL THE SUMMER SOLSTICE

Illustrations

PAGE 196: Rodney was directly behind her with the blade of his knife dangerously close to her throat.

PAGE 228: "Mr. Wise Owl, were you given a written decree by Sheriff Lone Wolf that your entire library was to be removed and taken to City Hall?" asked Phineas T. Fox, the new head of law enforcement.

PAGE 271: As they started to cross the clearing, the door of the dugout was flung open and a joyful rabbit bounded toward them.

PAGE 284: "Well I guess this is goodbye, old friend," the dog whispered, as he glanced over at the deer's unmoving back.

PAGE 295: "Without warning Billy Bones tackled him within a few feet of the opening of the rift."

Cast of Characters

BOOK TWO: IN THE SHADOW OF THE LYNX

HUMANS IN THE NINTEENTH CENTURY

Warren Nathaniel Stone – schoolmaster taking wagonload of books to Oregon Territory

Jimmy Stone – W. N. Stone's grandson

Ben Johnson and his wife – young couple going to Oregon Territory

HUMANS IN THE PRESENT

William Stuart Sr. (Will) – purchased land along old wagon trail

William Stuart Jr. (Bill) – son of William Stuart Sr.

William Stuart III (Billy) – grandson of William Stuart Sr.

Jake Williamson – owner of Wildlife Zoo

Danny Red Feather – Billy Stuart's friend

ANIMALS IN THE ENCHANTMENT'S PRAIRIE

Billy Bones (Bones) – Billy Stuart's shepherd dog who enters the Enchantment

Victor Running Deer – young buck who enters with Billy Bones

Winston Wise Owl – the wise gatekeeper, mentor to Billy Bones

Hester Groundhog – Winston's neighbor and confidant

Mayor George P. Beaver – mayor of the Prairie

Constance Beaver – Mayor George P. Beaver's wife

George (Georgie) Beaver– the mayor's nephew, guide for Billy and Victor

Justin and Gladys Beaver – parents of Georgie Beaver

Cornelius Van Mink – moderate councilor on City Council

Prudence Van Mink – his wife

Conrad and Priscilla Van Mink – grandchildren of Cornelius and Prudence Van Mink

Thaddeus P. Turtle – spiritual leader of the Old Meetinghouse

Percival (Percy) Gander – tailor and collector of used furniture

Brother Fabian Lynx – spiritual leader of the New Meetinghouse

Sister Sarah Mourning Dove – former spiritual leader of the New Meetinghouse

Rodney Wild Deer (the Rogue Deer) – Victor's rival for Melinda Doe
Melinda Doe – Victor Running Deer's love interest
Olen and Myrtle Buck – parents of Melinda Doe
Lester, Leon, and Leroy Coyote – friends of Rodney Wild Deer
Calhoun Coyote – father to Lester, Leon, Leroy and Lenny; has chicken
	farm
Leonard (Lenny) Coyote – Calhoun's youngest son
Sandy Antelope and Arnold Big Horn – running friends of Billy and Victor
Alvin Muskrat – friend of Billy and Victor
Dr. Muskrat – Alvin's uncle
Nolen (Nosey) Coon and Needles Porcupine – two rascals, friends of
	Billy Bones
Johnny Otter – swimming rival of Georgie Beaver
Phineas T. Fox – on board of councilors for the New Meetinghouse and
	City Hall
Philip P. Fox – brother of Phineas
Farmer Jason Crow – on board of councilors for the New Meetinghouse
Gwendolyn and Gerard Crow – wife and son of Farmer Jason Crow
Elmer Prairie Dog – proprietor of General Store, becomes mayor of the
	Prairie
Edwina and Patsy Prairie Dog – wife and daughter of Elmer
Irma Prairie Dog – sister-in-law of Edwina
Whiskers – old cat who had lived on farm with Billy Bones in the outside
	world
Wendell Red Breast – moderate councilor, baritone at Summer Concert
Melba Thrush – soprano at Summer Concert
Hosea Brown Thrasher – tenor at Summer Concert
Gloria Meadowlark – mezzo-soprano at Summer Concert
Walter Lone Wolf – sheriff of the Prairie
Harold Eagle – deputy of the Prairie and the Hill Country
Chester Hawk – assistant to Harold Eagle
Milton Brown Bear and Bison Bob – deputies to Sheriff Lone Wolf
Wiley Weasel and Rattlesnake Pete – two characters often in trouble
Mary McMink (Crazy Mary) – widow who has Irish furniture found
	along wagon trail
Ernest McMink – deceased husband of Mary McMink
Charlie Pheasant – councilor on City Council

Sylvester Turtle – moderate councilor in outgoing City Council
The Peccary Brothers – four brothers living in the North Woods

ANIMALS IN THE ENCHANTMENT'S HILL COUNTRY
Lucinda Vulture – spiritual head of the Hill Country
Felix, Festus, and Floyd Vulture – sons of Lucinda
Arthur Elk – guard of Tribal Council
Maurice Rabbit – painter on the Tribal Council
Omar Mountain Goat – chief of Tribal Council
Gaylord Cougar, Lucretia Lizard, and Orville Bat – on the Tribal Council

BILLY BONES

❧

Book Two

❧

IN THE SHADOW OF THE LYNX

PROLOGUE

Even if you were fortunate enough to hear about the mysterious rift from an old medicine man, late summer was not the time to find it. He had only mentioned that it occurred between two ancient trees along an old wagon trail that led up into the foothills. He also knew that it only opened for a few moments and that any creature who wandered too near its magic was immediately swallowed up. He did not know that on the twenty-first of June, a dog had chased a deer out of a cornfield and through that very opening. Unfortunately, all you could do on the second of September was stand near the old trees and imagine you had seen something.

PART ONE

THROUGH THE WINTER SNOWS

CHAPTER ONE

THE BOY AND THE OLD MAN

"Do you think Bones was kidnapped, or do you think the coyotes got him?" asked William Stuart III, as he and his friend, Danny Red Feather, rode home on Bus Number Twelve after their first day of school.

"My grandfather says that maybe he was swallowed up just like those other animals," answered Danny. "He said that when his cousin's father was a young man, he saw this hole open up between two trees. He said several animals wandered through it and just disappeared."

"You really think so?" queried Billy.

"Yeah, and his cousin's a medicine man, too. He said it's happened before, but white men don't want to believe it," concluded Danny.

"I know," agreed Billy. "My grandpa calls 'em fables. He says people like to believe stuff like that, but they're not really true. He says that Bones got lost chasin' that deer or was picked up by somebody."

"What do you think happened?" asked Danny.

"I don't know. I hope he got lost. 'Cause maybe then he'll find his way back," returned Billy. "Well, this is my stop. I gotta go…"

When the bus dropped Billy Stuart off at the end of his driveway, he could see Bones in his mind's eye, wagging his tail and running along beside him as they headed down the lane. He had been thinking about the dog all day, especially since coyotes raided his grandfather's chicken coop just the night before. Bones would never have allowed the coyotes to get that close to the farm.

Bones was a remarkable dog. Not only had he been a good watch dog and a loyal companion, but he always seemed to sense when something was about to happen and had saved Billy several times from serious injury.

Like many other shepherd dogs that populated the prairie states, Bones was actually a mixture of collie, German shepherd, and several kinds of sheepdog. In Bones' case, he favored his collie ancestry, since his coat was tan with white on the tip of his tail and on the front of his neck and chest.

As the young towheaded boy walked dejectedly down the lane, he heard his grandfather working on the little coop in back of the farmhouse. Will Stuart's farm was just east of a wildlife preserve that bordered the foothills of the Rocky Mountains. Billy had been sent to live with Will shortly after his mother's tragic accident. Although Billy got along well with his grandfather, it had been Will's dog Bones that finally lifted the boy's spirits and renewed his zest for living.

When the boy got to the front porch, he threw his books on the rocking chair, shoved his hands into the pockets of his overalls, and trudged slowly around the corner of the house. As soon as Will Stuart spied his grandson, he called, "Hey, Billy, how was school?"

"OK, I guess," replied the boy glumly.

"Well, I'm almost done here. I can't believe how smart those coyotes are. They manage somehow to break in every time," said the tall slender man, looking down from his ladder and sensing the boy's unhappiness. "What do you say we go over to the pond and see if the beavers have finished their winter home?" Will glanced down at the boy again. His stern face broke into a smile, and his eyes twinkled. "Well, how about it?"

"I don't know. I gotta write a paper for English tomorrow," answered the boy, kicking a loose stone at his feet.

"Already, wow, they don't give you much time to settle in, do they?" grinned Will again, trying to alter the boy's mood. "What do you have to write about, anyway?"

"I have to tell the class about somethin' exciting that happened this summer, and all I can think about is Bones," Billy replied, not looking at his grandfather.

"Oh," answered Will thoughtfully, as he climbed down from the ladder and put a hand on the boy's shoulder. "You really miss Bones, don't you, Billy. I've got an idea. Why don't I help you write something after supper? The two of us should be able to think of something else besides Bones' disappearance… Hey, I know. You can write about those blasted coyotes that just broke into my chicken coop and killed some of my prize hens!" When Will glanced over at Billy, he could see that he had failed to relieve the boy's sadness. "Well anyway, I think right now we could both use a good break."

The air around the old beaver pond just inside the wild-life preserve was very still, and the water shimmered like glass when Will pointed to the little island in the middle of the pond. "Well, I don't see any beavers out there. Maybe they've finished." He picked up a stone. "How's your arm today? I'll take you on." Before the sad little boy could answer, the old man skipped the stone three times across the water. Billy quickly picked up another stone and was able to skip it four times. "How about two out of three?" said Will, smiling and going for another stone.

By the time Will and Billy left for home, they were both laughing and joking with one another. When they reached the edge of the cornfield, Will put a hand on his grandson's arm. "Look! Over there!" Ahead of them, an old stag with a huge rack of antlers had stepped out of a row of corn. The late afternoon sun had just begun to sink behind the mountains, and the angle of its rays caused the tips of the antlers to sparkle like little diamonds. The man and the boy stood motionless, almost hidden by the edge of the cornfield. Finally the stag moved out of the field, glanced over toward Billy and Will, hesitated a moment, and then darted away.

"Wow!" said Billy quietly.

"Yeah, wow!" answered Will, as the two of them started walking back to the house.

"Grandpa, the deer that Bones was chasin' when he disappeared wasn't that big. I think he must have been only three or four years old," recalled the boy. He paused a moment. "Grandpa, do you remember when we were lookin' for Bones in the woods north of the pond? Remember when we thought we heard someone call my name? Remember?" The boy looked up at his grandfather. "I wonder what that was. We never did figure it out."

Will thought for moment. "I heard it too. It was probably a wild animal of some kind. It came from behind us somewhere."

"Well, I could've sworn it was a human," Billy insisted. "It sounded like it said, 'Wait, Billy, wait!'

CHAPTER TWO

SEPTEMBER THIRD

"Wait, Billy, wait! It's me, Bones!" mumbled the shepherd dog in his sleep as he twisted and turned in his little bunk. He had been dreaming again of Billy Stuart and the old man. "Can't you hear me? I'm trying to catch up with you. Wait for me!"

When the dog awoke on the morning of September third, he discovered it was still dark outside. Even though he tried to get back to sleep, memories of his first few days inside The Enchantment more than two months ago kept flooding through his conscious mind. He recalled chasing Victor Running Deer through a golden passageway and how the two of them had been mysteriously transformed when a kind of music had surrounded them and penetrated its magic into their very souls. After a time, they had awakened to a new clarity that allowed them to speak and walk upright like the human animals.

As the dog tossed about, he remembered trying to return to his humans' farm on that second morning. He had heard the old man and the boy call to him and had followed their shadows into the mist that surrounded his new world but was never able to catch them. While lost inside this hazy border, he had seen visions of the early pioneers leaving treasured possessions, those that were too heavy to carry over the mountains, along the old wagon trail.

The dog's next memories tumbled even faster as he recalled waking up inside the Hill Country halfway around the tiny world…and how they had imprisoned him for being a spy or a sorcerer…and how the Hill Country's spiritual leaders, Lucinda Vulture and Orville Bat, had come to his defense, declaring he was a highly spiritual animal… and how he had returned to the Prairie and tried to tell his story…and how the creatures from the Old Meetinghouse seemed to believe him, but the creatures from the New Meetinghouse had not—especially their spiritual leader, Brother Fabian Lynx.

When the dog finally fell asleep again, he dreamed he was back on Will Stuart's farm near the cornfield where he had chased the deer. Suddenly a great stag with immense antlers stepped out of one of the rows of corn. At the same moment a young buck appeared from the opposite direction and confronted the stag. The two began to fight. For a long time, they kicked and butted heads until tragedy struck. The antlers of the two males locked together and would not come apart. After much tugging, the old stag fell on his knees, exhausted. The younger deer tried desperately to pull away but could not untangle himself. Finally, he let out a huge bellow.

At the same instant the buck bellowed in his dream, the dog was awakened by a voice crying, "Billy, are you in there? It's me, Georgie! Let me in!"

The dog, who had taken the name of Billy Bones in honor of his human, hurriedly slipped on his blue shirt, homespun pants and suspenders, stumbled over to the Dutch door of his little cottage, and opened the top half. There stood his good friend, Georgie Beaver, wearing a red vest, a bow tie, and a pair of short pants. He had a toothy grin on his face and was holding a basket in front of him. "Look what I've got. Ma sent us a loaf of bread and some apple butter. It'll give us something to eat before we go over and see Mr. Wise Owl."

"I'm sorry, I seem to have overslept," said the dog, somewhat shaken. He knew that he had had one of his special dreams again—the kind Lucinda Vulture would have called *prophetic*. "Come on in. I'll get some knives and plates from the cupboard." Billy opened the bottom door and walked over to the hutch constructed in the north wall by the stone fireplace.

"I thought I heard you talking to someone when I passed by your window," said the beaver. "What was that all about?"

"I was dreaming about something that could have happened in the outside world," admitted the shepherd dog, "Sit down at the table, and I'll tell you about it."

After Billy finished his tale, Georgie peered quizzically over at his friend. "Do you think it means anything?"

"I don't know," admitted the dog.

"Do you suppose something is going to happen to Victor Running Deer or Melinda Doe's father, Olen Buck?" asked the beaver again.

"Gee, I don't know that either," confessed Billy. "I sure hope not. Maybe it'll amount to nothing, just like some of my other dreams."

"Well, hurry up and finish your breakfast, and let's get over to Land's End so you can tell Mr. Wise Owl about that personal message you got from Olen Buck."

CHAPTER THREE

JOURNEY TO LAND'S END

After Billy Bones and Georgie Beaver traveled a few hundred yards north on the East Wagon Trail, Billy glanced back at his snug cottage with its thatched roof, Dutch doors, and white-shuttered windows. He noticed that the purple and white petunias in the window boxes facing the sun were especially lush, their vines cascading almost to the ground. He was distressed to realize that he had started taking the beauty of The Enchantment for granted.

Today was different, however. Olen Buck had given Billy information after a chaotic City Council meeting the day before that renewed the dog's hope for the future, and he was seeing everything again as if for the first time, especially the rich colors.

When the two animals reached Beaver Dam Road, they headed east in the direction of Land's End. The first dwelling they came to was Percival Gander's shop on the south side close to the road. The eccentric gander favored the chicken-coop style of architecture from his memories of the farm he grew up in while in the outside world.

Just as the two animals reached the shop, Percival Gander poked his head out of the little window next to the door, and then in and out again. "Oh my, oh my, is that you, Billy Bones…and you too, Georgie Beaver? I thought I saw you coming down the road. I've been fitting Victor Running Deer with a new white shirt and tie. Yes, with a new white shirt and tie…" The long-necked bird stuck his head in and then out again. "…and a fine shiny tiepin. Yes, fine, very fine! Wait where you are and we'll come out and show you."

Billy frowned slightly. A strong bond of friendship had developed between Victor and him since their turbulent entry into The Enchantment. However, this bond had been strained lately when the dog discovered that the deer's mother had been killed by hunters in the outside world. While Billy had a strong love for the human animals, Victor hated them. Still, the two of them had made a special pact with Olen Buck, Sandy Antelope, and Arnold Big Horn after Billy came to Victor's rescue during yesterday's City Council meeting. And now he was on his way to Land's End with good news for Winston Wise Owl.

When Percival's door finally opened, both Billy and Georgie were taken by surprise. Instead of Victor Running Deer, the beautiful Melinda Doe, only daughter of Olen Buck, stepped out. She was wearing a white blouse buttoned closely around the neck and a long scarlet skirt with a matching ribbon in her straw bonnet. Billy rushed over to the ramp to take her hand. She accepted it politely, as the board walkway with its horizontal braces was quite steep.

"Thank you," said the doe coolly, as she reached the end of the ramp and withdrew her hand.

It concerned Billy that Victor was still enamored with Melinda Doe, especially since she seemed to encourage a rivalry between Victor and the unruly Rodney Wild Deer.

"Victor tells me that you came to his defense yesterday after Rodney attacked him during the City Council meeting," Melinda stated flatly.

"Well, it seemed rather unfair…" Billy began.

"Anyway, we are most grateful," interrupted the doe, as she turned her back on the dog and gazed up at the doorway.

At that instant Victor Running Deer emerged from the shop. Under his dark brown vest he wore a new white shirt and scarlet tie held in place by a shiny new tiepin. Billy noticed that the deer's left eye was still swollen, and he had a rather fat lip.

When Victor saw Billy and Georgie, he lowered his head. The shepherd dog could tell immediately that the deer was embarrassed about his new outfit. "I didn't expect to see you two this morning." The buck paused, smiled shyly, and then gestured to his clothing. "Melinda wants me to wear this on Sunday when we go to the New Meetinghouse."

"And right now we're going to lunch at the hotel," said the doe, smiling curtly. "Come, Victor, we don't want to be late."

As the two deer walked briskly off in the direction of Main Street, Percival Gander waddled down the long

ramp. He wore only a mustard-yellow vest with his trademark measuring tape around his neck. "Well, Georgie and Billy Bones, how did you like Victor's new clothes…yes, his new clothes?"

"Very nice, Percy, but he seemed a bit uncomfortable," commented the beaver.

"Well, perhaps the clothes are more for Melinda than Victor, Georgie…yes, more for Melinda."

"And his fat lip and swollen eye—did he tell you how he got those?" inquired Georgie.

"He said that Rodney Wild Deer attacked him after he made some remark yesterday at City Hall," returned Percy. "And then he said that Billy tried to pull Rodney off. And after that three of the Coyote Brothers jumped on Billy, and then Sandy Antelope and Arnold Big Horn came to Billy's defense…yes, yes, to Billy's defense. According to Victor, it was real pandemonium."

"All I can say is that we were lucky the council didn't punish us as well," admitted the shepherd dog. "Well, we must be on our way, Percy. We have an important message for Mr. Wise Owl.

"Well, if that's the case, off with you," responded Percival, as he climbed back up the ramp to his front door.

After Billy Bones and Georgie Beaver passed the four-way crossing that sent a road south toward the old wagon trail and north to the North Woods, they spied Jason Crow's farmhouse nestled snuggly into the fence row just ahead of them. Jason's son, Gerard Crow, was out in front rolling some sort of metal hoop. The young crow stopped playing when he saw the dog and the beaver.

"Hi Gerard," called the beaver, when he drew up even with the crow.

"Hi yourself," answered Gerard, as he walked past Georgie and timidly over to Billy. The crow had on a bright yellow vest and a straw hat that hung loosely around his neck. When he reached Billy, he reverently touched the dog's chest with the palm of his hand that stretched out from the tip of his black wing. "Are you a prophet, Mr. Bones?" he asked in a high clear voice. "I heard you speak about your adventures inside the mist, and about the human animals."

"Gerard, who are you talking to?" interrupted Gerard's mother in a shrill voice through the open doorway of the house. "Oh, Georgie, it's you and Mr. Bones. I'm sorry I didn't see you standing there."

"We're on our way to Land's End to see Mr. Wise Owl," returned Georgie.

"Is Gerard bothering you, Mr. Bones?" asked Gwendolyn Crow, coming out into the light. She had on a dust cap and a clean white apron. "I know he hasn't stopped talking about you since he and his father heard you speak at the Old Meetinghouse about your experience inside the mist."

"No, he's been no trouble," answered Billy, who smiled down at Gerard, who was now standing with both hands on his hoop.

"Gerard, are you still playing with that old metal hoop? You know your father won't like that," scolded Gwendolyn.

"Why is that, Mrs. Crow?" asked Georgie.

"Well, as you know, my husband is a guide at the New Meetinghouse, and he goes along with Brother Fabian Lynx on those things. He doesn't like Gerard playing with that hoop because it came off a wagon wheel that once belonged to the human animals," explained Gwendolyn. "Of course, I'm not much into that dogmatic stuff myself."

"What dogmatic stuff?" asked Farmer Jason Crow, who suddenly appeared around the corner of the house. The husband of Gwendolyn Crow wore only a sleeveless plaid shirt and an old straw hat and, as usual, was chewing on a stalk of wheat.

"I was just saying why Gerard wasn't supposed to be playing with that old hoop he found," explained Gwendolyn rather nervously.

"You still got that old thing?" questioned Jason, glaring over at the hoop. "I thought I told you to get rid of it."

"But I like it," insisted Gerard. "It makes me feel good when I touch it."

"Nonsense! Now throw it out back 'til I decide what to do with it," ordered Jason. As the young crow sulked behind the fence row, the older crow addressed Billy. "I'm sorry, but my son is very impressionable, Mr. Bones. I'm afraid he's somewhat taken with you and your stories." Jason Crow paused for a moment and then continued. "And Mr. Bones, I understand you still ain't been to see Brother Fabian Lynx like I requested some time ago. He really needs to talk to you about them visions you seen inside the mist."

"I just haven't had the chance," admitted Billy. "Besides, I've been attending the Old Meetinghouse."

"Well, you should at least give him the courtesy of explaining his point of view, don't you think?' returned Jason in an exasperated tone.

"I…I guess I could do that," said Billy hesitantly.

"Fine, make sure you do that soon! Well, I can't stand here gabbin' all day. Got to get back to work," cawed Jason, as he turned and tromped back behind the fencerow.

"Well, ah…good day to you, Mrs. Crow. We've got to be on our way," said Billy after an uncomfortable pause.

As Billy turned to go, he remembered again how he had imagined a yellow light glowing around Gerard and how the crow had started to shrink in size during the Grand Fair. It had been one of his strongest visions since entering The Enchantment. Earlier he had seen the same light around his friend Georgie Beaver and Patsy Prairie Dog. He had told the Hill Country's spiritual leader, Lucinda Vulture, about the visions. She had concluded that they were possibly harbingers of some future tragedy and that they would discuss them further at the next Tribal Council meeting during the Autumn Equinox.

"But maybe all that's changed now," thought the dog. "After all, this message I have for Winston Wise Owl makes everything all right again."

As Billy and Georgie started back up the path, the two great trees that made up Land's End rose majestically above the golden fields of corn and wheat. Behind the trees loomed the ever-present mist with its dark golden hue that stretched out on either side until it circled the entire Enchantment.

CHAPTER FOUR

A MEETING OF MINDS

"How much damage can he really do?" queried Cornelius Van Mink. "I mean, that's the question, isn't it?"

"Well, if we're to believe the speeches of our newly-elected mayor, Elmer Prairie Dog, he plans to eventually remove all the human artifacts from our homes. And I guess that includes my Oriental rug and tapestry and your library and grandfather clock, Winston," stated the Prairie's outgoing mayor, George P. Beaver.

"Of course, he's really speaking for Brother Fabian Lynx," said Winston Wise Owl, shaking his head. "We can't forget for one minute who's behind it all."

Winston Wise Owl glanced quietly over at his two friends in their formal attire. Because not much had changed since the first Great Rift, the citizens inside The Enchantment still dressed in late nineteenth century clothing. Mayor George P. Beaver's top hat and Councilor Cornelius Van Mink's derby lay in front of them on an old oak table, and their frock coats had been carefully placed behind them on chairs. Each animal wore dark pants, a vest, a high-collared shirt, and a black tie held in place by a large tiepin. Winston preferred tails with the sleeves removed in case he had to fly on a moment's notice. All around them, the bookcases in Winston's tree house at Land's End were stuffed with ancient leather-bound books that had at one time belonged to a human pioneer named Warren Nathaniel Stone.

The owl, the beaver, and the mink had gathered that morning to try to make sense of Mayor George P. Beaver's loss to Elmer Prairie Dog during the elections that had taken place only the week before. Just as devastating was Councilor Sylvester Turtle's loss to Olen Buck on the Prairie's City Council. Now, along with Phineas T. Fox and Charlie Pheasant, the strict constructionists would hold the majority in the Prairie's five-member council and the mayor's office. Starting January first, Cornelius Van Mink and Wendell Red Breast would be the sole representatives of the moderate cause.

"Under normal conditions, losing the race for mayor and control of the City Council wouldn't have been so catastrophic," said Winston Wise Owl, breaking the silence.

"You're referrin' to Brother Fabian Lynx's influence again, I suppose," chimed in George P. Beaver. "It's hard to believe those creatures over at the New Meetinghouse are so gullible."

A chill passed through Winston's body as he recollected Brother Fabian's quick rise to power. In only one year the lynx had convinced the guides at the New Meetinghouse to oust their old spiritual counselor, Sarah Mourning Dove and choose him instead.

"We must consider what would happen if Brother Fabian persuades the new City Council to destroy our human artifacts," hooted the owl finally. "As you know, members of the Hill Country's Tribal Council are convinced that some calamity would occur if that happened. And then of course, there's the matter of Billy Bones…."

"You're referring to his unique dreams, I take it?" questioned the beaver.

"Yes, they seem to indicate something similar," returned Winston.

"But we must be reasonable, Winston," interrupted Cornelius.

"All I know is that Billy has a special gift. After one of his dreams, he accurately identified the grandson of Warren Nathaniel Stone, who, as you know, left the books in the hollow of this very tree. I was the only one who knew that the grandson's name was Jimmy. The boy's name was written in the book of *Grimm's Fairy Tales* that I keep in my chest at the foot of my bed," said Winston with conviction. "You remember, George. I showed you the book at your home last July shortly after Billy's return from the Hill Country. I say we heed his visions, at least until we know our belongings are safe," concluded Winston, as he stood and moved to the large double window. Some commotion in the little courtyard below had caught his attention.

Across the pathway the old bird noticed that his good friend and confidant, Hester Groundhog, had just popped out of her house with a tray of tea and honey and several kinds of hot breads. As usual, she had on her dust cap, long patterned dress, and white collar and apron. Her little dwelling, built into the bottom of the huge tree just south of Winston's, had white Dutch doors, white shutters, and window boxes under the windows. All around the house were bushes and flowers of every sort, and in back stretched the groundhog's wonderful vegetable garden.

When Hester reached the long table outside of her tree house, she set the tray down in front of two guests and motioned up to Winston's window.

"Speaking of Mr. Billy Bones," the owl said, turning back to the beaver and the mink, "I believe he's down in the courtyard right now having tea with Hester Groundhog. And George, your nephew, Georgie, is with him. If you'll excuse me, I should go down and see what they want."

By this time, Mayor George P. Beaver and Councilor Cornelius Van Mink had already joined Winston Wise Owl at the window.

"Didn't you say earlier that Hester had invited us for lunch after our meeting?" questioned Cornelius, smacking his lips. "I say we all adjourn to the courtyard right now."

"And I second the motion," chuckled George P., "enthusiastically."

CHAPTER FIVE

THE IMPORTANT MESSAGE

Lunchtime at Hester Groundhog's was always a special occasion, so Billy Bones had not been surprised when Mayor George P. Beaver, Cornelius Van Mink, and Winston Wise Owl joined them. The dog decided to wait until he could speak to Winston alone concerning Olen Buck's request, since the important message was specifically for him. He thought that the owl could then pass the information on to whomever he chose.

After the meal of blueberry, apple, walnut, and pecan breads, and after Hester's exceptional tea and wild honey, the conversation quickly turned to the Prairie's City Council meeting the day before.

"Winston, you should have been at the council meeting yesterday. Rodney Wild Deer actually had the audacity to attack Victor Running Deer right in front of the council!" exclaimed Mayor Beaver.

"And then, Mr. Bones here came to Victor's rescue, and the Coyote Brothers jumped on him," continued the mink.

"All four Coyote Brothers?" asked Winston.

"No sir," answered Billy, feeling he needed to join the discussion. "Lenny Coyote wasn't involved in the altercation yesterday. And if you remember, during the Overland

Race, he was disqualified for stopping and helping me after his brothers tried to sabotage me. In fact, he even testified against his brothers at the trial. It took a lot of courage for him to come forward."

"Then it was just the three older brothers—Lester, Leon, and Leroy?" inquired Winston.

"Yes sir, and then Sandy Antelope and Arnold Big Horn came to my defense," said Billy, wanting to give his friends the credit they deserved.

"I couldn't believe what I was seeing," added the mayor.

"And what finally happened?" inquired the owl.

"Well, after Olen Buck and Sheriff Lone Wolf stepped in and Cornelius here finally gained some kind of order, Cornelius demanded apologies from everyone involved in the fighting," explained George P.

"But when it became Rodney's turn, the scoundrel tried to attack Victor a second time," said Cornelius.

"And Rodney had to be hauled out kicking and screaming!" exclaimed the beaver. "It was unbelievable!"

"So tell me: what was the outcome?" questioned the owl impatiently.

"Well, following that, Brother Fabian spoke on behalf of Rodney and Lester and Leon and Leroy. Needless to say, he surprised everyone when he informed us that they were willing to plead guilty to the charges of ambushing Victor and Billy and Nosey Coon before the Grand Fair," elucidated George P. Beaver.

"And what was the sentence?" asked Winston.

"The three older Coyote brothers got nine months' probation, and Rodney got three months jail time and six months' probation," answered Cornelius.

"Well, at least the Prairie is a bit safer," concluded the outgoing mayor.

"Let's hope so," said Winston, glancing at Billy.

After the owl's final statement, Cornelius Van Mink took one last sip of his tea and stood up to leave. "Well, enough talk. Thank you again, Hester. It was a most pleasurable lunch, but I must be going. Mayor Beaver, will you walk with me back to the pond?"

When Cornelius and George P. were out of earshot and while Hester and Georgie were removing the teapot and leftover breads, Billy escorted Winston slowly over to the circular staircase that led up to the owl's tree house.

"Olen Buck spoke to me yesterday after the City Council meeting," Billy began. "He asked me if I would be willing to give you an important message."

Billy could feel his heart thumping loudly inside his chest. After all, it had been Winston Wise Owl who had found Victor and him when they first entered The Enchantment. Since then he had learned to trust and respect the owl completely. He did not want to get Olen's message wrong, and he did not want to mention the special pact that he had made with the old stag, Victor Running Deer, Sandy Antelope, Arnold Big Horn, and himself. The five animals had secretly pledged to protect Winston and his books and the other citizens who had human artifacts in their homes.

"I didn't want to tell you about Olen's message in front of the others. I thought you should decide when to do that," explained the shepherd dog.

"Well, you certainly have my attention, Billy," said Winston. "For heaven's sake, what did he say?"

Again, Billy chose his words carefully. "He said that he was against going into citizens' homes and removing their human valuables without their permission, and he said that included your books."

"Why…why that's wonderful! What a tremendous relief! I just hope that Brother Fabian doesn't get to him and change his mind," continued the owl. "At least it gives us something to hope for."

"Mr. Wise Owl, it's good that the books will remain safe, isn't it? I mean, without them, how would we know what went on before us? It would be a great loss, wouldn't it?" asked Billy.

"Yes, that's true, Mr. Bones. The books are our link to human knowledge. We have a collective memory that has been passed down to us since the Great Rift and, of course, *The Great Book of Rules,* but we really have nothing else."

"I'm sure you're aware that the human animals' achievements surpass ours in many ways, Mr. Wise Owl. I mean, like the lights that turn on magically, and the wagons that are drawn without animals to pull them," commented the shepherd dog.

"You've been blessed, Mr. Bones. Most of our citizens no longer remember what they saw in the other world.

Even Brother Fabian Lynx seems to have forgotten that outside of The Enchantment only human creatures have clarity…"

The owl stopped speaking for a moment and then glanced up at his tree house. "That's why the information in my books is so important. It's a link to that clarity. It's all I…we have."

"Ah…Mr. Wise Owl, there is one more thing I must talk to you about. You see, Jason Crow asked me some time ago to visit Brother Fabian at the New Meetinghouse. Apparently he wants to question me about what I saw inside the mist. I'm afraid I've been avoiding it—I suppose out of loyalty to you and the Tribal Council. But this morning when I was passing Jason's house, he confronted me again, and I'm sorry to say I…I finally agreed to go through with it," admitted Billy, looking down the path toward town. "Perhaps, well, perhaps I can influence him in some way…I mean, about the books."

"My dear Mr. Bones, I understand why you feel you must do this. But I must warn you—Brother Fabian has a powerful charisma. You'll be drawn into his way of thinking."

"Yes, I know…but I will try to remain strong. I know what's at stake. Perhaps if I went today…"

"Would you like me to go with you?" asked the owl.

"No, I think this is something I must do on my own," concluded the dog.

"I see. Very well then, may The Great Spirit be with you," declared the owl, starting up the stairs. Before he reached his door, he turned one last time. "But be very vigilant!"

As Winston Wise Owl entered his tree house, Billy and Georgie thanked Hester Groundhog for the wonderful meal and started hiking back to their respective homes. When they reached the East Wagon Trail, Georgie continued on to the beaver pond, and Billy turned south toward the New Meetinghouse and the uncertain task before him.

CHAPTER SIX

BROTHER FABIAN LYNX

The New Meetinghouse stood at the foot of Main Street just beyond where the road divides into its eastern and western branches. To Billy Bones it looked very plain and squat. Unlike the Old Meetinghouse with its elegant steeple and pained windows or the beautiful clock tower over City Hall, the steeple on the New Meetinghouse was shorter and thicker and had no embellishments.

Even though Brother Fabian's study and sleeping quarters were in the rear, Billy felt it was wiser to enter the New Meetinghouse by the front door. "Well, here goes," he thought as he pulled the heavy door open and cautiously stepped inside. To his amazement he discovered that the interior of the hall was much roomier than it appeared to be from the outside. Although the ceiling was lower than the one in the Old Meetinghouse, the partially shuttered windows admitted enough light to see the room clearly.

As Billy nervously glanced around, he felt strangely relieved that no one seemed to be inside. He walked slowly up the center aisle and looked at the plain benches covered with blue pads for more comfortable seating. "Well, some good soul has been looking out for this gathering," he whispered to himself.

When Billy reached the front of the hall, he stepped onto the raised platform and walked over to the lectern. It was adorned with a delicate white lace cloth and a copy of *The Great Book of Rules*. Without thinking, he reached down and turned one of its pages.

"Yes, Mr. Bones, may I help you?" sounded a resonant voice behind him.

Billy quickly turned around and beheld Brother Fabian Lynx standing in a doorway that apparently led to his private rooms. The big cat was wearing a pair of home-spun pants and a white long-sleeved shirt open at the collar instead of the white monk's robe he wore in public.

"Oh, Brother Fabian, I...I didn't expect you without your robe," stammered Billy, promptly turning the page of *The Great Book of Rules* back to where it was. "I prom-ised Jason Crow that I would come and talk with you... and well...I realize that was a number of weeks ago, but here I am."

"Yes, it was in late June, I think, and again just before the fair. But I'm glad you finally came," answered the lynx, holding out his hand.

Billy did not immediately react. He had shaken hands twice with Brother Fabian, and on both occasions unpleasant visions of abuse by humans had flashed through his mind.

"You hesitate to take my hand, Mr. Bones. I wonder now, are you afraid of what you might see with that prophetic mind of yours? I could tell from the way you withdrew your hand the last time we met that something unexpected had occurred," began the lynx. "Come now, I've been informed of your visions. Take my hand. Perhaps we will both discover a new truth about each other."

The shepherd dog looked directly into the lynx's eyes. Winston was right. The handsome cat with the extraordinarily white teeth and winning smile was indeed charismatic. "I thought you doubted my visions, Brother Fabian. At least that's the impression I got from some of your followers. When I explained what I saw inside the mist during my talk at the Old Meetinghouse, I got the sense they didn't believe me."

"You misunderstood, Mr. Bones. Between you and me, I have no doubt that you are a highly spiritual animal, especially if Lucinda Vulture vouches for you. What I do say is that you've misinterpreted what you've seen, and I will prove it to you. Now shake my hand and tell me exactly what that gifted mind of yours perceives," admonished Brother Fabian.

"No, I'm sorry. I'm afraid I made a mistake coming here," mumbled Billy, as he turned to leave.

"Wait, Mr. Bones," called Fabian, before the dog could step down off the platform. "Please, it's important that you do this—for both our sakes. I understand you see more clearly than the rest of us do. So, you'll do me a great favor by staying."

"I'm sorry, Brother Fabian, but I have no control over these visions. I don't know when or where they'll come," admitted Billy, still averting the lynx's gaze. "Perhaps nothing will happen at all."

"Mr. Bones, I implore you. You must see for yourself what I've had to endure. I'm not without some powers of my own in this regard, and I have a strong feeling that something will come to you. Now shake my hand!"

In spite of his best intentions, Billy Bones finally did exactly as Brother Fabian Lynx commanded. As soon as their hands clasped, the vision of two humans coming at him with a whip and a long prodding pole immediately shot through his conscious mind. "Ah!!!" screamed the dog, trying to pull his hand away. In response, the lynx took hold of the dog's arm with his other hand and would not release it.

"Tell me, Mr. Bones! Tell me what you see…what you feel," ordered Brother Fabian.

"I'm very sorry, Brother Fabian. I realize now how painful it must've been for you!" winced the dog, as he felt the sharp sting of the human's cruelty vibrate through his body.

"But what do you see? Tell me exactly what you see!" pleaded the big cat a second time.

"I see two men…and they have a whip and a long pole…and they're attacking us…I mean, they're attacking you!" exclaimed Billy.

"And what do they look like, these men?" insisted the lynx, squeezing the dog's hand and arm even harder. "Describe them to me."

"Well, the one with the whip has black hair and a kind of beard, and the other one is fat and bald."

"And what else do you notice about the one with the beard?"

"Well, it isn't a full beard. It's sort of wild and sparse."

"And what is he wearing?" demanded the lynx.

"He has on a tee shirt and a black vest."

"And how about his arms? Do you notice anything about his arms?"

"They are covered with drawings made of ink," responded the dog.

"Yes, that's them. You've described them perfectly. And now you can appreciate what I lived through and why I hated them. They did this to me day after day after day… after day."

"But the humans I knew were kind to me," retorted Billy, pulling free from the lynx's grip. "They loved me. They were not like the humans you knew at all."

"Well then, they were the exceptions," responded Fabian. "Ask your friend Victor Running Deer. He will tell you how these '*loving*' humans killed his mother for sport. The list of their atrocities goes on. Only a few of you *pets* were treated well. Now you see why we must rid ourselves of this collective memory. The human animals have been the curse of our existence!"

"No, I cannot accept this," said Billy, backing away from Brother Fabian. "And how about their books, their knowledge? You must realize how important that is. The humans have given us an understanding of what went on before we came into existence. Surely you can appreciate that this knowledge must be protected."

"After the cruelty I endured, I see nothing good in saving anything that belonged to them. Our *Great Book of Rules* that you so reverently touched and our collective memory are all we need," rebutted the lynx, grabbing the dog by both shoulders. "The human animals are evil. Even you must see that now!"

"But the pioneers who left their priceless treasures along the wagon trail; we may owe them our very existence," rebutted the dog.

"Ah, you're referring again to those visions you had inside the mist. Has it ever occurred to you that what you saw might be dangerous to our little society? Read the *Prairie Dog's Appendix!* Remember those evil creatures who attacked me and Victor's mother," cried the lynx.

Filled with frustration, Billy Bones whirled around and bolted right into the arms of Lester, Leon, and Leroy Coyote who had heard the commotion and had rushed into the meetinghouse. They had their sleeves rolled up, as if they had been working.

As Billy backed away from the coyotes, he felt the lynx's arm go around his shoulder. "Do not fear Mr. Calhoun Coyote's sons, Mr. Bones. They're working for me today, and I promise, they won't hurt you."

"I...I must go now Brother Fabian. If it's any consolation, I won't forget what was said here today," stated Billy, trying to regain his confidence.

"Can I convince you then to come to our gathering on Sunday? I believe you owe me one more time. After all, I should get equal billing with the likes of Thaddeus P.

Turtle—unless of course, you're afraid of what you might hear?"

"No, no, it's not that…" began Billy.

"Then promise me you'll come. After all, you've seen into my past like no one else. We have a connection now. Even I can't remember what happened to me with such clarity," reasoned the lynx.

"I will consider it. That's all I can promise. If…if not this Sunday, maybe another time. Yes, that I will do," proclaimed Billy. "But you…you must think carefully about what I said concerning Winston Wise Owl's books. That…that you must do for me."

In order to leave by the center aisle, Billy had to brush past the Coyote Brothers, but they did not try to stop or detain him. The shepherd dog was ashamed that he had not been stronger in his resolve. Winston was right. The lynx had a powerful way of drawing creatures into his confidence, and the dog would have to do some real soul-searching before their next meeting.

When Sunday came, Billy Bones did not go the New Meetinghouse. Sandy Antelope had invited all the witnesses who had testified against Rodney Wild Deer and the Coyote brothers to his dugout to celebrate their victory in court. He had to pick up Nosey Coon on his way, and besides, he knew in his heart that he was unprepared to face the lynx again so soon. Billy was excited to attend the supper but did not want to discuss how weak and ineffective he had been during his confrontation with Brother Fabian Lynx.

As the dog started down the embankment toward the raccoon's tree house, he noticed that a dark bank of clouds had collected on the western horizon. "We're in for some nasty weather," he thought out loud, "and it looks like we might get good and soaked. Well, that's fine with me. It will serve me right!"

CHAPTER SEVEN

THE FLOOD

Torrential downpours were quite a rarity inside The Enchantment, especially those that lasted all afternoon and into the evening. North of Sandy Antelope's little dwelling, the rising water quickly filled the old creek bed that the natives called Dry Gulch. By the time Billy Bones and Nosey Coon finally arrived, it had begun to spill over its banks. Inside the cozy little dugout, Sandy's guests, Billy Bones, Nosey Coon, Victor Running Deer, and Arnold Big Horn, were drenched from the storm. Sandy had built a fire in the stone fireplace to make a pot of stew and to help the animals dry their clothes and their natural coats.

Billy was intrigued with Sandy's dugout. It was built into the hillside of one of the smaller foothills west of the little town that ran through the center of the Prairie. The antelope had reinforced the inner and side walls with stone to hold back the sandy soil. The front wall with its two connected windows was fashioned of long vertical boards, and the roof was a single slab of rock that emerged directly out of the hill.

Sandy usually wore a collarless shirt and home-spun pants with suspenders. Like Victor and Billy, the soft-spoken Sandy Antelope had been born in the outside world. However, the antelope had entered The Enchantment eight years ago when he was only a year old before he had reached his full size.

Toward evening after the guests' clothes finally dried out, the antelope gathered enough bowls to serve them. As the companions sat around the room eating stew and telling stories, the conversation finally got around to Sandy's closest neighbor.

"If the creek gets any higher, we're going to have to keep an eye out for Mary McMink," stated Sandy, absently glancing out the window and noticing the rising water. "She lives across the road, you know. You can see her roof line if you look down toward the creek."

As the others strained to look, Nosey Coon scampered off the bed, across the Big Horn's lap, and onto the table that sat in front of the windows. This sudden motion nearly knocked Arnold's bowl out of his hands.

Unlike his friends, the no-nonsense Arnold Big Horn had been born in the Hill Country. Some dispute with his family had caused him to move to the Prairie. Arnold preferred overalls to pants and wore a collarless plaid shirt only on special occasions.

As for the mischievous raccoon, he and his friend, Needles Porcupine, had come through the golden portal five years ago. The pants he had on had been patched a number of times and were held up by a single strap, and his red shirt resembled the top of an old union suit.

"Hey, watch it there, Nosey! What are you doin'?"

complained the ram, as he managed to catch his bowl.

"You mean Crazy Mary?" said the wide-eyed raccoon, completely oblivious to Arnold's complaints. He twisted nervously to look at his host. "Is it true, Sandy, that she's a witch? That's what I've heard. That she comes out only at night and then casts spells on anyone who accidentally crosses her path."

Sandy laughed, "Whew, Nosey, where did you ever hear a story like that? That's just plain silly."

"I heard that too," exclaimed Arnold unexpectedly, adding credence to the young raccoon's story. "They say her house is full of exotic things, maybe even a crystal ball."

Nosey pressed his nose even harder against the windowpane, trying to get a better view of the old house. In the meantime, his bushy tail became more and more agitated, forcing Victor and Sandy to pick up their bowls also. "Wow, a crystal ball!"

Billy quickly got up off the rocker, pulled Nosey down from the table, and tossed him back onto the bed. Seeing this playful action, Sandy decided it was time to tell what he knew about his mysterious neighbor.

"Well, it's true that Mary rarely comes out except in the morning. I've often seen her just after sunrise workin' in her garden or gatherin' herbs along the creek. Sometimes I even call to her, but she always ignores me or runs inside her home."

"Is she related to Cornelius Van Mink on the City Council?" inquired Billy Bones.

"They're actually brother and sister. I think Cornelius and the rest of the mink families don't have much to do with her though. I know Mary stopped goin' to the Old Meetinghouse or seeing any of her friends or relatives in town," explained the antelope.

"Has she always lived alone?" asked Billy, sensing there was more to her story.

"No. She used to be married. Apparently her husband, Ernest McMink, disappeared twenty years ago."

"Do they have any idea what happened to him?" asked the deer, who had leaned back from the table as the story became more interesting.

"Some thought he might've gotten lost inside the mist," continued the antelope. "After all, his hobby was exploring, and he was constantly askin' the Tribal Council for permission to poke around inside the Hill Country."

"Some thought there might've been foul play on her part!" said Arnold, leaning across the table to Sandy.

At that precise moment when all five animals were contemplating the possibilities of Mr. McMink's disappearance, the front door opened, and a wild disheveled creature appeared in the doorway.

"My things! My beautiful things! They're going to be ruined! You must help me save my things!" said the distraught creature, glancing frantically about the room.

Instantly Sandy realized who it was. "Mrs. McMink! What?"

Mary suddenly spotted the one animal she knew. She lunged across the room and began tugging at his arm.

"Help me, Mr. Antelope, please. The water—it's coming into my home!"

Once Mary was inside the hut, the companions got a better look at their unexpected guest. The nightgown she wore was soaked and clung haphazardly to her body, and her nightcap was smudged and pushed back on her head in general disarray.

Billy Bones was the first to assess the situation and headed for the open door. "Come on, we've got no time to waste!" The distraught mink followed closely at his heels, dragging the unsuspecting antelope in her wake. Arnold and Victor came soon after, but the little raccoon, hiding behind the bedpost, had not yet worked up the courage to move. As Billy dashed out into the weather, he noticed that the rain had lessened in its severity. The wind had picked up, and it blew smartly against his face, making it difficult to see.

When Billy finally reached Mary McMink's front door, he had to wade across a small gully of water before stepping into the house. Mary had left the door slightly ajar, but now it took some effort to move it even further so that the others could enter. The stone floor had about two inches of flood water already, and they could see that it was rapidly rising. The last one to arrive was the still-frightened Nosey Coon, who splashed through the gully and then slipped and came crashing through the front door on his stomach.

As Billy reached down and picked up the soaked raccoon, the little creature suddenly pointed a wet finger in amazement as he gazed about the house. "Oh my goodness, look! Look at all the beautiful things! It's like a fairy tale!"

The others also paused to look at Mary's house. The great room was filled with stately, eighteenth-century furniture. Halfway up the staircase was a partially rolled-up, braided oval rug that Mary hauled up out of the water.

"We need to get all of this up to the second floor!" commanded Billy, breaking the momentary paralysis. "Victor, help me with this rug! Sandy, you'd better get Mrs. McMink up there too!"

Victor and Billy moved the rug upstairs and placed it against the wall in the bedroom. Fortunately, the old carpet had gotten damp at only one end. Sandy was also successful in getting the frazzled mink upstairs and seated on her bed. To try to stop her shaking, he found a blanket and wrapped it snugly around her. The rest of the furniture was carefully stacked around the bedroom and in the nearby hallway, and the legs of each piece were wiped clean.

By the time the lower cupboards were emptied, the rain had abated, and everyone found a spot to curl up for the night. After Mary stopped shaking, she managed to find a blanket or wrap for each animal, and the long watchful night began. Gradually the water receded below the level of the ground floor, and the anxious creatures were able to get some sleep.

In the morning the sun rose in a clear cloudless sky. Victor and Arnold hauled some wood over from Sandy's dugout and started a fire in Mary's fireplace to help dry out the first floor. Billy and Sandy swept the debris out the front door and washed the stone floor and walls. Mary put on hot water for tea and found some cornbread that was still dry and tasty in a higher cupboard. After breakfast Sandy and Arnold promised Mary to return later that afternoon and carry the furniture back downstairs.

When the five friends finally got back to Sandy's dugout, Arnold blurted out what was on everyone's mind. "Well, we know one thing. She's no witch!"

Later that evening Sandy and Arnold dropped by Billy's cottage with some disturbing news concerning Mary McMink and Brother Fabian Lynx.

"Poor Mary's beside herself!" stated Sandy, showing genuine concern. "Brother Fabian came by to see if she was all right just as we were movin' her furniture downstairs. Mary tried to explain to him that her highboy and her big dining room table and chairs had probably belonged to humans 'cause 'McNeil from Ireland' was written underneath some of the chairs. Since Mary was the oldest in the Van Mink family, her father had left the best pieces to her."

"For some reason, Brother Fabian started scoldin' the poor mink!" continued Arnold, anxious to take up the story. "He told her it was against the teachings of *The Great Book of Rules* to hold on to things that once belonged to the human animals. As you can imagine, Mary was really upset. She said she couldn't understand why Sister Sarah had been visitin' her for twenty years and never once got after her for havin' the old pieces!"

"When Arnold and I came downstairs for the last time, Brother Fabian had left, and Mary was cryin'," said the antelope. "Apparently he'd warned her that in January he'd get the laws changed, so she'd have to give up her stuff."

"Well, I guess that's clear enough," sighed Billy, knowing firsthand the lynx's powers of persuasion. "Even if Olen Buck keeps the new City Council from taking the human artifacts out of citizens' homes without their permission, it won't apply to Mary McMink if she gives up her antiques voluntarily. What do you think Brother Fabian will do with the human antiques? Try to have them destroyed? What a tragedy that would be and such a trauma for Mary! All I can suggest is that we'd better see Winston Wise Owl right away. Maybe there's something he can do."

CHAPTER EIGHT

THE THIN LEATHER BOOK

Without Sandy Antelope's help, Winston Wise Owl would not have gotten in to see Mary McMink the next morning. Before he left his tree house, he retrieved a thin leather book that had drawings of English and Irish furniture of the eighteenth century. He was hoping to use it as a pretext for seeing the mink.

Winston had not talked to Mary in almost twenty years, but she still considered him part of the company at the Old Meetinghouse that had ostracized her. Now, however, she considered Sandy a trusted friend, and she even baked him a loaf of bread and placed it on his doorstep earlier that morning. Although she was still hesitant to see Winston, she allowed him in when he appeared outside her door with the young antelope.

"When I heard about what almost happened to your furniture, I remembered this old book. I thought you might want to look at it. I noticed that your highboy is described on one of the early pages," commented Winston in a gracious manner.

Mary looked carefully at the ancient leather book with its elegant drawings but said little. She did smooth down each page lovingly with her finger, and tears moistened her eyes. Finally, she looked up at the old bird. "My father told me how precious they were. Why did Brother Fabian tell me that it's a crime to keep them?" she whispered.

"Because he's interpreted *The Great Book of Rules* to support his own personal opinions," explained the owl.

"But how do you know this?" responded Mary with a frightened look in her eye. "What if he's right?"

"Will you at least be willing to speak to Counselor Turtle at the Old Meetinghouse?" the owl suggested. "Perhaps he can give you more insight."

"No!" Mary quickly looked away. "My friends and family at that place deserted me! They acted as if I had something to do with Ernest's death. I will never forgive them for that, and I will not talk to their counselor!"

"Will you talk to Sarah Mourning Dove, then? I think she might be willing to advise you on this," suggested Winston hopefully.

Mary McMink paused and looked over at her furniture. Winston could see that she wanted a way out of her dilemma, but she was torn. "Yes, I will listen to Sister Sarah."

"Then I'll send her to you," said Winston with some relief. "Just promise me one thing. Promise me you'll never give your furniture over to Brother Fabian Lynx. We're afraid of what he might do!"

Mary turned slowly away from Winston once again. "I can promise you nothing, but I will talk to Sarah. That much I will do."

After Winston left the old stone house, he was terribly concerned that Brother Fabian had already frightened Mary beyond all hope of redemption. The mink had pleaded with Winston to borrow his book with the drawings of English and Irish furniture. Reluctantly, he left it with her. He hoped that he had not made a mistake.

CHAPTER NINE

RAINBOW FALLS

Before dawn on the twenty-second of September, Billy Bones and Georgie Beaver made their way across Main Street with its many-colored Victorian-style buildings and west onto Rocky Route. Billy's destination was Echo Canyon in the Hill Country for the quarterly meeting of the Tribal Council, but Georgie had persuaded him to visit Rainbow Falls first. The unusual phenomenon was located on the border between the two states.

"It's The Enchantment's most glorious natural wonder," the beaver enthused, "'specially when the first rays of the sun hit the top of the falls."

Just before the two animals reached the Hill Country, they took a little path that led down to the foot of the falls. The route ended at an opening between the trees where several benches were strategically placed so that visitors could enjoy the view in quiet comfort. Fortunately for the two friends, they reached their objective at about six in the morning just as the sun's beams touched the highest point of the tumbling water.

For the next hour the dog and the beaver watched the early sunlight move slowly down the cascading water into the valley below. The natural gold that augmented the atmosphere, the deep wondrous green of the foliage, and the glory of the wild flowers that dotted the area added to the majesty of the scene. Billy Bones felt somewhat abashed that he had waited so long to see the spectacular sight.

"Georgie, you didn't exaggerate. I don't think I've ever seen such splendor!" admitted the shepherd dog. "Now I see why they call it Rainbow Falls. Not only are there little rainbows in the water when it's churning, but there are so many colors all around us. It's nothing short of miraculous!"

"I thought you'd like it. I used to come here often with my Mom and Dad, but now everyone's caught up in this big turnover at City Hall." Georgie paused and looked sadly at the ground. "I just wish things would go back to the way they were!"

"Well, they're not going to for a while I'm afraid. But thanks for showing me this wonderful place," smiled Billy, putting a hand on the beaver's shoulder. "As I told you before, I never saw colors until I came to The Enchantment. It's one of the gifts you natives take for granted."

"I can't imagine what it'd be like not to see color, but then, what do I know?" laughed the young beaver, returning to his naturally good disposition.

"I think it's one of the things I'd miss most if I ever had to leave," said the dog thoughtfully, not meaning to spoil the moment.

"Well then, don't ever leave!" rejoined Georgie simply.

For the next couple of hours, Billy and Georgie climbed to the plateau above the falls where the Hill Country began and then back down and behind the rushing water to the other side of the river. When they finally returned to the two benches, Georgie took out the hot cross buns his mother had packed and shared them with the hungry dog.

Soon after their breakfast, the two explorers hiked back up to the main road so Georgie could take his leave. When they reached the top of the path, they spotted a huge bird gliding in from the foothills to the south. The bird circled several times above them and then landed heavily in front of them. Billy could tell from the plaid swag across its chest and its immense wingspan that it was the deputy who served both the Prairie and the Hill Country, Deputy Harold Eagle. The great bird had his headquarters on Eagle Butte at a spot called Lookout Point. From his office he could observe all the Prairie and a great deal of the Hill Country.

"Ah, so it's you, Billy Bones. I suppose you're wantin' to go into the Hill Country for the Tribal Meetin' durin' the autumn equinox. Well, since you're one of the few creatures from the Prairie that can cross without special permission, I won't waste your time," said the eagle, who spoke with a Scottish brogue.

"Deputy, it's good to see you again. I guess you heard about the uproar we had during the City Council's special session a while back?" said Billy, smiling.

"Well, at least they did somethin' about that rogue deer, Rodney, and his coyote buddies. But I'm thinkin' it's not the last we've heard from them," complained the eagle. "It will be interestin' in January though, takin' orders from Elmer Prairie Dog. It's funny. I guess before the Great Rift I would have been his worst enemy. Well, I won't detain you any longer. I hope the session goes well. I'm sure they'll be some talk about the new mayor and his promises."

As the two friends watched, Deputy Harold Eagle lift effortlessly into the air on his powerful wings, Georgie gave Billy one last warning. "So long, and be careful. I still don't completely trust those Hill creatures."

CHAPTER TEN

THE AUTUMN EQUINOX

When Billy Bones finally reached Echo Canyon deep inside the Hill Country, it was nearly noon. He had arranged to meet his friend, Maurice Rabbit, just outside the old lodge, but when the jolly rabbit saw Billy coming, he raced down the narrow valley and threw his arms around the shepherd dog. As usual, Maurice wore a painter's smock and a felt cap at a jaunty angle.

"Billy, I hoped you'd arrive early. Come over to my house before the first session starts so you can get rid of your backpack. You're staying with me the next couple of days," said the rabbit jubilantly, patting the dog's back.

Maurice's home, like many in the valley, was built into the wall of one of the foothills. Because he was a painter, he chose to live across the stream the locals called Spirit Moves, and dug his hole into the hillside facing south. Along the front wall to the left of his doorway, he put in large windows in order to catch as much daylight as possible.

Inside the rabbit's single room was a large table under the window with a number of canvases, brushes, and other articles used in the artist's trade. His easel and a high-back chair sat near the middle of the room facing the windows. A cupboard, an old painted bed, and a colorful dresser with the bottom drawer perpetually open completed the rabbit's furniture. A number of unfinished paintings sat around the room, and many completed ones crowded the walls.

"You can drop your bedroll there," said Maurice, pointing to a spare mattress he had placed against the northeast corner. "I've got some bread and honey for lunch. We've just enough time to grab a bite to eat before the opening ceremony begins. Come on over to the table while I clear off a space for us to sit down and make ourselves comfortable."

The opening ceremony, which celebrated the autumn equinox, took place inside the old log lodge at the west end of Echo Canyon. For the occasion, the Tribal Council took their usual seats in a semicircle facing the door. Maurice Rabbit sat on the far right, wearing a multicolored robe. Next to him, Billy Bones wore the light blue Robe of Truth that had been given to him when he joined the council three months earlier. The seat next to Billy had been left vacant for the Tribal Council's spiritual leader, Lucinda Vulture. The patient Tribal Council chief, Omar Mountain Goat, dressed in a robe of deep purple, took the center position. The handsome and outspoken Gaylord Cougar sat to the tribal chief's left in a robe of gold, and Lucretia Lizard and Orville Bat, wearing robes of green and deep red, finished the semicircle.

Two white candles in silver candlesticks and a large handwritten booklet had been placed on an old oak table in the center of the circle. Billy recognized the candlesticks from the Sacred Chamber located behind the lodge's main room.

At two o'clock in the afternoon, Lucinda Vulture entered from the back of the room. She was dressed in a black robe and carried a large lighted candle in an equally large wooden candleholder. She carefully lit the candles on the table and placed the one she was holding in the center. With great deliberation she read several passages from the old book that dealt with the crossing of the sun into the autumn months, the coming of shorter days, and a special time for grave reflection. After she finished she took her seat, and Orville Bat continued the process. He was followed by Lucretia Lizard, who hissed out the final traditional readings.

During the ceremony Billy noticed that a small number of local inhabitants had congregated to witness the event. The gathering was considerably short of the throngs that he remembered during the summer solstice. After the official opening was concluded, the room was cleared of everyone except the council and Arthur Elk, who stood guard in the doorway like a giant warrior in his dark blue shirt and trousers held up by suspenders. Maurice grinned as the dog questioned him about the audience.

"Where was the crowd? I expected to see a lot of your citizens here!"

"They're never as interested in the fall. Wait until the

winter solstice when this place is decorated in greenery and the old songs are sung. This lodge will be packed," answered the rabbit good-naturedly. "I'm afraid it's business as usual for now."

"What book were Lucinda and the others reading from?" asked Billy, trying to understand the meaning behind the ritual.

"That's our copy of *The Vulture's Appendix*. It's the only part of *The Great Book of Rules* we use. It's the backbone of our code," explained the painter.

The first session of the Tribal Council lasted most of the afternoon. Many disputes from the previous three months were heard, debated, and decided, and from time to time, Omar Mountain Goat asked Billy for his input.

On the twenty-third of September, the routine was almost the same as the first day, and by the fourth day Billy felt quite comfortable as an invited judge. Even Gaylord Cougar decided to befriend him. After the final day's agenda, the dog, the rabbit, and the mountain lion spent quite a bit of time together over supper at the local tavern, laughing and reminiscing about the races during the Grand Fair—especially the Overland Race.

"I'll never forget the expression on Lester Coyote's face when he looked over and saw Maurice and me passing him by. He was so busy trying to force you off the trail that he completely ignored us!" howled the cougar, slapping the shepherd dog on the back. "It was worth the whole struggle."

"Did they ever find out who Wiley Weasel and Rattlesnake Pete were workin' for when they laid those two traps for you and Victor during the Great Medley?" inquired Maurice.

"We had a pretty good idea that it was Rodney Wild Deer and his coyote buddies, but we never pursued it," returned Billy, "especially since we won the race. I think Georgie was the hero though. The way he caught up to Johnny Otter was nothing short of a miracle!"

"Well, you didn't do so badly yourself after you were tripped," added Maurice. "That was no small feat!"

Billy glanced around the tavern's log walls and rough-hewn tables and chairs and thought about how much he enjoyed the camaraderie of the rabbit, the cougar, and many of the other free-spirited citizens of the Hill Country. Even Arnold Big Horn's brothers took time to come over and sit with them awhile.

"You should come up and live with us?" stated Gaylord, suddenly. "You need to get away from those stodgy Prairie creatures and all their rules!"

Billy was pensive for a moment. "Maybe this would be a better place, especially with Fabian and his bunch taking over," he thought to himself. "Then again, I'd have to leave Georgie Beaver and Winston Wise Owl and of course, the two rascals, Nosey Coon and Needles Porcupine. I don't know…. And as for Victor Running Deer, well, he spends most of his time with Melinda now. And I don't think she cares for me…or Georgie, for that matter."

After Billy, Maurice, and Gaylord returned later that evening for the final ceremony, Omar Mountain Goat approached the dog while he was putting on his blue robe.

"Lucinda told me about your visions on the day of the Prairie's elections and their possible repercussions. Tomorrow we're having a special session with Winston Wise Owl and Thaddeus P. Turtle concerning the distressing turn of events in the Prairie. Before that happens, Lucinda wondered if you would consider going back to my home after the ceremony. There's something we'd like to show you." Omar hesitated and then stared straight into Billy's eyes. "And we have a specific task for you if you're willing to undertake it. There's some danger involved but we can take precautions. We're hoping it will clarify these visions. Maurice can be there too if you like."

Billy stared back at Omar with some anxiety. He could tell from the old goat's tone of voice that the proposal was of a serious nature and that it would call for a sacrifice on his part. The dog suddenly realized that he had allowed himself to be lulled into a comfortable space. He now knew that he could not escape his concerns about Brother Fabian or his friend Victor Running Deer by moving to the Hill Country. He would have to face those troubles no matter where he lived. Finally, he turned to Maurice for further clarification.

"What is this, Maurice? I don't have a good feeling about it."

"Lucinda wouldn't ask you to do anything dangerous unless it benefited both our communities. Why don't you see what she wants before making a decision?" suggested the rabbit.

Billy Bones knew in his heart that Maurice Rabbit was right. After all it was Lucinda who had convinced the council members that he was a highly spiritual creature and belonged on their Tribal Council.

"Anyway, you must see Omar's cave. It's like no other inside The Enchantment," concluded the rabbit, bringing the shepherd dog back to the reality at hand.

CHAPTER ELEVEN

INSIDE THE SACRED MOUNTAIN

Later that evening Billy Bones followed Omar Mountain Goat, Lucinda Vulture, and Maurice Rabbit up to Omar's cave. The natural orifice that led into the mountain called Spirit Dwells was near the mist that made up the western border. A wall made of horizontal boards, several small windows, and an old wooden door covered the opening of the cave and created a room in front.

By the time Billy stepped inside, Omar Mountain Goat had lit several lamps so that the dog could make out a high-poster bed, a table, and several chairs. About twenty feet into the cave was a boarded-up entrance that led into the depths of the cavern. Billy observed that there was just enough room underneath the boards for an animal to crawl through. Beyond the barricade, the dog was immediately aware of a familiar density that could only mean the start of the golden mist. Lucinda wasted no time as she explained her plan.

"Billy Bones, neither Omar nor I have been able to decipher your powerful visions that you had before the Prairie elections. We think that for the welfare of our two states, further clarification is necessary. Therefore, we've devised an experiment that we hope you'll accept."

"What would you have me do?" questioned Billy with some trepidation.

"We would like you to enter into the mist at this point for a couple of hours," explained the mountain goat. "Of course, you'll have a rope tied around you at all times so you can find your way back. As you are probably aware, neither candles nor lamps work in the dense atmosphere of the mist."

After a moment of silence, Lucinda continued, "You will be inside Spirit Dwells. We know of no way out except back through this opening. Unfortunately, you must go by yourself. The channel to the spirit world is much stronger that way. If you're meant to get another message, this is the best way of finding it. Of that, I am sure."

"I was hoping I would never have to go into the mist again," declared the dog uneasily. "As you know, I've been severely criticized in the Prairie for my previous attempts."

"I know this is difficult for you," said Omar again, "but Lucinda wouldn't make such a request unless she felt it was warranted. She has great faith in your gifts."

"But what if it fails? I have no control over my dreams or my visions," admitted Billy, hanging his head. He had no desire to experience the dense fog again, especially in an unfamiliar dark cave.

"I know you'd prefer not to do this, but if anything can trigger the process, entering Spirit Dwells will," explained the old vulture empathetically. The dog did not answer. He did not want to appear cowardly, but an ominous feeling was starting to rise in him.

"We certainly don't want you to think this is a command," assured Omar, aware of the dog's discomfort. "Here in the Hill Country every creature has free will." As the goat paused for a reply, Billy looked away from him. He was suddenly ashamed of his fear.

"We understand if you're not willing to undergo this trial," consoled Lucinda in a softer tone. "I know it's a frightening experience, and I don't ask it of you lightly."

Slowly the dog turned back to them. "All right, I will do as you wish. Tell me how to go about it."

Omar picked up a long rope over by the barricade. "Tie this around your waist and also around your wrist. Do not remove it even for one second or for any reason. If you do, you could be lost forever. Once you're inside, it's confusing and you'll get turned around. Without the rope you'll find it nearly impossible to find your way back, especially in the dark. We'll secure the rope to one of the boards that covers the entrance and then to one of us. After a couple hours, we will pull on the rope for you to return."

As Billy Bones prepared for the perilous journey, Maurice offered to tie the rope around his own waist. "If you want to bail out at any time, please do so. We'll understand. And trust me, I won't let go of this end of the rope."

The shepherd dog smiled weakly at the well-intentioned rabbit but could only remember Georgie's final warning: "I still don't completely trust those Hill creatures." Billy considered backing out but after studying the faces of the three Tribal Council members, he decided to take their offer—even in this strange dreamlike scenario in the middle of the night.

Cautiously Billy Bones crept under the old boards and started walking into the cave. The pungent odor of the mist immediately filled his nostrils, and he wanted desperately to turn back. Instead, he gritted his teeth and continued on into the absolute darkness. Soon he heard again the strange singing, the fluttering sound, and the gush of wind that he had experienced the first time he entered the mist. As in his previous experience, he soon found himself turned around and walking away from the sounds until he stumbled hard into the mountain wall. He tested the rope and found it was still secure. Finally, when he felt he'd gone far enough, he sat down with his back against the cold stone and waited for the two hours to pass.

At first he tried to sense anything around him. Several times he crawled off in various directions. All he could feel was the unevenness of the ground and the cold dampness of the cave. He shivered slightly and wished he had brought his blanket with him. Finally, he worked up enough courage to stand up and start out across the open floor of the cave.

All of a sudden, the floor of the cave dropped off in front of him, and he fell down into what seemed to be a hole or pit, landing hard on his right arm. After he got back up on his feet, he stretched to his full height but could not reach the top of the cavity. He cautiously got back down on his hands and knees and inched forward until he came to another drop-off. He felt around for a stone and threw it into the extended pit. It bounced off several surfaces until it finally rested on solid ground far below him.

After studying the extent of the wall of the crevice, Billy Bones devised a plan. He pulled the rope toward him until it was taut and then used it to balance against the side of the drop-off. He wished he had tested it before he had entered the cave. He could only hope that it was strong enough to hold his weight.

Cautiously the shepherd dog pulled himself up and out of the strange pit and then began to follow the rope back toward its source. Suddenly and without warning, he felt a hand touch his as he clasped the rope. He jerked his hand violently away. "Ah…! Who's there?" he cried sharply, as another voice answered almost simultaneously.

"It's only me, Billy! Are you all right?" Happily, the dog recognized Maurice Rabbit's voice.

"Yes, yes, I'm all right!" panted the dog, "but be careful! There's a whale of a drop-off just behind me!"

"But the rope—you gave it such a yank. I thought I'd better come in after you."

"That's because I fell down a hole of some sort and had to pull myself out."

"Do you want to come back with me?" asked the rabbit, still clutching the rope.

"Are the two hours up yet?" returned Billy.

"No, you've been here only about forty-five minutes."

"Well, then go back and tell them what happened. I'm going to return to the wall and finish this thing," said the shepherd, "but be careful; it's real easy to get lost in here!"

As Billy Bones felt the rabbit move back along the rope, a new feeling of loneliness swept over him. He wished, at least for the moment, he had not been so foolhardy in his effort to finish his assignment. Slowly he continued to shuffle over to the wall of the cavern, making sure the ground under him was always solid.

Just as he got to the wall, he was again mysteriously cognizant of another presence close to him. "Maurice, is that you?" He stretched out his hand hoping to touch his friend but found nothing. Again he groped the darkness around him but still felt nothing. Suddenly a cold wisp of air passed in front of him. He grabbed after it and almost lost his footing. He wished he could see something, but the darkness inside the mountain was absolute.

After several more feeble attempts, the dog finally gave up and slid down the damp wall onto the ground. For a while he remained alert but eventually lost his concentration and dropped off to sleep.

After what seemed like only moments, Billy was again strangely aware of something moving toward him. This time however, it did not frighten him. Miraculously the small creature seemed to slide out of the darkness and stop only a few feet in front of him. He was amazed that he was able to see the thing when all about him was pitch black. After careful examination he realized that the animal was a mink dressed conservatively in a dark suit, vest, white shirt, and black tie with a large emerald tiepin.

"Who are you and what are you doing in here?"

inquired the dog sluggishly.

The well-dressed mink looked at him sadly for a moment and then shook his head. "Tell Mary that I got lost in here and never found my way out," cried the creature, as if from a great distance. "Tell her I still love her, and that I'll always be true." Slowly he started to retreat back into the darkness.

"Wait, don't leave! You can follow me out. I have a rope. Here, see…" entreated Billy, as he tried to speak clearly without slurring.

One last time the little mink moved toward the shepherd dog and wailed, "Tell her I love her and give her this so she'll know!" With those words the frantic creature grasped the emerald tiepin on his black tie and thrust it into Billy's shirt pocket.

Billy reached out after the handsomely-dressed animal but seemed unable to rise. "Wait, come back! Let me help you!"

At that instant, the young dog was jolted again by a tugging at his waist. He realized that the councilors at the other end were trying to rouse him and get him to return. He shook his head several times until he revived enough to stand. As he made his way back to the barricade, he realized that he must have been dreaming and that the mink had been part of it.

"Maurice said you fell into a hole of some sort," said Omar Mountain Goat, as he and the rabbit untied Billy's ropes. "I'm sorry. I guess no one has ever wandered that far away. I hope you didn't hurt yourself."

"No, I think I'm fine," said the dog, still a little drowsy from his short sleep, "just a sore arm but nothing serious."

Lucinda Vulture suddenly stood before him again and stretched out a crooked finger at Billy. "What did you see? Something happened to you, I know. I could feel it in my bones."

"No, I'm afraid I failed. I don't think I saw anything that will help our two states," sighed the shepherd, shaking his head.

" Think again! You did see something, I felt it," snapped Lucinda with much authority. "Answer me! What did you see?"

Billy stared vacantly into the old vulture's eyes and then related his dream to her as accurately as he could. When he finished, he made a final addition. "Also, before I fell asleep, I thought I felt someone pass close to me. I reached out a number of times but found no one."

Lucinda finally turned away from Billy and talked hastily to Omar. "So that's what happened to Ernest McMink. He got lost in the mist inside this cavern."

"I wonder what Ernest was doing there?" questioned the mountain goat. "Of course, he always did like to explore."

Lucinda faced Billy once again. "Be sure and tell Mary exactly what Ernest told you. Don't leave anything out!"

"But will she believe me?" asked the dog with great concern.

"Probably not, but you'll have tried," assured Lucinda, as she put the black hood of her robe over her head. "Well, at least we found out something. If anything more comes to you, let us know before tomorrow's conference with Winston and Thaddeus."

After Lucinda Vulture made her quick exit, Maurice took Billy back to his dugout in the mountain so they could get some much-needed sleep. It was important for both of them to be fresh for tomorrow's special session.

CHAPTER TWELVE

THE SPECIAL SESSION

When Maurice Rabbit and Billy Bones finally got back to the rabbit's dwelling, it was in the wee hours of the morning on the twenty-sixth of September. Both animals were so exhausted that they fell headlong onto their mattresses. It was at that moment that Billy felt something prick his chest. He quickly turned over, reached inside his shirt pocket, and pulled out a green pin of sorts. Instantly he sat up and observed the strange object more closely.

"Maurice, come here! I don't believe it! Look at this!" Billy handed the expensive-looking jewel up to his friend.

"What do you think it is?" asked Maurice, turning it over in his hand.

"It's a tiepin! It looks just like the one Ernest McMink put in my pocket during my dream," determined the dog, "the one he was wearing on his tie…but how?"

"Maybe it was more than a dream after all," surmised the rabbit.

"Well, there's one animal who will know for sure," decided Billy again, "and that's Mary McMink herself."

Maurice gave Billy a small pouch to carry the pin in, and the dog put it in the pocket of his trousers. Although both animals were excited by the discovery, their lack of sleep soon caught up with them, and both fell into a deep slumber.

Shortly before dawn Maurice was awakened by shouting. When he looked over at Billy's mattress, he realized that the dog was crying out in his sleep. The rabbit quickly jumped out of his bed and crossed over to the disturbed animal.

"Billy, Billy, wake up! You're havin' a bad dream!" he yelled, as he shook the dog by his shoulders. The canine sat up with a jolt, almost hitting the good rodent's head.

"What…what's the matter?" asked the dog, still somewhat dazed.

"You've been shouting in your sleep. I think maybe you were having a nightmare," determined Maurice, as he sat back on the floor. "Do you recall anything at all?"

"Yes, yes, I remember now. I think I was havin' the dream that Lucinda hoped I would have inside the mountain," admitted Billy. "It was about Brother Fabian Lynx and the human artifacts."

"Well, for now you'd better get some more sleep. I'll wake you up about nine. We'll go to the meeting early so you can tell Lucinda about your dream and the tiepin before the others get there," decided Maurice, trying to form the best plan of action.

Lucinda Vulture was pacing back and forth in the main room of the lodge when Billy Bones and Maurice Rabbit arrived. "I've been waiting for you for over an hour! Why didn't you come to me sooner?"

Maurice, who was used to Lucinda's temperamental outbursts, smiled and approached her immediately. "I thought Billy should get as much rest as possible so he'd have a clear head for today's session."

"I want you to know that I've been awake since before dawn when I first felt Mr. Bones' distress!" complained Lucinda, venting most of her anxiety on the rabbit. "So, Billy Bones, you've finally had the vision we hoped for. Tell me, what did you see?"

For the next few minutes, Billy related his dream to the old vulture and the rabbit. Lucinda had him repeat certain sections over until she seemed satisfied that every detail was absolutely clear in the young shepherd's mind.

"Well, that's certainly an ill wind off the mountain! I want you to relate that dream as precisely as possible for the Tribal Council and for Winston Wise Owl and Thaddeus P. Turtle. I want them to be positively convinced about the immediate dangers facing both our communities," Lucinda insisted.

"We have one more thing to show you, madam," smiled the jovial rabbit. "Billy, where's the pouch? Show Lucinda what you found when we got back from the cave this morning."

Cautiously the young shepherd took the jeweled pin out of the pouch and handed it to the vulture. "What...? Why, it's a tiepin! Mr. Bones, where did you find this?"

"In my shirt pocket. I felt it stick me when I tried to lie

down. It's the same one that the mink tried to give me in my dream. I'm sure of it. I don't know how…but…" The young dog was unable to continue. He was convinced in his own mind, but reason told him that it was impossible for a dead animal to pass on such a thing.

"You're thinking that such an action is beyond the realm of possibility, is that it? Well, it is possible when the spirit's caught on this earthly plain and is unable to continue its quest. It's just one more proof that your visions are authentic. You must show this to the council and Winston and Thaddeus at the end of today's meeting," stated Lucinda, whose feelings for the dog had again mellowed. "And think what it will do for Mary McMink. It might even save her in the end."

The special session of the Tribal Council did not convene until almost eleven o'clock in the morning. The members of the council knew that Thaddeus P. Turtle, the spiritual counselor of the Old Meetinghouse, would find the journey to Echo Canyon slow and laborious, especially the ascent from the plateau into the Hill Country. Therefore, they waited patiently. Winston Wise Owl, of course, flew in and reached the sacred lodge in a matter of minutes.

Billy Bones took his seat between Maurice Rabbit and Lucinda Vulture and thought, "It's interesting that the Tribal Council trusts Counselor Turtle and Mr. Wise Owl more than the outgoing mayor and the moderate members of the Prairie's City Council. It must be that there's a spiritual connection. Anyway, the choice seems obvious to them."

Chairs for Winston and Thaddeus had been placed between Maurice Rabbit and Orville Bat so that the circle of confidence was complete. The good turtle wore only a white stole around his neck because of the thickness of his shell. After Omar Mountain Goat made some introductory remarks, he turned directly to the issues in question.

"As you know, this special session has been called because of the results of the election in the Prairie at the end of the Grand Fair. We heard certain arguments set forth by the strict constructionists during their debates, and comments made by their spiritual leader, Brother Fabian Lynx. We are especially concerned about the fate of their human artifacts. Brother Fabian has consistently spoken of the evils inherent in these objects and has suggested they be confiscated and ultimately destroyed. Since our code and *The Vulture's Appendix* upon which it is based warn of disaster if this should happen, we are naturally concerned."

"*The Vulture's Appendix* is only one of the supplements of *The Great Book of Rules*," interrupted Thaddeus politely. "The other appendixes and *The Great Book* itself do not prophecy such catastrophic events."

"We hold no credence in the rest of your *Great Book of Rules*," hissed Lucretia Lizard. "Only *The Vulture's Appendix* is relevant to our way of life."

"Nevertheless Lucretia, in order to convince the sitting City Council, I'm afraid we must come up with evidence outside that single appendix," continued the terrapin.

"Then how about using your own Billy Bones? You've seen proof of his prophetic visions," declared Lucinda, rising from her chair. "Remember that he told you the name of the grandson who left Winston's books in the hollow of the great tree at Land's End. He also knew the name of his grandfather and the pioneer who took him away. Remember his dream of the Ancient Ones and the wind blowing away their children after the destruction of the human artifacts found along the wagon trail. Some of those first offspring are still alive today!"

Billy recalled that the 'Ancient Ones' were what they called the original animals who were transformed when the Great Rift occurred.

"Still, it'll be hard to convince even the moderate councilors at City Hall," replied Winston. "Members of the Old Meetinghouse have been taught to use only reason in making their decisions. To them dreams, prophecies, and ghosts are matters of a fantasy world."

"Then you must persuade them to put aside their prejudice this time," warned Lucinda, "and get them to act before they turn over their power to the strict constructionists!"

"It's not that we disagree with you, Lucinda," said the wise owl. "At present we're trying our best to persuade Mary McMink to keep her furniture intact. We've even asked for assistance from Sarah Mourning Dove. However, Brother Fabian has already had a powerful influence on Mary, and it may be too late to gain her allegiance."

"Then you must think of another way to solve the problem!" snapped Orville Bat. "This is not a time for reason but for action. If a calamity does occur, it'll be too late to go back and change things!"

The august body sat quietly for a few moments considering the bat's last remarks. Billy was especially intrigued. From his conversations with Maurice, he knew that Orville was considered to have prophetic powers of his own, especially when it came to the darker side of things. Finally, Lucinda Vulture rose again and turned to Billy Bones. "I think it is now time that we hear from our newest councilor. He's had another dream of great importance after visiting inside the sacred mountain we call Spirit Dwells. I asked him to share his dream with you. Mr. Bones, stand before us and tell us what you saw."

It was nerve-racking for Billy, but he tried to relate his story as simply and directly as possible without any embellishments.

"I remember in my dream that I was standing in front of Mary McMink's old stone house. All the furniture that we'd saved from the flood was for some reason sitting out in the front yard. I soon discovered that Brother Fabian Lynx and a group he called his 'lieutenants' were responsible for carrying them there. Brother Fabian had this long, sort of wand-like stick in his hand, and he began waving it in the direction of the old human pieces."

"A wand!" interrupted Gaylord Cougar. "Come on, Billy, how are we supposed to take you seriously? That sounds like wizardry."

"Hush, Gaylord!" Orville squealed, turning to the handsome cougar. "Prophetic dreams are often symbolic.

Let Mr. Bones finish his story."

"Yes, what happened then?" queried Omar.

Billy was taken aback by Gaylord's interruption. He glanced over at his newfound friend. The cougar seemed more puzzled than disturbed. The dog finally continued. "Well, amazingly enough, the furniture started to rise and circle like…like…well, like smoke rising out of a chimney. Finally, it flew through a hole in the sky that took it up and out of our little universe. I remember yelling for them to stop, but Brother Fabian's helpers held me back as they laughed and pointed toward the heavens. It's strange, but I turned at that moment and saw Mary standing in her doorway. She was sobbing uncontrollably and…and she was still wearing the disheveled nightcap and gown that she had on during the flood."

"You mean the flood you were telling Maurice and me about?" interrupted Gaylord again, deciding to be more helpful.

"Yes, Gaylord," answered Billy, "the one we had earlier this month."

"And then what happened, Mr. Bones?" asked the mountain goat patiently.

"So, after finishing with Mary's stuff, the group moved to the mayor's castle. Brother Fabian and his crew seemed to take pleasure in removing the mayor's tapestry from the wall and his Oriental rug off the entry floor, while members of the community just stood around and stared as if they were hypnotized. Seeing these treasures floating up into the sky was like watching flying carpets in one of those human fairy tales that Mr. Wise Owl is so fond of."

"Flying carpets? Now, Billy, really!" broke in Gaylord a third time.

"Mr. Cougar, will you be quiet? Orville has already explained that to you! How many times does it take?" screeched Lucinda. "Please, Mr. Bones, what happened after that?"

The shepherd dog found himself a little shaken by the cougar's interjections but gathered his wits about him and continued. "Well, finally Fabian and his lieutenants came to my cottage. I knew they were after the old corner cupboard that had belonged to Alvin Muskrat's grandmother. Alvin and Georgie Beaver and I tried to save the cupboard, but Brother Fabian's wand was too strong, and we couldn't hold the old thing down. In fact, it started pulling me up with it. When Georgie tried to interfere, he too was lifted off the ground. After that several other animals tried to help, but each in turn was taken up until there was a whole chain of us hanging from the old cupboard. I remember Cornelius Van Mink's granddaughter, Priscilla, in partic-ular. She was letting out blood-curdling screams as she hung on to Georgie's webbed feet. When I finally worked up the courage to look down, I noticed that a storm was gathering…and families were crying out for their loved ones…and reaching up towards us…but it was no use. They couldn't stop us!"

The young dog halted momentarily and gazed around the circle. All eyes were on him as if his last narrative had mesmerized everyone, even Gaylord and Thaddeus, the two skeptics in the circle. He also noticed that he had allowed his voice to rise to an emotional pitch. After a brief pause he was able to calm himself and finish his story. "Fortunately I was awakened at that moment by Maurice, who was shaking my shoulders."

"What should we make of all this?" asked the turtle after a few moments of silence. "The objections that Mr. Cougar raised will certainly be brought up again by the City Council. I'm afraid it will only sound like a frenzied dream to them."

"From someone else maybe," agreed Lucinda, "but from Billy they might take heed. They all know that he survived inside the mist, and it's up to you to tell them about his other visions. This foreboding omen of some sort of disaster cannot be ignored."

"But another sign from Billy that he really does have these spiritual powers would be helpful," implored Thaddeus, still trying to play the devil's advocate.

"Wait! He has one more experience to relate to you," stated Lucinda firmly, "something that he saw and felt inside the goat's cave where the great mist starts. Listen closely to what he discovered and the undeniable proof that was given to him."

As Billy told the incredible story of Ernest McMink, he captured the imagination of the entire group. Everyone had heard the story of Ernest's disappearance, and they were also aware of the lonely exile that Mary had forced upon herself. After they were shown the tiepin with the dark green emerald, every animal was convinced that the ghost of Mary's husband was indeed wandering inside Omar's cave, especially when Orville Bat took the tiepin and held it in his thin, black hand. "Mr. Bones is right! I can feel Ernest McMink's vibrations on this tiepin. But don't take my word. Show it to Mary. She'll know if it belongs to Ernest!"

At the end of the session the two parties agreed to keep in constant contact with one another, and Winston and Thaddeus were to do everything in their power to keep the human treasures out of the hands of Brother Fabian and his councilors, especially those belonging to Mary McMink. Billy Bones, for his part, made a secret pact with Maurice and Lucinda to find a way to move Granny Muskrat's cupboard out of harm's way as soon as possible.

When Billy finally stepped outside the sacred lodge, Gaylord was waiting for him. The big cat put a large paw-like hand on the dog's shoulder. "I didn't mean to doubt you, Billy. But you must admit…that was a pretty wild dream. However, if Lucinda and Orville believe it's prophetic, I'll go along with it. After all, they know about such things. It's just that I tend to be a doubter…nothing personal."

As Billy said goodbye to the cougar, he understood the misgivings in the cat's eyes. "Why am I having these dreams anyway?" he thought to himself. "They seem preposterous even to me! I've got to get back to my cottage and work all this out somehow. But first I've got to see Georgie Beaver and his dad about my corner cupboard!"

CHAPTER THIRTEEN

RETURN TO THE PRAIRIE

For his return to the Prairie, Billy Bones decided to go the northern route along Winding Walk. It was still only early afternoon, and he wanted to follow the path that led between the huge pine trees. Their great size and wonderfully scented needles let him lose his problems momentarily and forget the pressures of the previous five days at the Tribal Council. Along with the sense of freedom from stress, a sweet nostalgia came over him.

Following a sudden whim, the dog veered off the path and ran helter-skelter up into the thick pine trees until he found a small open space. Noticing that the ground was covered with a soft bed of pine needles, he decided to lie down on his back so that he could gaze up at the sky through the thick branches of the surrounding trees. He let his mind wander back to Billy Stuart and the many happy adventures he had enjoyed with him in that very grove.

In this contented state, the shepherd dog recalled how he had worshiped the boy almost like a god in the other world. Even now, his love for Billy Stuart was surprisingly unconditional and absolute. As a light breeze swept through the pine trees and caressed the hairs around his muzzle and on the crown of his head, it gradually dawned on him that if the two of them were together inside The Enchantment, he would be the older, more mature creature. It amazed him how the old memories had treated his approximate age in canine years. To the animals that inhabited the Prairie and the Hill Country he was considered a young adult, but Billy Stuart was still considered a young boy.

After indulging himself for the better part of an hour, Billy finally returned to the path. He wanted to stop by Georgie Beaver's home on the beaver pond by late afternoon. He hoped to discuss a plan with the young beaver and his father, which he had formulated with Maurice Rabbit and Lucinda Vulture before leaving the sacred lodge in Echo Canyon.

When the shepherd dog reached Beaver Dam Road, he knelt down and gazed between the trees. Nestled on the far side of the pond was Justin Beaver's little beam house with its white-washed mud and stick siding glistening on the water. The trees surrounding the pond were thick gnarled giants whose rich canopies reached hungrily toward the heavens, almost every one a home for one or more woodland creatures. On an island in the center of the pond was an even more resplendent sight, Mayor George P. Beaver's house, whose castle-like towers and white-washed siding sparkled brightly in the afternoon sun.

By the time Billy Bones reached the beaver dam, Georgie Beaver was already taking his daily swim. The beaver saw him coming and waved from the middle of the pond. "Come on in! The water's great!"

The sight of the happy rodent and the desire for a cool dip after his long walk prompted the shepherd dog to immediately throw off his clothes and dive into the water.

"It's a lot easier diving off the dam than trying to enter through that underwater passage of yours. At least, I don't have to worry about half drowning myself!" laughed Billy, as he splashed the unsuspecting beaver.

"You never were any good at duckin' that big head of yours under water. It's amazing to me how hard it is for you," chuckled Georgie, avoiding the spray.

"Well, not everyone is part duck," returned the young dog, glancing around the pond. "By the way, do you ever run into Johnny Otter? Maybe it's about time the two of you made up."

"After what he tried to do to me during the Great Medley…I hardly think so!" responded Georgie, his demeanor changing slightly.

At that instant the otter's head popped out of the water between the two friends. "That wasn't my idea! I had nothin' to do with that net."

"Then why did you trip it?" inquired Georgie, who was slightly taken aback by Johnny's sudden appearance. "And don't tell me you didn't. There was no one else around!"

The otter looked up and away from the beaver and was silent for a moment. When he spoke, he stared more in the direction of the dog than the beaver. "Because I panicked," he said softly. He looked back at Georgie. "Rodney Wild Deer and Lester Coyote told me about the net, but I wasn't plannin' to use it, honestly. It's just that I was gettin' winded and didn't know what else to do." He lowered his head slightly. "I'm sorry."

Georgie also looked away from the otter who had teased him so relentlessly all of his life. "Well, alright. I'm glad you told me the truth anyway."

As Johnny Otter started to back away, Billy quickly intervened. He did not want the moment to pass without some resolution.

"Wait, Johnny, don't leave yet!" the dog called out.

The otter was stayed by the shepherd's urgency. "What do you want, Billy? Ain't I said enough?"

"I just wanted to say that it took a lot of guts for you to do what you just did," declared Billy sincerely, "and I think a handshake is in order. What do you say?"

"OK by me," said the otter, looking over at Georgie.

"Well, OK," agreed the beaver hesitantly.

The two swimmers cautiously approached each other and shook hands. Afterwards Johnny backed off again. "But this don't mean I'm gonna let you win again, Chubby. So put that notion out of your mind!" grinned the otter, as he splashed the surprised beaver, dived under water, and swam quickly out of sight.

"Well I'll be darned! I let him do it to me again," sputtered Georgie, looking over to the shepherd. "And it's all your fault!"

"Yep, I certainly hope so," laughed Billy. "At least things are back to normal. You wouldn't want to go around hating him forever, would you?"

"No, I guess not," admitted Georgie with a toothy grin.

"Now come on back to the house. I'm sure Mom will want you to stay for supper."

Later that evening Billy Bones told Justin and Gladys Beaver about the mysterious events surrounding Omar's cave and the concerns that the Tribal Council and Winston Wise Owl and Thaddeus P. Turtle expressed in their special session.

Justin and Gladys's house consisted of one large room with a stone fireplace and a small room on the west side where Georgie slept and where the passageway under the water was located. Because of his profession, Justin wore a brown carpenter's apron over his collarless shirt and pants held up by suspenders. Gladys wore a large white apron over a long patterned dress and a dust cap on her head.

"I've a great favor to ask of you both," said Billy to Georgie and Justin after Gladys excused herself to putter around the pantry. "I'd like to duplicate Granny Muskrat's cupboard as close as possible. Mr. Beaver, what do you think? Is it feasible?"

"Well, you can make something that looks almost like it. You can't come up with the same wood and the patina and wear of an old antique come only through aging."

"But can you reproduce it close enough that a novice wouldn't know the difference? I mean, if he didn't inspect it too carefully?" questioned Billy with an air of mystery.

"Perhaps, but why would you want to do such a thing?" inquired Justin.

"Lucinda Vulture and Omar Mountain Goat are concerned that Brother Fabian might confiscate the human artifacts in January. They think my corner cupboard is especially vulnerable since it belonged to Granny Muskrat, a member of the New Meetinghouse. Perhaps if you just showed Georgie and me how to build a duplicate, we could take it from there."

"I'm afraid neither of you has the experience for such fine work," said Justin, shaking his head. "No, I'm going to have to work closely with you on this one."

"Then you'll help? I'm afraid it's going to have to be done as soon as possible. I have to smuggle the real one into the Hill Country before anyone is the wiser," confessed the dog, fully trusting the two beavers.

"Of course we'll help!" said Georgie emphatically. "I can start tomorrow if you like."

"In the morning the two of you can look through the available wood I have and find something close to the same color and grain," proposed the older beaver. "I suggest that no one else should know about this. Word travels fast in this little town!"

"That means I'll have to keep Nosey and Needles away for a while," declared Billy, nodding his head, "and that won't be easy. I'll have to pretend I'm mad at them for something."

After plans were more fully formed, Billy took leave of the loyal beavers.

"Are you sure you wouldn't like to spend the night?" invited Gladys. "We still have the hammocks hanging in the picnic area."

"No thanks," said the dog gratefully. "Nosey and Needles have been staying at my place, and there's no tellin' what it looks like. I better get home!"

CHAPTER FOURTEEN

THE COTTAGE IN SHAMBLES

It was quite dark by the time Billy Bones arrived back at his cottage. Before he went inside, he peeked through the open window by the Dutch door. Nosey Coon was sitting cross-legged on the table eating an apple, and Needles Porcupine was lying on the floor munching on a piece of bread covered with honey that was dripping down his face. Like Nosey, Needles wore pants that had been patched a number of times, but he wore no shirt over his prickly chest.

Billy could see at a glance that the room was in shambles. "Do you mind telling me what's going on here?" he hollered through the opening. "I thought I told you to keep this place tidy!"

There was a sudden scurrying inside as the raccoon fell off the table and the porcupine tipped over the honey pot resting beside him on the floor.

"In the name of The Great Spirit, slow down! You're just making things worse!" shouted the dog as he entered the room. He noticed that the candle on the table and the one on the floor where Needles had been lying were nearly used up. "Hold on! You'll burn the place down!" Billy picked up the small piece of candle on the floor and put it on the table. After that, he looked slowly around the room. Needle's nose was sticking out from under his blanket next to the old corner cupboard, and Nosey's masked face was poking through the rungs of the ladder that led up to the loft above the dog's bunk. "Well, come out, for heaven's sake. I'm not going to hurt you!"

"We didn't expect ya' back 'til tomorrow," said Needles shyly, uncovering his head. "Nosey said that if you wasn't home by dark, it'd be at least another day!"

"Well, you tell Nosey for me that I need this place cleaned up right now," scolded Billy, "and get some water to wash up that honey. It's dripping all over the floor!"

Slowly Nosey came out from behind the ladder and started sweeping the area in front of the hutch cupboard. "And what's this business of sitting on top of the table? When you're in this house, you sit at the table!" said the dog more sternly. He knew that if he was going to be successful in keeping the raccoon and porcupine away for two weeks, he would have to come up with some pretty harsh criticism.

"Sorry," pouted Nosey quietly. "You don't have to get so mad! After all, we was keepin' the place safe."

"Looks to me like you were wrecking it at the same time. Now let's get to work!" yelled Billy, continuing his tirade.

After about a half hour of careless attempts, the dog took the broom from the unhappy raccoon. "It's not that I don't appreciate your staying here, but I can't have you tearing the place down. Now I want you two out of here tonight, and I don't want to see you for another two weeks. Is that understood?"

"Two weeks! But how about Sunday night at our usual time?" complained Nosey. "That's not fair!"

"Two weeks!" repeated Billy, as determined as he could be. "And one other thing: I'll come get you when the time's ready. I don't want you peekin' through the windows. Now off with you!"

When the two little creatures started to shuffle out, they seemed quite crestfallen. Billy could see by their demeanor that they did not believe he would be so cross with them. They glanced back several times, but the dog did not swerve from his purpose. After they were gone, Billy felt strangely guilty. He knew that he needed to keep the two scamps away while he was working on the new cupboard, but he wished he could have been more open and honest about his plan. After all, they were completely loyal to him. Perhaps he had made a mistake. Perhaps he should have taken them into his confidence.

CHAPTER FIFTEEN

THE UNEXPECTED VISITOR

Before he went to bed, Billy Bones swept the floor again and dusted off the table and hutch cupboard. He noticed that his bed had not been slept in, and he was thankful for that. To his dismay, the blanket on the top mattress was half off the rafter, and crumbs were all over the quilt that covered the mattress. He took both covers off and shook them outside. The mattress was then re-covered and the blanket folded neatly and placed at the foot of the top bunk. Lastly, he cleaned the remaining wax out of the candlesticks and inserted fresh candles.

Billy was just about ready to blow out the candle by his bed when he heard a soft rapping at the door. He froze for a moment and waited. In a few moments it sounded again. Cautiously he picked up the candle and crossed to the door.

"I bet it's those two imps back to stay the night," he muttered to himself. "I'll just have to be firmer with them!" He carelessly threw the top door open expecting to chastise the two little animals. Instead to his surprise, Lenny Coyote was leaning against the door frame, obviously hurt and in quite a bit of pain.

"Lenny, for heaven's sake, let me help you! What in the world happened to you?"

"I'm sorry, Billy, I don't mean to bother you. It's just that I don't know where else to go," uttered the coyote with some difficulty.

"You're not botherin' me at all. Sit down at the table and let me look at those wounds." Billy reached quickly for the other candle, lit it, and placed both lights on the pine table.

"In the name of all that's holy, look at you! Your face and shoulders are a mess!" exclaimed the shepherd dog, as he got a basin of water and a cloth. "Here, let me clean out those wounds before they get infected."

The young coyote was silent throughout most of the process and only winced from time to time as the dog bathed his injuries.

"Do you want to tell me about it? Did your brothers do this?" Billy asked in a steady voice, as he gave the coyote a drink of water. Billy remembered how Lenny's older brothers, Leon, Lester, and Leroy Coyote, had tried to sabotage Billy during the Overland Race at the time of the Grand Fair and how Lenny had lifted him back up and encouraged him to continue with the race.

"I ain't goin' back there! Not while they're still around, 'specially after they visited that deer in the jailhouse!" gritted Lenny between his teeth, as he finished gulping down the last of the water.

"Who's that? You mean Rodney Wild Deer?" inquired Billy, even more concerned.

"He's a bad one! I never thought he'd get my brothers to turn on me like that!"

"Here, let me make you some tea. I've been away for a couple of days, but I think I can find somethin' to eat," offered the shepherd, after he finished cleaning the coyote's cuts and abrasions.

"Please, don't go to no more trouble. If I could just lie down for a bit, I think I'll be all right," said Lenny, getting up and crossing to the ladder.

"No, not up there. Take my bed," commanded the dog, as he helped the coyote lie down. "Now let me see if I can find something to eat."

The worried dog went back to the cupboard and found an apple and a couple slices of bread. He cut up the fruit, put jam on the bread, and returned to the coyote's bedside, but Lenny had already fallen asleep. He quietly placed the food back on the table and covered it with a cloth. When he returned, he pulled up the blanket from the foot of the bed and covered the coyote as carefully as he could.

The next morning when Georgie Beaver arrived to examine the wood on the corner cupboard, Billy explained what happened the night before. After deciding to wait a couple days before starting to build, Georgie returned to the pond to start looking through his father's woodpile. Lenny slept until almost noon. Before he finally awoke, Billy had brewed some tea, and Georgie had returned with a pot of soup that his mother had made.

"I guess I must've put on quite a show last night," said the young coyote, as he tried to stretch out his stiff arms and shoulders. "I'm really sorry. I didn't mean to barge in on you like that. I just didn't know where else to go. I'll see if the boardinghouse will take me in."

"No, you're not going anywhere," said Billy, smiling as he placed the soup on the table. "You're going to stay right here until your wounds are better, and then we'll decide what to do."

"But I can't just…" Lenny started to protest again.

"Nonsense! It's the least I can do. After all, I'm the reason your brothers are so angry with you. Now eat your soup. It's all settled," stated the dog firmly.

For the rest of that day and most of the next, Lenny Coyote recuperated in the home of Billy Bones. The shepherd dog decided to bandage the deep gashes on the coyote's left shoulder and around his forehead. When Lenny's father, Calhoun Coyote, finally found him, the young coyote was sitting on a bench by the southwest side of the cottage. Billy had positioned the seat there so that the wounded animal could catch the rays of the afternoon sun.

When Lenny saw the old coyote coming up the path from the south, he lowered his head.

"Let me have a look at you, son. I've been just about everywhere trying to find you. Lester finally told me what happened," Calhoun began softly.

Gradually Lenny let his father raise his face so he could get the full effect of the beating. "Good heavens, son, why didn't you come to me right away?"

"I ain't goin' back with you, Dad. Not as long as they're there. I don't care if they are my brothers; enough is enough!" declared Lenny, as his father sat down beside him. Billy Bones heard the conversation through the south window and decided to join them. When he saw the two coyotes sitting side by side, he waited over by the corner of the house.

"I've asked your brothers to leave, at least for a while," admitted Calhoun. "Brother Fabian's decided to allow them to live in the shed next to the New Meetinghouse. They're making sort of a barracks out of it. Because they're on probation, Sheriff Lone Wolf decided to send his deputy, Bison Bob, over there to keep them in line. He's a pretty tough customer. I think he'll do a good job!"

Billy Bones suddenly jerked his head toward Lenny's father. He realized that he had in a roundabout way contributed to the making of the crew that Fabian would later use to do his dirty work. Now they were even living together in a barracks-type situation. "You say they're staying with Brother Fabian full time?" the dog questioned out loud.

Calhoun saw the dog for the first time and rose to shake his hand. "I want to thank you, Mr. Bones, for taking care of my son. I'm sorry if we inconvenienced you in any way."

"Lenny is welcome here anytime, sir," said the dog graciously.

"Well, I'll take him off your hands now, if you don't mind," stated Calhoun. "He's the only one left to help me now, and we've got a lot of work to catch up with. I'm afraid he's the only one of my sons that I can really count on." The old coyote turned back to his youngest son. "That is, if it's agreeable to him?"

Lenny Coyote sat for a moment and meditated on his father's words. Finally he nodded his head affirmatively. "All right, Dad, let's go. But I'll have to take my time. I'm still really stiff." After a couple steps, Lenny turned back to the kind shepherd. "If you should ever need me, Billy, just give me the word."

Calhoun put his arm carefully around his son's shoulders, and the two canines started the slow journey back to the chicken farm. Billy could see that there was a special love between them, and it gave him some consolation. However, his mind turned quickly back to the barracks and the making of Brother Fabian's lieutenants. He was afraid that his vision was becoming more and more a reality. "Now I've got to get back to Georgie and Justin," he thought out loud. "We've got to get that corner cupboard copied as soon as possible. I only hope that Winston Wise Owl and Thaddeus P. Turtle are deciding what to do about Mary McMink's furniture. If it gets into Brother Fabian's hands, it could be disastrous!"

CHAPTER SIXTEEN

THE COUNCIL'S DILEMMA

Procrastination was the biggest stumbling block that Winston Wise Owl and his friend Thaddeus P. Turtle seemed to be having. Even after a number of days, they had still failed to approach the outgoing City Council about the problem of Mary McMink's furniture.

Finally, to Winston's embarrassment, it was Cornelius Van Mink who brought up the subject of his sister's furniture during the October meeting of the City Council. His wife Prudence had heard that Mary was planning to hand over her Irish antiques to the New Meetinghouse. To settle the matter, Mayor George P. Beaver asked Winston, Thaddeus, and Sarah Mourning Dove to join them during the afternoon session.

"I really think I've failed," sighed Sarah as she looked around the council. Because she was no longer the spiritual leader of the New Meetinghouse, she had taken off her white bonnet and robe and replaced them with a light blue shawl and a straw bonnet. "I truly believe that Brother Fabian has persuaded Mary to give up all her Irish antiques. In fact, I strongly suspect that she's already signed them away to the New Meetinghouse."

"When…how long ago?" asked Cornelius rising to his feet. "She can't do that! That furniture goes to me if something happens to Mary! She can't just give them away to someone else!" He glared over at Mayor Beaver. "Well, can she?"

"Well, that's a difficult question. Even though you're next in line, the things have always been in her possession. I'm afraid we'll have to make a ruling."

For the next few minutes both Thaddeus and Sarah read to the council from *The Great Book of Rules* all the contradictory material they could find that either agreed or disagreed with Brother Fabian's hard line. The first reading came from *The Prairie Dog's Appendix*:

"The hoarding of articles left by human pioneers should be strictly forbidden," began the terrapin, pushing up his spectacles that rode perpetually halfway down his beak. "These items are highly dangerous and should be kept away from the general population. This is the reading that Brother Fabian Lynx is using to support his presumption."

"But here is another reference that seems to contradict that passage. It's from *The Vulture's Appendix*," countered Sarah Mourning Dove. "Furniture and other discarded items that belonged to the human animals are highly sacred and contain the strongest spirit. They should be gathered into one holy place and safeguarded for all time."

Winston Wise Owl interrupted the two readers at this point and addressed the council. "That's what the Tribal Council up in the Hill Country believes. That's why they keep their human artifacts in a special chamber inside their sacred lodge."

"Now let's try *The Mink's Appendix* and see what it has to say," continued Thaddeus. "'Artifacts found along the Old Wagon Trail are of the highest quality and must be safeguarded at all costs.'" He looked over his glasses at the City Council. "According to this reference, Mary McMink has done nothing improper by keeping the treasures passed on to her by her father."

At this point Winston intervened and enunciated the Tribal Council's concern. "*The Vulture's Appendix* also predicts that great tragedy will strike The Enchantment if something adverse happens to any of these artifacts. Therefore I believe that none of Mary's furniture should go to the New Meetinghouse. We cannot take the chance!"

"But if Mary leaves the artifacts to the New Meetinghouse, the Hill Country would have no say in the outcome!" clucked Charlie Pheasant, ruffling his feathers.

"Mr. Pheasant, you're not listening to me!" continued the owl. "The Hill Country's councilors are concerned about their citizens as well." Winston paused for a moment. He knew that he must bring up Billy's prophetic insight, but he also realized that this would put him on shaky ground with the City Council.

"And then there's the matter of the shepherd dog, Billy Bones," the owl began slowly. "Because of his survival inside the mist and the visions he witnessed there, the Tribal Council believes he's a highly spiritual animal. As some of you know, he's already had several dreams about impending disaster if any of the artifacts are confiscated.

This along with the Tribal Council's concerns should be enough to stop this foolishness!"

"Surely you're not going to have us make a ruling based on the hallucinations of a young dog who's been in The Enchantment for only four months?" scoffed Phineas T. Fox, "especially since journeys into the mist are strictly forbidden by *The Great Book of Rules.*"

Before Winston could respond, Sheriff Walter Lone Wolf, who had been guarding the outside door, burst into the entrance hall with the animal in question, Billy Bones. The wolf addressed the mayor immediately.

"I don't mean to interrupt your discussion, your honor, but Billy Bones here insists that he has news of great importance for the council."

"Well, Mr. Bones, what have you to say?" asked the beaver sternly.

"I'm sorry to disturb you, sir, but I've just come from Mary McMink's place. I wanted to show her a tiepin that belonged to her late husband. When I got there, all of her antiques were sitting out in front of her house, and three of the coyote brothers were taking her dining room table and four of her chairs away. I tried to stop them, but just then Bison Bob came out of the house. He showed me a piece of paper with Mary's signature. He said that Mary had given Brother Fabian permission to take all the pieces to the New Meetinghouse!"

"I demand a cease-and-desist order be taken to Deputy Bison Bob immediately and the rest of the furniture be brought to City Hall until this thing is resolved!" shouted

Cornelius Van Mink. "All in favor of the order say Aye!" With that instruction, Cornelius gave Wendell Red Breast and Sylvester Turtle such a vicious glare that they immediately shouted "Aye," and the order was written up and handed over to Sheriff Walter Lone Wolf.

"Now get over to Mary's house right away, sheriff, before everything's hauled away. Billy, you stay here! It seems we'll need your personal testimony on this matter!" huffed Cornelius, as he almost pushed the sheriff out of the large double doors leading from the building.

For the better part of a half hour, Billy Bones answered questions concerning his two prophetic dreams. Neither he nor Winston mentioned the two visions regarding Georgie Beaver, Patsy Prairie Dog, and Gerard Crow, since they were harder to defend. Although the moderate councilors were intrigued by the dog's premonitions, they had difficulty accepting them, as Thaddeus Turtle had earlier predicted at the special meeting with the Tribal Council. As for the two strict-constructionists, they were downright belligerent.

"These dreams are highly critical of our beloved counselor, Brother Fabian Lynx. The idea of him waving some sort of magic wand and furniture flying through a hole in the sky is just preposterous!" barked Phineas T. Fox. "It's simply nonsense!"

"These images are symbolic, Phineas," explained Winston. "But then I think you know this. You can't be so naïve!"

When the ruling concerning Mary McMink's furniture was finally made, the four councilors decided to compromise on the grounds that both Mary and Cornelius had legitimate claim to their father's antiques. The table and four chairs that Billy saw being carted away would go to the New Meetinghouse. The rest of the chairs and the highboy would go to Cornelius and Prudence Van Mink.

Billy Bones, who was waiting patiently next to Winston, jumped to his feet when he heard the decision and glared incredulously at the council. "You don't understand! You can't allow Brother Fabian Lynx to have any of the human artifacts! Don't you know that he'll seek to destroy them? He's already threatened to burn Mr. Wise Owl's books! You must reconsider! You must!"

The mayor and the five councilors were quite startled by Billy's sudden outburst. They believed that common sense had dictated their decision and that a calamity like Billy predicted would most likely not occur. They determined that Billy's warnings fell into the category of superstition, the kind of thinking that belonged only in the Hill Country.

As for Winston Wise Owl, he truly believed that there was much truth in what the young dog had envisioned, and he was quite certain that Thaddeus felt the same way. However, he also knew that prophetic utterances held little sway over the members of the City Council. Subsequently the owl rose from his chair and put a restraining hand on the dog's arm and led him from the hall.

"I'm afraid we've done all we can here, Billy. It's no use trying to convince them any further. Their minds are closed to your world of the spirit, I'm afraid. We'll have to find another approach."

"If it's not too late," whispered the dog, "if it's not too late!" As Billy stepped outside the large double doors of the City Hall that led to the outside, he suddenly stopped and turned back to his old mentor. "Perhaps there *is* something I can do, Mr. Wise Owl, and it involves our good friend, Victor Running Deer. But I can't promise he'll listen to me. I think he still believes my visions are wicked. But I've got to give it a try!"

"Would you like me to go with you, Mr. Bones?" inquired the owl.

"No, I think this is something I've got to do on my own…if I can only catch him when he's away from Melinda Doe!"

As fortune would have it, Billy caught up with Victor as the deer was trotting over to Olen Buck's lean-to, where Melinda Doe was waiting for him. He had just crossed the ford in the stream where the path changed from the East Wagon Trail to the Old Wagon Trail. "Victor, I'm glad I caught up with you. Do you have a minute?"

"Yeah, of course I've got a minute. What's up?" the deer smiled. "I don't think we've talked since the flood. Is everything all right?"

"Well, not exactly. I was on my way to Mary McMink's to tell her about something I'd found that belonged to her late husband, and I…well, I discovered that she'd given Brother Fabian permission to take her Irish furniture away.

In fact, Bison Bob and three of the Coyote Brothers have already removed her dining table and four chairs from her house. I…I hurried over to City Hall where the outgoing City Council was having its October Session. They ordered Bother Fabian to leave some of the furniture at Mary's, but allowed him to keep the table and four chairs that were already at the New Meetinghouse." The shepherd dog stopped for a second and took a deep breath. He realized he was rambling on but wanted the deer to understand what was transpiring as quickly as possible.

"I see," said Victor, turning toward Melinda's place. "Well, I guess that settles that. So what did you want to talk to me about? If she gave the artifacts of her own free will, that's not part of the pact we made with Olen."

"But you don't understand, Victor. I…well, the Hill Country's Tribal Council and I believe that it will be a disaster if Brother Fabian tries to destroy that furniture."

"Now Billy, I know you've had these dreams, but I hardly believe…."

"But if there's a chance… What I'm trying to say is… could you talk to Olen Buck and try to convince him to vote against destroying those pieces when the New City Council convenes?" Billy hesitated again. "How can I make you understand, Victor? You've got to believe that there's a good chance something terrible will happen if we don't do something!"

The young buck hung his head for a moment. Then he looked squarely into the shepherd's eyes. "I don't know how to tell you this, Billy, but you know my feelings toward humans. You also know that Olen and I are against taking their artifacts out of citizen's homes without their permission…but if they're freely given…well, that's a different story."

"Then you don't believe in the truth of my visions?"

"Well…I know they seem real to you, but I've got to be honest, Billy…I'm with Brother Fabian when it comes to the humans' artifacts and their importance, or the power they may have over us."

"But if I'm right, Victor, can you take that chance?"

"I'm sorry, Billy, I just can't help you," said the deer sadly, lowering his eyes again.

"I see…." blurted the dog, as he abruptly turned and headed up the path toward his little cottage.

CHAPTER SEVENTEEN

THE NIGHT JOURNEY

As for keeping the building of a new cupboard a secret from Nosey Coon and Needles Porcupine, Billy Bones might as well have been barking at the moon. In fact, the two rascals were spying on the shepherd dog from the edge of the bluff the next afternoon.

By the time Justin Beaver joined his son and the young dog, the two inquisitive creatures worked up the courage to start peeking in through the south window. After catching a glimpse of Nosey's bandit eyes, Billy Bones finally shook his head in a gesture of defeat and crossed to the open window.

"All right, you two, come on in here. You might as well see what's going on."

"We was worried about you!" Nosey proclaimed, as he slipped through the opening.

"We knew you couldn't really be mad at us," Needles confessed, as Billy helped pull him up over the window sill. "We thought somethin' must be really wrong!"

"Well, I'm sorry I tried to deceive you. It's just that we wanted to keep our building project a secret," the dog confessed. "You see, the fewer animals that know, the better."

"What are ya' makin' anyway?" Needles asked, as he looked at the pile of lumber on the east wall. "Are ya' buildin' a second cupboard?"

"Well, something like that." Billy looked over at Justin who smiled and shrugged his shoulders.

"You might as well tell them the whole story and swear them to secrecy," the older beaver conceded.

"It's a secret?" the raccoon inquired excitedly. "And you're gonna let us in on it?"

"We won't tell no one, honest!" the porcupine promised.

"Well, if you do, it could go badly for your friend Billy," Justin warned, eyeing them seriously, "and you wouldn't want that, would you?"

"Oh, no!" both creatures exclaimed simultaneously. "We wouldn't want that!"

Billy seated the two curious animals at the pine table and went over the entire plan with them, including the proposed undercover trip into the Hill Country with the original cupboard. Both Nosey and Needles listened with wide-eyed excitement and offered to help.

Instead of the two weeks anticipated, building the replica took more than five weeks to complete. Although the counterfeit had been carefully distressed and aged, it did not have the same warmth and feel of the original. However, to the average observer the switch would go undetected. Justin Beaver had done a remarkable job. And to Billy's amazement, the two snoopers kept their word and managed to tell no one about the fake cupboard or the planned night journey into the Hill Country.

On the evening of the exchange, Billy Bones, Georgie Beaver, Nosey Coon, Needles Porcupine, and another friend of Billy, Alvin Muskrat loaded the two halves of the old cupboard into different carts. Since the cupboard had once belonged to Alvin's grandmother, Billy felt that the muskrat should be in on its transfer to the Hill Country. As far as Victor Running Deer was concerned, Billy had not asked for his help and had avoided any contact with him whatsoever since their meeting five weeks earlier.

After spreading a piece of canvas over each section, the five amateur smugglers placed light boards over the top to make it look like they were hauling lumber. They decided to take the long way around the little community and follow the old Timber Trail to the north. This would eventually lead into Winding Walk, which in turn would take them to the Hill Country. The northern roads were less traveled, especially at night, and they were unlikely to meet any resistance.

Sandy Antelope and Arnold Big Horn had agreed to meet the early transporters at the old bridge north of town where Timber Trail and Winding Walk intersected. Billy was aware that the hardest part of the journey would be the steep ascent into the Hill Country, and he knew he would need their help. At the border, Maurice Rabbit would be waiting to escort them the rest of the way.

Shortly after dark, the five animals started out on their risky adventure. The first part of the trip was fairly uneventful. Charlie Pheasant's son hollered a greeting to them from his front porch but did not inquire about their destination. The third-quarter moon gave just enough light to keep them safely on the path, and the carts were well-greased and fairly easy to manage.

When the travelers turned north into the wooded district, the trees blocked out much of the moonlight, and the path became more difficult to follow. Gradually the quintet realized that the moon had disappeared behind a bank of clouds, and the breeze had picked up considerably.

Feeling his way along the darkened path, Billy soon became aware of one contingency he had not planned for—rain. It started with large droplets and quickly developed into heavy sheets of water. The wooden wheels of the carts began to bog down in the mud, and Billy called for his helpers to park their loads under some large trees until the worst of the storm passed.

As the companions concentrated on their task, they soon realized they were being approached by four ominous-looking creatures. Although one of these creatures carried a lantern, it was impossible to determine who they were because of the storm and the darkness of the night.

As the strangers slogged closer, Billy finally made out the features of the beast holding the light. He had one of the ugliest faces the dog had ever seen. He resembled one of the pigs the dog had seen in the outside world, only he had small tusks growing out of either side of his upper lip. The leader and his swarthy friends all wore patched trousers held up by ropes and dirty bandanas around their thick necks.

"Hello there," yelled Billy in a controlled voice. "We're sort of bogged down here, as you can see!"

"Hello yourself!" the leader grunted, as he held up his lantern so he could study Billy, Georgie, and Alvin. "What're you doin' up here in the middle of the night, and what do you have in them wagons?"

"We're carryin' some wood to a friend in the Hill Country," said Billy, trying to sound reasonable.

"But it's after dark! That seems like an odd time to me!" snorted the leader, while his motley crew shuffled about and snickered to one another.

"Well, we had moonlight until a short while ago," returned the dog. "Then we had all this rain, and our carts got stuck."

"I see. Then you'd better follow me. Our shed's a short distance from here. You can keep your stuff in there until the rain passes," ordered the homely creature, as his companions began pushing the two carts off toward the right. Billy, Georgie, and Alvin started to protest but decided to simply follow along and try to protect their carts. When Georgie looked around for Nosey and Needles, he discovered they had mysteriously disappeared.

"Why those little cowards...!" the beaver began.

"Sh!" warned Billy with a slight shake of the head. "Don't let them know there are more of us."

True to his word, the pig-like leader led them to an old shed that was large enough to shelter the two carts and all seven animals. After the wagons were safely under cover, the four tusked creatures wallowed together in the entryway, making escape from the old building impossible. As for Billy, Georgie, and Alvin, they sat up against the wheels of their carts and listened to the rain splashing against the roof. Eventually they became weary and fell asleep.

In the morning when Billy Bones awakened, he felt an uncomfortable strain on his chest and arms. He tried to rise but soon discovered that his hands had been tied securely behind him and then to the wheel of his cart. He glanced over at the beaver and the muskrat and saw that they were in a similar predicament. He twisted himself around just far enough to see that both carts were empty, but he could hear his abductors snorting and complaining just outside the shed. Through the open door, Billy could see that the rain had stopped and that an early morning sun was shining ribbons of light between the trees.

"Georgie, Alvin, wake up. I think we've been tricked!" Billy whispered. Luckily Alvin Muskrat opened his eyes immediately and was able to nudge Georgie Beaver awake with his foot.

At that moment, another voice from just behind the dog murmured, "Hey Billy, it's me, Nosey."

"Nosey, what…?" mumbled Billy in response.

"Sandy let me down through the back window. He wants me to untie you so we can all charge the pigs at the same time!" the raccoon continued with great excitement.

"Nosey, am I glad to see you," the dog whispered again, as the raccoon loosened his bonds and then crawled over to do the same for the beaver and the muskrat.

After all three animals were untied, Billy glanced back at the window and saw Sandy Antelope motioning for them to rush their hostile hosts through the open door of the shed.

Within a few seconds the freed prisoners and Nosey heard Sandy and Arnold give out high-pitched war cries as they attacked the unsuspecting wild pigs with heavy sticks they had picked up off the forest floor. Shortly thereafter, Billy, Georgie, Alvin, and Nosey fell upon their captors from the opening in the shelter.

After several sound beatings from the larger antelope and the Big Horn sheep and added reinforcements from the shed, the peccaries quickly scattered with much squealing and kicking. Fortunately, the two sections of the old antique were undamaged. Quickly the seven animals loaded them back onto the carts, camouflaged them, and started west through the woods.

"When Nosey and Needles told me you had run into the Peccary Brothers, I knew you were in for trouble," said Sandy, as they hurried through the pine trees. "They're so mean even their own parents won't let 'em come home. We've got to get out of here as soon as possible. I'm sure they won't do anything that will bring the law down on them, but it's no use takin' any chances."

Billy and his accomplices stayed off the main path until they reached the border. This made the journey more tedious because of the uneven terrain. Fortunately, there were many hands available to move the carts.

It was late morning by the time the tired animals finally arrived at the steep hill that curved up into the Hill Country. On cue, Maurice Rabbit came rushing down the path to meet them.

"I was afraid the rain would slow you down," the jolly rabbit called cheerfully. "Come on. It's not too far from here. I've got lunch waiting for us."

As soon as the corner cupboard was carefully placed in the northeast corner of Maurice's studio, the animals ate and talked happily about the perilous journey. Later, the rabbit escorted the little group around the hidden canyon and inside the main part of the lodge. Arthur Elk even showed them the cage in his shed where Billy, Georgie, and Victor Running Deer were held captive before the shepherd dog's big trial in front of the Tribal Council. By late afternoon the relieved adventurers headed back to the Prairie.

When the good friends reached Paradise Trail and before the antelope and the ram took their leave, Billy asked Sandy for one more favor. "I need to try to see Mary McMink again and return her husband's tiepin. The last time I tried, I ran into the three Coyote brothers and ended up warning the City Council about the removal of her furniture. Do you think you can arrange it for me?"

"Why don't we try on Monday morning? Mary's taken to her bed, you know, ever since Brother Fabian and his crew took her furniture. They tried to replace them with furnishings from Percival's shop, but she won't have anything to do with 'em," Sandy said sadly, shaking his head. "Sarah Mourning Dove looks in on her while I'm away. I'm afraid Mary won't see anyone except Sarah and me. But I think she'll make an exception when she finds out why you've come."

CHAPTER EIGHTEEN

ERNEST'S TIEPIN

Gloria Meadowlark was in rare voice on Monday morning. Billy enjoyed hearing the mezzo-soprano practice as he prepared himself for his meeting with Mary McMink. For the Winter Concert at the Old Meetinghouse, Gloria had been working on a medley of songs honoring the coming of light during the winter solstice. For some time, Billy Bones had been thinking of asking the songbirds to perform for the Hill Country's celebration as well. He thought it would be a wonderful way of renewing old ties between the members of the Old Meetinghouse and the citizens of the bordering state.

Billy found Gloria on her front porch and suggested the idea to her. The good lark seemed receptive to the plan and said she would pass the proposal along to her colleagues.

After leaving the meadowlark's farm, Billy traveled west along the Old Wagon Trail until he arrived at Lonesome Road. Sandy Antelope was waiting for him in front of Mary McMink's stone house.

As Billy approached Sandy, he became aware of a subtle change in his friend. The antelope seemed somehow taller and more massive.

"Billy, we're in luck! As soon as I mentioned Ernest's tiepin, Mary perked right up. She wants to see you as soon as you arrive!" yelled the young antelope hopefully.

When Sandy and Billy entered the house, the dog was shocked when he looked around the large downstairs room. The once magnificent interior had been completely transformed by the plain, rough-hewn furnishings that had been scraped together by Brother Fabian's compatriots.

Before the antelope and the dog entered the bedroom, Sandy rapped gently to let Sarah and Mary know they had arrived. The good dove had been sitting at the mink's bedside trying her best to get the old animal to take some porridge. Several pillows had been propped up behind Mary's back so she could eat and receive company.

"Mary, Billy's here! He brought the tiepin I was tellin' you about," called Sandy softly across the room.

"Bring him over," replied Mary barely above a whisper. "Let me see what he has."

As Billy approached Mary, Sarah got up from her chair and motioned for the dog to sit by the bed. Deliberately he drew the pouch out of his pants pocket and pulled out the emerald jewel. He wiped it carefully on his shirt pocket and handed it to Mary. "Watch it. The pin is still sharp."

Mary McMink was silent for a few minutes, and then tears began to roll down her cheeks. "Yes, it is his! My dear dog, wherever did you find it?"

"I first came into contact with it inside a cave. Well… actually it's a long story, but I would like to tell it to you, with your permission of course," said Billy hesitantly.

"Oh yes, oh yes, please do!" cried the old mink, clutching the newly found tiepin and pressing it lovingly to her lips.

For the next few minutes, Billy Bones recounted the whole incident. After he told Mary of Ernest's request to "tell her I love her and give her this so she'll know," she wept softly for a few moments. Finally, she turned to Billy and grasped his hand tightly.

"And you found it in your shirt pocket later that night?"

"Well, actually it was early the next morning, but yes, I lay down on it, and it pricked my skin."

"Then he didn't leave me after all, and he said he loved me?" asked Mary, wanting to hear the words again.

"Yes, he said it twice, and he also said that he would always be true."

"Oh, Ernest, all those years of blaming myself and thinking the worst—all those wasted years!" The regretful mink turned to the wall, still shaking her head. "And now I've foolishly given away all my furniture. Why was I so easily persuaded?"

Sarah Mourning Dove, who had been listening quietly along with Sandy Antelope, stole cautiously over to Billy. "Is it possible that Omar Mountain Goat or one of the other councilors could have slipped the tiepin into your pocket?"

"Yes of course, it's possible but highly unlikely. And why would they? It would serve no purpose. Besides, I remembered it vividly in my dream," confirmed the dog.

"Well, this is my husband's tiepin, of that I'm sure, and you've described Ernest exactly," said the mink, turning apprehensively to Billy. "Didn't you also dream that something catastrophic would happen if my father's things were destroyed?"

Billy hung his head but did not answer. Finally, Sarah intervened, "We can only hope that Brother Fabian doesn't try anything foolish, but it's out of our hands. For now, we must depend on the will of The Great Spirit."

As soon as The Great Spirit was mentioned, a rude knock was heard at Mary McMink's front door, followed by the sounds of a door opening and the footsteps of several creatures. Sandy Antelope immediately bounded out of the bedroom door.

By the time Billy Bones and Sarah Mourning Dove reached the landing, Sandy was most of the way down the stairs and was successfully blocking the ascension of Brother Fabian Lynx. A short distance behind the lynx, Leon, Lester, and Leroy Coyote and a newly released Rodney Wild Deer stood like combatants waiting for their captain's orders.

This sudden confrontation marked the first time Billy had seen Brother Fabian since his visit to the New Meetinghouse in early September. The shepherd dog was still amazed by the handsome lynx's dazzling smile and the splendor of his robe of office.

"I'm sorry, Brother Fabian, but Mary doesn't want to see you. She's still upset over losing her father's things," explained Sandy resolutely.

"Perhaps Mary should tell me herself how she feels. Naturally she's upset, but I have carefully explained to her that she's done the right thing."

"Has she?" called Sarah Mourning Dove from the top of the steps. "It seems to me you explained only one appendix to *The Great Book of Rules*. You conveniently left out the others."

"Still trying to be a spiritual counselor, is that it, Sarah? Don't you realize that I am now the authority? It seems you haven't learned when to give up!" snarled Brother Fabian, changing his demeanor and glaring up at the dove.

"As long as Mary needs me, I'll keep advising her. I think you've done enough damage. Now perhaps you'd better go!" responded Sarah, raising her little chin contemptuously.

"Not until I see Mary, thank you," said Brother Fabian, trying to regain his poise.

"What is it you want?" called a voice behind Sarah. Slowly Mary McMink shuffled forward and clasped the banister at the top of the stairs. "I have nothing else to give you or my brother. Now please, go away and leave me alone!"

"I know you're still feeling the loss of your father's things, but one day you will thank…" began the big cat.

"No!" interrupted the mink, hanging her head in defiance. "You've already bled me dry!"

"But you promised all the artifacts, my dear, and there is still one that neither I nor the sheriff retrieved," smiled Fabian, showing his full white teeth.

"And what might that be?" asked Sarah, as she moved over to help support the weakened mink.

"That book that belonged to the humans, the one that describes Mary's precious furniture," returned the lynx.

"You mean this one?" shouted Lester Coyote suddenly, raising the ancient book above the mantel piece in the main room.

"Wait! You can't take that!" cried Billy, joining Sandy at the foot of the stairs. "That book belongs to Winston Wise Owl!"

"Ah, the famous Billy Bones! So we finally hear from you. After our last meeting, I hoped we could be on the same page by this time, but it seems you are wary of meeting with me again. Well anyway, let me try to explain to you my claim to this book. You see, it was in Mary's possession when she signed the agreement to turn over all her human antiques, and the sheriff said nothing about it going to Cornelius Van Mink. That means it should go to us."

With extreme quickness, Billy rushed to the fireplace and snatched the book out of Lester's hand. "No, you can't have this book! I told you, it's the property of Mr. Wise Owl. It was only on loan to Mary."

"Get that book, you fools! Don't listen to him!" shouted Brother Fabian, completely losing his composure.

"Stop!" hollered the shepherd, as the deer and the coyotes tried to corner him. "Brother Fabian, what's the matter with you? I've tried to explain to you about the books. What could you possibly want with this one?"

"Because it was written by humans, and it's as evil as all the others, and you'll be damned if you continue to defend them!" screamed the big cat in return, letting out all his venom. "You must come over to the right side on this Billy Bones—before it's too late for you!"

Billy was momentarily stricken with both the shock and bitterness of Brother Fabian's words. He quickly came to his senses as the lynx turned again to his followers and cried, "Now take that foul thing from him before he worms his way out of here!"

Reacting instantly, Billy threw the ancient relic to Sandy who was standing on the first step of the landing. "Sandy, take the book to the sheriff. I'll meet you there as soon as I can!"

Before Brother Fabian or any of his aides could react, Sandy was out the door and headed across the field in the direction of Main Street.

"Rodney, he can't outrun you! Catch him before he makes it to Lone Wolf's office! The rest of you—be there when he falls. I want that book!" ordered the frustrated cat.

Brushing past Brother Fabian, Billy ascended the stairs to help Sarah put Mary McMink back to bed. "I thought maybe I could reason with you, but I see that your hatred has taken you beyond reason, Brother Fabian," the dog barked, turning back to the big cat, who now stood alone in the middle of the room. "And as for Sandy, they'll never catch him. Haven't you noticed? He's had a growth spurt. I'll wager that now he's the fastest animal in The Enchantment. They don't have a chance!"

CHAPTER NINETEEN

ANDY'S NEW STATURE

True to Billy's prediction, neither Rodney Wild Deer nor any of the three coyote brothers was able to catch Sandy Antelope. When Billy Bones arrived at Sheriff Walter Lone Wolf's office on Main Street next to the saloon, he found Sandy sitting in the front room, grinning from ear to ear. As usual, the well-built wolf was dressed all in black and his badge was freshly polished.

Because of Sandy's new size, the two straps of his pants had both snapped in the chase, and he was holding them in his left hand. Fortunately, the sheriff had been working in his office when the young antelope arrived and allowed him immediate entrance. Billy soon learned that Rodney and the three coyotes had apparently accepted their failure and returned to their barracks and the sure wrath of Brother Fabian Lynx.

"Good morning, sheriff. I guess Sandy has explained to you about the book. It was on loan to Mary McMink, but we knew it belonged to Winston Wise Owl," explained Billy, repeating the antelope's story.

"As I told Sandy, this issue's too hot for me! I'm going to keep the book until the council meets in December. I'll let them handle it," announced the wolf resolutely.

"Do you mind if we tell Mr. Wise Owl what happened?" asked the shepherd dog.

"No of course not, and tell him I'll keep it in a safe place," returned the thoughtful sheriff, turning the pages of the ancient book. "Who would have thought that a thing like this even existed?"

When the two friends finally stepped back into the street, Billy turned to Sandy, who was still holding his pants up by their straps. "I thought you'd grown these last three months, Sandy. I'm anxious to see what you'll do against those two deer in the race on May Day!"

"Well, something's happened to me," laughed the antelope, tying the straps around his waist. "For one thing, I've gotten too big for my britches!"

"We'll stop by Percival Gander's shop on the way to Mr. Wise Owl's place and see what he can do for you," chuckled Billy. "Come on. We'll catch him before lunch."

On the way to the shop, Sandy told part of his story. "I came through the golden portal nearly eight years ago. Somehow, I got separated from my herd. I must've been only a year old or so and hadn't achieved my full growth. Anyway, once I got inside The Enchantment, it seemed I almost stopped growin'. I guess I'm just now getting to my full size."

"Well, it seems that I'm the only one who's noticed it so far," observed the dog.

When Billy and Sandy reached Percival's Shop, they walked up the ramp and knocked several times on the door. Finding it slightly ajar, the shepherd dog pushed it open and heard the gander honking and humming to himself in another part of the long coop. They finally found the strange bird sitting in the fitting room to the right of the main gallery. He was sewing what seemed to be a black vest. Several other similar vests of various sizes were lying about the little room along with an assortment of other half-finished costumes.

"Percy, do you have a minute?" called the dog softly, hoping not to frighten the high-strung gander.

"Billy, Billy Bones, oh my, oh my," sputtered Percival, hopping to his feet, "and Sandy, Sandy Antelope, what a surprise…what a pleasant surprise!"

"You see, Sandy here has developed a little problem. He…" began the dog.

"Oh yes, yes, I see, I see!" interrupted Percival, as he walked around the young buck, inspecting his new size. "I wondered how long those trousers would last when I was making your white shirt last August. Even then you'd gotten somewhat bigger, but these last three months, oh my, oh my…"

As Percival Gander removed his measuring tape from around Sandy's waist, Billy questioned him about the uniform clothing. "What are all the black vests for, Percy? Is someone getting married?"

"No, no, my good dog, that's a special order from Brother Fabian Lynx. He wants vests all alike for the young animals under his guardianship…oh, yes, and for Deputy Bison Bob, too, who's watching over them. It's funny, but he called them his 'lieutenants.' Did you ever hear of such a thing? Sounds like an army, doesn't it? Yes, yes, just like an army!"

Suddenly Billy felt his head spinning. He turned around and kept himself from falling by putting his hands against the little table where the extra vests were lying.

"Are you all right, Billy?" inquired Sandy, as he put a comforting hand on the dog's shoulder.

"No, no, it's just that…well, that's what Brother Fabian called them in my dream…his 'lieutenants'!" the dog answered ominously. "It's such a coincidence, as if something terrible might really happen after all!"

The antelope and the gander were pensive for a moment. Finally, Percival broke the momentary gloom. "Well, well, come on, Sandy. Let's go into the showroom and find you a pair of pants that fit. And I think a shirt might be in order too. Yes, yes, I think definitely another shirt. This one's bursting at the seams!"

After some careful searching, the gander came up with dark, gray-striped trousers held up by a pair of suspenders and a loose yellow shirt that could be worn every day. Sandy seemed pleased and more comfortable.

After Percival dismissed them, Billy and Sandy hurried down the long ramp and turned east toward Winston Wise Owl's tree house. They did not find the owl at home so they crossed the path to the other great tree where Hester Groundhog had her cottage.

The old groundhog poked her head out of the window as they approached. "I hoped you would call on me. Make yourself comfortable while I brew some tea. It's a little nippy, so I've placed the table in the sunlight. I also have a fresh loaf of walnut bread that needs eating!"

"Well, we can't say no to that," smiled Billy, as Sandy nodded in agreement. "I'm afraid we haven't eaten all morning."

"What brings you back here? I know it's more than just a visit to an old groundhog!" chuckled Hester, as she brought out the steaming bread and butter and strawberry jam.

"We've got some news about Mr. Wise Owl's book. We were hopin' you might pass it on to him," said Billy, reaching for a slice of the fresh bread.

"As you well know, I'd be only too glad to assist you," answered Hester with a twinkle in her eye, "and I want all the details, if you please! Winston's attending a meeting with George P. Beaver and Cornelius Van Mink at the castle. I think they're discussing what to do with Winston's clock, Mary's Irish furniture, and the mayor's tapestry and rug. Now just a minute while I fix tea. I think I hear the water boiling."

After telling Hester Groundhog the exciting adventures of the morning and after enjoying the bread and hot tea, the two comrades expressed their thanks and headed homeward.

"I hope Mr. Wise Owl doesn't forget about his books. I know Brother Fabian Lynx hasn't," mused Billy, as he started down the path.

"Well, there's still three weeks before the old year

ends," consoled Sandy. "At least they're startin' to make plans."

"Well, let's hope so," said Billy with some trepidation.

The two animals walked in silence until they came to Beaver Dam Road. Billy had been deeply affected by the morning's events, and he felt the antelope had too. Finally he broke the stillness. "Sandy, race me back to my place. Let's see what you can really do!"

The antelope watched the dog jog a little ahead of him and then grinned, "OK, you're on!"

Billy was amazed at how quickly and easily Sandy outdistanced him. The buck was waiting calmly in front of the little cottage when the young shepherd finally arrived. Billy smiled broadly as he leaned his arm against the door frame, trying to catch his breath. "Sandy, you're even faster than I imagined. I can't wait until May Day and the Spring Race. You'll change the whole notion of running around here!"

Billy felt better now that he could share a newfound happiness with the good antelope, and in some ways, it made up for his estrangement with Victor Running Deer. He also hoped that he could keep his mind off his dreams and visions for a time...especially since the deer had expressed such doubts about them. He had seen something at Walter Lone Wolf's office that deeply troubled him, however. For a brief moment when the sheriff was glancing through the ancient manuscript on Irish antiques, the book had seemed to glow and sprout wings.

CHAPTER TWENTY

THE WINTER SOLSTICE

The City Hall had already been decorated with greenery and ribbons in honor of the Winter Solstice when the outgoing City Council met for their last session in December. Both Winston Wise Owl and Brother Fabian Lynx had been invited as special witnesses to discuss the fate of Winston's book on Irish and English furniture. Mary McMink was also asked to attend but declined, as expected. However, she sent Sarah Mourning Dove as her personal representative.

"Mary has asked me to inform the council that she changed her mind about her father's furniture and requests that it all be returned to her," announced Sarah. "She feels that Brother Fabian gave her bad advice and that *The Great Book of Rules* does not necessarily forbid the personal possession of human artifacts."

After much discussion, Wendell Red Breast suggested placing all the furniture in a neutral place like the City Hall until a special session to review the matter could be arranged. At this proposal, both Cornelius Van Mink and Brother Fabian Lynx took umbrage.

"My wife has already incorporated the furniture into our home. To ask her to give up my own father's things would be unthinkable on my part," argued the mink.

"With your permission, I would like to agree with Chairman Van Mink, for once. Besides, the furniture we were given is in the back room of the New Meetinghouse which, as you all know, is a place of sanctuary," stated the lynx smugly. "And as you are all also aware, the paragraph on the sanctuary of the meetinghouse is in the main body of *The Great Book of Rules* and is not up for debate."

After a brief discussion, the council decided to let the old ruling stand, and shortly thereafter, Winston was given possession of his ancient book on furniture. The owl noticed however, that Brother Fabian gave him a wry smile as he left the entrance hall with his good friend, Phineas T. Fox. He knew that the lynx was only biding his time until January first.

Suddenly the big cat stuck his head back into the room and announced, "Winston Wise Owl, there is something that I forgot to tell you. Victor Running Dear and Melinda Doe are announcing their engagement on Sunday at the New Meetinghouse. I thought you and your friend Billy Bones might like to know. Olen and Myrtle Buck have invited everyone who goes to the New Meetinghouse to stay afterwards for a party in their honor."

Brother Fabian flashed another dazzling smile and ducked back out the double door at the rear of the hall. Winston turned and looked out the great windows with their many panes. He knew of Billy's failure with Victor and was aware that the two animals had stopped seeing each other. He wanted to shout out his frustration but restrained himself. When he turned back, Cornelius Van Mink gestured for him and Mayor Beaver to join him up on the stage.

"It seems that Brother Fabian has opened a can of worms for himself," suggested the mink. "By declaring that Mary's furniture is untouchable at the New Meetinghouse, he's given us a way to protect our own artifacts if worse comes to worse."

Regarding Victor's engagement, Winston decided that he would inform Billy Bones of the news when he joined him in the Hill Country. The owl was invited as a special guest to a concert the songbirds were planning at the Great Lodge on the night of the winter solstice. Billy Bones had arranged for Winston to sit with the Tribal Council, who would be just finishing their quarterly adjudication.

On the evening of the winter concert, Winston Wise Owl flew in with only a couple of minutes to spare. The lodge doors were decorated with large wreaths of pine boughs, cones, and various gold-painted fruits and nuts. When the old bird entered the large hall, he was even more amazed at the wealth of swags, ribbons, and wreaths around the room.

As the owl looked around, he suddenly became aware of Billy at his side. "Mr. Wise Owl, they're about ready to start. Come on, I've saved a place for you."

Winston knew that Gloria Meadowlark, Wendell Red Breast, Melba Thrush, and Hosea Brown Thrasher were filled with some misgivings about performing for the less refined citizens of the Hill Country. After the first ensemble number, any fears they had were dispelled as the ovation was immediate and enthusiastic.

At the end of the evening, Winston waited around to congratulate the four songbirds. As he was about to leave, a shrill voice rang out from the other side of the room. "Mr. Wise Owl, a minute of your time, if you please!" Even though the figure was hooded, Winston knew from the commanding voice and black robe that it was Lucinda Vulture. She swiftly crossed the room with short determined steps and stopped a few feet from the old owl. Then she angrily threw back her hood and pointed a crooked finger in Winston's face. "Mr. Wise Owl, it seems to me that you haven't held up your part of the bargain! You've allowed some of Mary McMink's furniture to fall into the hands of Brother Fabian Lynx!"

The stunned owl was at a loss for words, especially in front of the group of singers. Finally he regained his composure. "Madam, as you know, I tried to persuade the old council, but Brother Fabian had already moved some of the furniture into the New Meetinghouse."

"That's because you waited almost six days after our special meeting to go before the Prairie Council," countered Lucinda. "Your failure to act immediately may be the cause of great misfortune! You do realize what you've done, don't you?"

"Madam, I assure you that our council has done everything in its power to stop Brother Fabian from any further

actions. Chairman Van Mink himself put out an immediate cease-and-desist order and was able to save at least half of the pieces," rebutted the owl.

"Half is not enough, you doddering old fool! You must find a way to save them all, even if it means stealing them back!"

"But Madam, I am a law-abiding bird!" stammered Winston.

"The law be damned! You still don't comprehend the seriousness of this situation!" the old vulture shrieked, as she pulled up her hood and swished out of the building.

Winston Wise Owl was mortified. He had been concerned about his failure to act promptly but found it awkward to convince others in the Prairie that a dog's dreams had so much significance. Now, however, the likely consequences of his inaction hit him like a bolt of lightning. Without meeting anyone's gaze, the old owl left the lodge without looking back and flew to his tree house in the semidarkness. He felt the cool chill of the December air on his wings, which reminded him that the New Year, with all its promised uncertainty, was fast approaching.

CHAPTER TWENTY-ONE

THE JANUARY SNOW

Snow started falling on the twelfth of January. It came down quietly in huge flakes that seemed to immediately blanketed everything in a mantle of white. In the afternoon, Georgie Beaver appeared outside the cottage of Billy Bones. He had gathered a huge sack of provisions and waded down from the beaver pond.

"I thought maybe you could use some food, and I could help you gather firewood," chuckled Georgie. "Dad says we're in for a big one."

By the time Billy and Georgie had a roaring fire going in the fireplace, Nosey Coon and Needles Porcupine were knocking on the door. At the sight of the two rascals with their bundles of belongings, the shepherd dog shook his head and laughed. Georgie, for his part, just scratched above his eye and resigned himself to the added company.

"The snow was coverin' our doors, so we decided to head up here," explained Nosey.

"Yeah, where it's nice and warm!" added Needles.

By the end of the next day, the snow finally stopped after over two feet had piled up outside Billy's Dutch door, and the weather remained cold for another two days with no signs of melting. Inside Billy's cottage it was warm and cozy. When they were not gathering wood or preparing a meal, the four housemates took turns telling stories or reminiscing about the Grand Fair and Billy's adventures inside the Hill Country.

On the fourth day as the four animals enjoyed a good hot bowl of soup and some of Gladys Beaver's wheat bread, Nosey got around to the subject of the shepherd's past life. "Billy, tell us another story about you and Billy Stuart."

Billy Bones leaned back in his chair. The dog had thought a lot about the young boy when the snow started to fall. He remembered how thrilled the boy had been last year when he was able to make a snowman and build part of a snow fort. He also recalled how he kept knocking down part of the fort's walls with his clumsiness.

Just as Billy was about to begin, there was a loud knocking at the door. "Who do you suppose that could be in this weather?" he wondered out loud. He got up from the old pine table, crossed hesitantly to the door, and opened the top half. Deputy Bison Bob's head and shoulders filled almost the entire opening. He wore a short black jacket with a red wool scarf over his black vest. A little ways behind him, Billy could just make out the "lieutenants" that Percival Gander had mentioned with their black vests visible under their winter coats.

"Deputy Bob, what a surprise to see you out in this weather! Please come in," invited the shepherd somewhat hesitantly, "and bring your friends too."

"Ah, thank you, Billy, but we'd bring in half the outdoors with us!" laughed the big buffalo. The deputy and his crew were carrying bags of what appeared to be foodstuffs.

"No, no, come in, all of you, and warm yourselves by the fire. You can have some of our hot cider if you wish."

"All right, if you insist, but just for a minute. We've got lots of places to go today, and we don't want to be travelin' after dark," declared the buffalo.

After Bison Bob, Rodney Wild Deer, and Lester, Leon, and Leroy Coyote all trooped in and were standing with their backs toward the fire, the deputy continued explaining their mission. "Mayor Elmer Prairie Dog wants to make sure that no one in the Prairie is sufferin' from want of food or shelter. He's especially concerned about the elderly, as you can imagine. Brother Fabian offered to send us as a gesture of good will. All the foodstuffs, of course, come from the new mayor's General Store." He looked around at the raccoon and the porcupine. "Seems we don't have to look in on Nosey and Needles since you've taken them in. How are you fixed for food?"

"We seem to be holding out OK. You better save what you've got for those who might really need it," said Billy, as he and Georgie served cider to the five helpers. "The mayor's doin' a fine thing here. Sounds like a good way to start his term of office!"

"And don't forget Brother Fabian!" barked Lester, looking around the room. "We're workin' for him, you know!"

Billy Bones was surprised at how loyal the coyotes were to Brother Fabian Lynx. In just a short period of time the crafty cat had thoroughly won them over. Rodney Wild Deer seemed to be another story, however. Since he lost his chance to impress Melinda Doe after being defeated by Victor Running Deer in the Great Medley, he seemed to carry a terrible grudge that permeated his entire being. Billy could not help noticing that even with his friends, there was a dark, vacant look about him, as if he were just biding his time.

Although Bison Bob seemed to enjoy his new role as leader of the motley crew, Billy wasn't sure where the buffalo's loyalty lay. The dog smiled to himself. He could not visualize another time in which that particular group would have a friendly drink together. He hoped that it was a harbinger of better days to come but knew in his heart that it possibly was not.

"Well, we gotta be goin'. We gotta finish the whole east side by this afternoon. Here, at least take some bread. I think we got plenty," offered the buffalo, as he took a loaf out of Leon's sack and placed it on the table. "And thanks for the cider and lettin' us warm our backsides!" The other lieutenants grunted their appreciation, and the strange visit ended as the bison and his four lieutenants trudged out the door and turned north.

"Deputy Bob, just a minute," called Billy suddenly, darting out the door.

The large buffalo stepped back through the high snow. "Yeah, what is it, Billy?"

"When you passed by Victor Running Deer's place, was everything all right there?"

"I think he's stayin' with Olen Buck and his family until the snow melts," answered the deputy, shrugging his shoulders. "At least that's what Olen indicated. Actually, they didn't invite us in. He just yelled to us from his doorway." The huge buffalo gestured with his head back toward Rodney Wild Deer. "I don't think he wanted a confrontation."

As Bison Bob trudged back to the head of the line, Billy looked over at Rodney, who was staring straight at him. His eyes had a strange hollow look that caused the dog to shudder and look away. The dog knew that the deer had only been out of jail for one month, and he wondered how Brother Fabian was able to control him. He also wondered what kind of influence he was having on Lester, Leon, and Leroy Coyote and whether Lenny was still safe. But above all, he found he was still worried about Victor Running Deer, even though he had tried to put him out of his mind. He knew that the deer was never completely safe as long as Rodney was still around.

CHAPTER TWENTY-TWO

THE DARING RESCUE

The next week a warming breeze swept in from the southwest and quickly melted most of the snow cover. On Thursday Georgie Beaver went home to check on his parents, and on Friday Nosey Coon and Needles Porcupine hiked down the bluff to make sure that the rising water had not damaged their little homes.

By the time Saturday evening came, Georgie returned with more provisions, since Billy Bones' houseguests had pretty much cleaned him out of food. The dog in turn invited the beaver to stay overnight so he would not have to slosh back through the muddy paths in the dark.

That same night, Billy had another dream. For some reason he was back in Omar's cave. He was wandering about in complete darkness as before, but this time the image of Victor Running Deer appeared before him, much like the image of Ernest McMink had four months earlier. The young buck reached out to him and called, "Billy, Billy, help me. I'm being dragged away, and I can't seem to stop! Help me…please…please, help me!"

The shepherd dog suddenly sat up in his bunk. He poked the straw mattress above him as he hopped out of bed and threw on a coat and scarf. "Georgie…Georgie, get out of bed! Victor's in trouble! Get your coat on and follow me!" Before the beaver could jump out of his bunk, the dog was out of the door and heading south toward the deer's lean-to.

Billy was thankful that the sky was clear and the moon was full. He stayed on the dead grass just off the muddy path, which made running considerably easier. When he got to the area of the bluff close to Victor's place, he could see a thick unnatural smoke rising from the vicinity of the deer's dwelling. He immediately left the high ground, leaped over the bluff, and crashed through the thicket down below. Finally, after many scratches and a few tumbles, he reached the lean-to. The outside of the structure was smoldering all around its base with flames flickering here and there. Fortunately, the wet timber was hindering the fire, but billows of smoke were already coming out of the windows and around the door.

Without hesitating, Billy tried to shove the door open but found it locked. Quickly he moved to the window. Luckily Victor had left the inside shutters slightly ajar, and the dog was able to force them open and dive through without much trouble. Once inside he found the door, unbolted the crude lock, and pushed it open so he could see around the little lean-to. Since it was a fairly small space, he soon found the unconscious buck.

When Billy tried to drag Victor out of his bed, he was shocked at how heavy the young deer really was. It was all he could do to pull him down onto the floor. The smoke was also starting to choke the dog, and he began coughing uncontrollably. At that very moment he heard Georgie calling from the doorway. "Billy, Billy, where are you? Are you in there?"

"Georgie, thank goodness," the dog sputtered, "I'm right ahead of you on the floor. Help me pull Victor out of here. This smoke is really getting to me!"

Once outside, the two animals began slapping the young deer about the back and chest until they revived him. After a great deal of coughing and spitting, the deer finally rolled his eyes open and glanced over at Billy. "What happened?"

"I don't know, Victor. I'm just glad you're still alive! Now let's see what we can do about this fire."

Victor showed his two friends where the tools were in his little shed, and the three animals were able to throw enough dirt, mud, and leftover snow onto the walls to smother the flames. "Even though the wood down here is still wet, it looks like I'll have to rebuild most of my lean-to."

"All it really did was make a huge smoke pot," chuckled Georgie, showing his teeth. "But it looks like most of the branches will have to be replaced all right."

As the three animals leaned against their shovels, Victor finally turned to Billy. He found it difficult to thank the dog because of his innate reserve but knew he had to say what was on his mind.

"I remember now, Billy," said the deer, hesitating for a moment. "Before you came, I kept trying to wake up, but I couldn't. I kept dreaming that I was in a dark hole, and I was being pulled backward into nothingness. I kept trying to reach out for someone to help me, but no one was there. And then I saw your face above me, and I knew that somehow you'd find me."

Billy Bones was deeply moved that Victor had called to him in his despair. Somehow it redeemed their friendship, which had taken such a sullen turn in the past few months. "We saw the smoke from the top of the bluff, and Georgie and I rushed down here and pulled you out. It was not an easy task, I tell you. You weigh a ton!" Billy laughed in relief.

"Don't let him fool you, Victor! It was Billy who found you. Somehow, he knew you were in trouble. He jumped up out of a sound sleep and started runnin' down here!" said Georgie, not wanting to take any credit for the rescue. "I don't know how he knew."

"He heard me, that's why," said Victor, looking back at Billy. "I don't know how, but he did. And Billy, I…I don't know quite how to tell you this, but I want to say how sorry I am. No one else could've done what you did. And after tonight, well, I'm convinced, that you really do have special gifts and that we need to listen to your dreams. And I want you to know that I've decided to talk to Olen Buck, as soon as I can. I'm sure now that I can convince him to protect Mary's furniture. I…well…I just hope that you'll forgive me for being such a foolish friend."

"I don't have to forgive anything, Victor. I know that it must have been terrible for you after your mother was killed. I can't imagine what you must have gone through!

But I really appreciate your willingness to talk to Olen. You don't know how much that means to me," said Billy, smiling and putting a hand on Victor's shoulder.

After putting his shovel back into the shed, Billy started looking around the perimeter of the lean-to. "I'm afraid we've probably wiped away any clues, but maybe if we searched a little farther off, we could find something."

"Here are some tracks headin' down toward the stream," called Georgie excitedly. "It looks like hoof marks of some kind.

"Could they be Rodney's?" suggested Victor, supposing the worst.

"No, I don't believe so," Billy surmised, getting down and observing the tracks. "They seem smaller than a deer's, and besides, it appears there were three or four of them." Suddenly he put his nose to the ground and used his exceptional sense of smell. "Pigs! It's those wild pigs, the Peccary Brothers. I'd know their scent anywhere!"

"But why?" asked Victor. "Why would they want to burn my place?"

"I don't know, but I think we'd better get the sheriff. Georgie, why don't you see if you can wake him up and bring him down here? Victor and I will guard the place."

When Sheriff Walter Lone Wolf arrived, he came to the same conclusion that Billy did. Fortunately, Walter's sense of smell was as good as Billy's, and neither one of them had any doubts about who was to blame. The pungent odor of swine was undeniable, as were the distinct hoof marks of four peccaries.

Later that week Billy learned that the Peccary Brothers were arrested, and during the first meeting of the new City Council, they were found guilty. To the dog's chagrin, after two months in jail, they were added to Brother Fabian Lynx's lieutenants. Billy also learned that Sheriff Lone Wolf asked Deputy Milton Brown Bear to come down from his home in the woods and help Bison Bob supervise the larger group on probation. Although Rodney was suspected of masterminding the arson attack, he was never accused, since the wild pigs never confessed.

The new City Council moved very slowly on Elmer Prairie Dog's reforms, which were, of course, directives from Brother Fabian Lynx. To Billy's delight, Olen Buck proved to be the sticking point. He voted against going into citizen's homes and confiscating their human artifacts and also against destroying Mary McMink's furniture. Although going into the mist was finally deemed a crime, Olen also insisted that this not be made retroactive, sparing Billy needless harassment.

Billy knew that Olen's steadfastness stemmed in part from Victor Running Deer's influence. Since the fire, the deer had strengthened his friendship with the shepherd dog. "I'm here if you ever need me," he declared one afternoon, while both animals were surveying the damage done by the fire. "And Billy, I want you to tell me truthfully. Were any of the human animals ever cruel to you, like Brother Fabian's zoo keepers?"

"No, Victor, none of the humans were ever unkind to me. But I imagine they're the same as creatures everywhere.

Some are good and some are not so good. I think perhaps that's the nature of all things," answered Billy.

"Yes, I'm beginning to think you're right," admitted Victor. "There's certainly a great difference between the likes of Olen Buck and Rodney Wild Deer. As you pointed out, I imagine it's the same with the human animals."

When it came to Brother Fabian however, Billy realized that the big cat was greatly frustrated by Olen's refusal to follow his suggestions. Of course, the lynx did not know about the pact that Olen had made with Victor, Sandy Antelope, Arnold Big Horn, and Billy after the election. The five animals had promised to do all they could to protect Winston Wise Owl's books and the other human artifacts that still remained in the homes of citizens living inside the Prairie. The dog also hoped that the lynx did not suspect that Victor Running Deer had influenced the old stag's vote on Mary McMink's artifacts, because if things got suddenly worse, Billy knew he would still need Victor's help in dealing with Brother Fabian Lynx.

CHAPTER TWENTY-THREE

THE SNOW FORTS

After the second heavy snowfall of the New Year, Billy Stuart asked Danny Red Feather to come over to his grandfather's farm for building snow forts and all the other pleasurable activities that surrounded such endeavors. The two young boys worked together for over an hour, building opposing three-sided, chest-high walls for the forts themselves. Then they toiled separately on the stocks of personal ammunition needed to fight the battles royale that would follow.

The barnyard of Will Stuart's farm with its view of the foothills leading up into the Rocky Mountains was the perfect setting for such an important event. After several hours of exhilarating yet exhausting engagement, both boys were wet beyond belief. Will called to them from the porch of the farmhouse, "OK, you two, I think it's time to come in and dry off before you catch your deaths of cold!"

"Ah, come on, grandpa, we're just gettin' started!" yelled Billy in protest.

"Danny's dad will never forgive me if I let you both get sick. Now come on! Besides, I've got hot chocolate and marshmallows!"

The mention of hot chocolate and marshmallows turned the tide in favor of Will Stuart and his warm farmhouse. For added comfort, Will placed several fresh logs in the fireplace and set three comfortable armchairs in front of it.

"How did it go, boys, and who won?" asked Will, taking their wet coats and placing them close to the fire.

"Well, I caught Danny good at least five times! One snowball hit him right on the kisser!" laughed Billy.

"Yeah, but I got you a couple a' times on the side of your head, and you slipped and fell, remember?" bragged Danny.

"Well, maybe it was more like a draw," admitted Billy, as Will Stuart poured the satisfied boys a cup of the tasty brew.

"If you ask me, I think the snow forts really won. We did too good a' job buildin' 'em. It was really hard to get a decent shot off!" concluded Danny, taking a long drink of hot chocolate and getting marshmallow all over his upper lip.

"Better than last year!" interjected Billy. "Remember how Bones kept jumpin' up on the walls of the fort and knockin' 'em down before we could get anything built? I think he thought the blocks of snow were just for him…" At the memory of the shepherd dog, the towheaded boy's voice suddenly caught in his throat. Even after eight months, the recollection of happy times in the snow with the missing dog still evoked sorrow.

Billy's melancholy was soon broken as the sound of a horn outside the farmhouse, signaled the arrival of Danny's father.

"Maybe next time you can stay all night," said Will, while Danny slipped on his cap and coat. "Don't you think that would be a good idea, Billy?"

"Yeah, that would be swell," agreed the young boy, trying not to let his feelings for the lost dog spoil the moment. From his demeanor, both Danny and Will knew how much he still missed Bones.

"Well, goodbye," called Danny, as he started for the door, "I had a great time."

"Yeah, so long," answered Billy. "Thanks for coming."

As the sound of the car faded into the late afternoon, the boy and his grandfather sat quietly together and watched the logs in the fireplace crackle and burn and stir up old memories.

PART TWO

UNTIL THE SUMMER SOLSTICE

CHAPTER TWENTY-FOUR

A STRANGE CONFRONTATION

During the spring equinox, Billy Bones again stayed with Maurice Rabbit while the Tribal Council was in session. The council members had become reconciled to the fact that some of Mary McMink's furniture had fallen into the hands of Brother Fabian Lynx. They decided to pin their hopes for solving the problem on Olen Buck, chairman of the Prairie City Council. The stag had become somewhat of a hero in the Hill Country since he had tempered most of the lynx's radical plans and kept relations between the two states on an even keel.

Since going into the mist had become a crime inside the Prairie, Lucinda Vulture and Omar Mountain Goat did not ask Billy to reenter Spirit Dwells. Omar caught Billy after the final ceremony and gave him some parting advice. "If for some reason things turn out badly for you, you must return to the Hill Country at once. Your first contact should be Maurice, of course, but if there isn't time, come straight to my cave."

After Billy returned to his own little cottage, he learned that Sandy Antelope, Arnold Big Horn, and Victor Running Deer planned to enter the Spring Race on May Day. The three hoofed animals worked out almost every morning and afterwards helped Olen Buck rebuild and enlarge Victor's damaged lean-to. Billy and Georgie Beaver also offered their assistance. When the old stag realized their exceptional carpentry skills, he was happy to have them and, in a short time, grew even fonder of them.

One week before May Day, the extended lean-to was finally completed to the satisfaction of all the workers, and Olen invited Sandy, Billy, Georgie, and Arnold to attend Sunday meditations at the New Meetinghouse.

"I think it would be a good thing for the community to see us all together," Olen began. "And maybe it will ease some of Brother Fabian's concerns when he witnesses our friendship."

Although Billy had misgivings, especially after his confrontation with Brother Fabian Lynx at Mary McMink's home, he promised to attend one of the lynx's meditations.

"I accept," said Billy finally, "and then perhaps next week we can all attend the Old Meetinghouse."

"Splendid idea!" answered Olen happily. "We'll show these two feuding communities how to get along."

On Sunday morning Billy, Victor, Sandy, Arnold, and Georgie put on their clean white shirts and met Olen and his family at the stag's lean-to. Olen felt it was important for them to attend the New Meetinghouse as a group. When Brother Fabian spotted them all sitting together, he immediately came over and greeted them. When he reached Billy, he acted as if their altercation at Mary McMink's home had never happened.

"Ah, Mr. Bones, you finally kept your promise. It's good to see you."

For the first part of his meditation, Brother Fabian lectured on the importance of strict adherence to *The Great Book of Rules.* As before, Billy was struck by Brother Fabian's magnificent white robe, his charismatic smile, and his exceptionally white teeth.

Even though Brother Fabian did not mention that going into the mist was now considered a crime, he made direct eye contact with Billy when he remarked, "When creatures wittingly or unwittingly break the rules found in *The Great Book,* they must give back to the community in some way, as my lieutenants are doing." The lynx then smiled over at the three coyote brothers sitting with Bison Bob on the far right. "Lester, Leon, and Leroy, for example, are happily making restitution for their misdeeds."

As the hour passed, Billy was relieved that Brother Fabian made no mention of the human artifacts. But to the dog's chagrin, the lynx addressed the subject just before the hour ended. "Mr. Bones, since you've spoken about your unusual experiences inside the mist at the Old Meetinghouse, perhaps you'd give us equal time. Would you mind joining me on stage?"

The lynx's request caught Billy completely off guard, and he felt trapped. He quickly glanced over at Olen who only smiled and nodded his approval. The old stag seemed unaware of the lynx's ability to twist anyone's words around to suit his own purposes.

With great trepidation, Billy climbed over Sandy and Arnold and stepped forward onto the stage. The lynx put his arm on the dog's shoulder as he began his questioning.

"Now, Mr. Bones, when you found yourself inside the mist up in the Hill Country, I understand that you saw the ancient human animals taking some of their belongings out of their wagons. Is that correct?"

"Yes, that's correct. They were removing what was too heavy to carry over the mountains."

"And aren't these belongings now known to us as the human artifacts?"

"Yes, that's true," affirmed Billy.

"And after that, didn't these human animals haul the rest of their belongings up into the foothills?" questioned Fabian.

"Yes, that's what I understand," answered Billy.

"And tell me, just how were they managing to accomplish this feat?" asked the lynx.

"What do you mean?"

"I mean, how were they getting their wagons up into the hills?"

"Well, they were urging their horses up the steep slope," said Billy.

"So their horses were doing all the work?"

"Well, yes, but…"

"And didn't you say that one team of horses tripped, and their wagon came crashing down the hill?"

"Yes, that's what I saw," agreed Billy.

"Tell me, why weren't the humans pulling the wagons?"

asked Fabian, glancing around the room.

"Well, the horses were used for that purpose. They were much stronger."

"So the horses were really slaves to the humans, were they not? Isn't that the way it is in the outside world?" questioned Brother Fabian.

"That's not exactly the case. You see, in the outside world, horses can't reason clearly."

"And so it's OK to make slaves of them?" pursued the lynx.

"No, I didn't say that," said the dog, trying to clear up the cat's assumptions.

"Now Mr. Bones, if you don't mind, let's go on to a slightly different subject. When you visited me earlier, something happened when you shook my hand. Is that correct?"

"Well, yes, I guess you could say…."

"And as I understand, you are renown for your prophetic gifts, are you not?"

"Well, I wouldn't exactly say that…"

"Come now, Mr. Bones. Why don't you let the gathering know precisely what happened that afternoon?" interrupted the lynx. "Tell them what you saw with that rare insight of yours."

"Well, I would rather you…."

"No, it must come from you," demanded the big cat.

"Well I…."

"Go on," insisted the lynx, smiling down at Olen.

"I thought I saw two humans. They were coming

straight at you…with a whip…and a pole," answered Billy solemnly.

"And you even described them to me, did you not?"

"Well, yes, but…."

"They certainly embodied evil, wouldn't you say?"

"I…I guess you could say that, but I also said that the humans I lived with treated me well," countered Billy.

"Ah, but you belonged to them too, didn't you, Mr. Bones – your human <u>masters</u>?"

"Well, they took care of me, if that's what you mean, but I was certainly not their slave," answered the shepherd dog.

"So, they treated you well. How nice for you," concluded the cat, taking his hand off the dog's shoulder. "Well, thank you, Mr. Bones, I think it's quite clear what you were to them. You were their pet! The rest of us creatures weren't so fortunate in the outside world. We can only hope, Mr. Bones, that in time, you'll come around to our way of thinking."

After this caustic comment, Brother Fabian Lynx quickly turned away from Billy Bones, faced his gathering, and flashed a smile in the direction of Sandy Antelope, Arnold Big Horn, and Georgie Beaver. "Ah, but it's getting late. Thank you for coming, and be sure to greet our guests. I believe we can honestly say that we've come to a better understanding this morning."

With these parting remarks, the lynx quickly stepped down to Jason Crow and shook hands with him and his family. He continued on to some of his other faithful followers, leaving Billy standing awkwardly alone in the center of the stage.

As soon as the eight friends got back to Olen's house, Myrtle Buck and Melinda Doe prepared a special meal to celebrate the completion of Victor's lean-to. After the meal Victor finally touched on Sandy's new size and speed. "Sandy, I don't know exactly what's happened to you, but you're bigger and faster than you were last summer. I have a feeling that on May Day you're going to give Rodney and me the hardest race of our lives."

Billy glanced over at Melinda after Victor's statement, and saw the doe looking confused and disgusted. From her past behavior, Billy suspected that her pride would not accept any remark that hinted at a possible defeat for Victor in the Spring Race.

CHAPTER TWENTY-FIVE

MAY DAY

The Spring Race on May Day ushered in the biggest festival day of the season. For the occasion, booths had been set up with various kinds of flowers, food, crafts, and games.

Winston Wise Owl watched with great interest as Victor Running Deer arrived with Melinda Doe and her parents. The young buck left the three of them on the steps of City Hall where Mayor Elmer Prairie Dog and his new City Council and their families would sit. Winston and Deputy Harold Eagle would monitor the race from the air as usual, and Farmer Jason Crow and Justin Beaver would officiate on the ground.

Unlike the other races, the Spring Race started on Court Street in front of City Hall and ran southeast over Beaver Dam and around the pond on River Road. The path then crossed the two bridges on either side of the island before heading back to Court Street and the finish line.

Rodney Wild Deer reached the warm-up area shortly after Victor Running Deer with a large support group that included Bison Bob and all the other lieutenants. The two deer eyed each other apprehensively as they removed their shirts and began prancing up and down in preparation for the race. Soon afterward, Sandy Antelope and Arnold Big Horn came in from the west before the other hoofed animals trickled in. From what Winston could tell, the only other animals to challenge the two deer, the antelope, and the Big Horn were Arnold's two brothers and two smaller deer who came down from the Hill Country.

At a few minutes before ten, Farmer Jason Crow blew the whistle that called the eight runners to the starting line. Winston perched himself on the Court House roof just above the runners so he could see the start of the race clearly. The owl shuffled his feet back and forth restlessly as Victor lined up next to Rodney and then glanced over at Melinda Doe. The owl noticed with some amusement that Victor did not ask for her scarf. Apparently, Rodney noticed it too.

"Afraid to take Melinda's scarf, eh?" snarled Rodney, as he placed his fingers carefully on the starting line. "Not so sure of yourself today, is that it?"

"Mind your own business, Rodney!" retorted Victor out of the corner of his mouth. "Melinda no longer concerns you!"

"Unless I'm the winner, you fool. I think I know her better than you!" snapped Rodney in return.

"I'd like to start now if I might have your attention!" cawed the crow loudly, interrupting the two deer. "On your mark…get set…go!"

Winston took to the air as soon as the race started. He suspected that the large crowd wanted more fireworks at the starting line between Victor and Rodney. They seemed to forget their disappointment as the two bucks shot off to an early lead. By the time the animals reached South Court Street, Sandy Antelope moved in cleanly behind them, and the tenor of the race was set.

As the two front-runners crossed Beaver Dam, Rodney tried to jostle Victor into the water with his elbows. On the second try, Winston swooped out of the sky and scraped the top of Rodney's head with his sharp talons. "Keep that up, and you'll be disqualified, Rodney! Keep it clean! Keep it clean!" the owl hooted, as Victor took a slight lead.

Three quarters of the way up River Road, Winston observed that the bumping and shoving continued, especially when the two bucks were under a heavy canopy of leaves. The owl tried to fly closer but was turned back by the low-lying branches.

At the junction of Shady Lane where the path widened, Winston noticed that both Rodney and Victor were suddenly jolted into a new reality as Sandy Antelope shot past them. The owl could just hear Victor as he turned to Rodney. "Thought this was between you and me, didn't you? Well, guess again!"

As the antelope forged ahead, Rodney nudged Victor as they neared the first bridge to the island, causing Victor to go too wide and miss the entrance. By the time the buck stumbled back onto the bridge, the crafty rogue had opened up a twenty-foot lead, and one of the fleet-footed deer from the Hill Country had passed Victor.

As soon as Sandy reached the other side of the pond, he reached for all of his pent-up energy. Without looking backwards or sideways, he seemed to be caught up in the full joy of running. From Winston's position in the air, he almost collided with Deputy Eagle as the two birds witnessed the debut of a new hero with the utmost respect and amazement.

When the large group of spectators that lined North Court and Court Streets saw Sandy steaming toward them all by himself, they turned to one another in disbelief. The owl guessed they had expected to see Victor and Rodney running head to head at this point. When the onlookers realized the tremendous speed at which the antelope was traveling, their bewilderment turned to awe.

CHAPTER TWENTY-SIX

THE CONSEQUENCE

Billy Bones and Georgie Beaver had positioned themselves near the end of the Spring Race. Immediately after the race, the two friends and a crowd of well-wishers gathered around Sandy Antelope. As soon as Victor Running Dear crossed the finish line, he also made his way over to Sandy to congratulate him. Victor had never been able to catch Rodney after his misfortune at the bridge but did manage to finish third after nosing out the little deer from the Hill Country. Coming in third was a hard pill for Victor to swallow, but he seemed genuinely glad that the win had gone to his friend Sandy and not to Rodney Wild Deer. As for Rodney, he was nowhere to be found.

When Billy and Georgie finally got around to speaking with Victor, he was wandering around the seats in front of City Hall.

"Have you seen Melinda?" the deer asked anxiously.

"I thought I saw her leave earlier with her father and mother," answered the dog.

"Was she angry?" inquired Victor, looking toward Main Street. "I thought at least Olen would stick around."

"I'm afraid she was," said Georgie, joining the discussion.

"After the race, she just started marchin' down Main Street. Olen tried to call her back, but when she wouldn't stop, he ran after her. And before long, Myrtle followed them."

Just as Georgie mentioned Olen's wife, Billy spotted her running wildly up the street towards them. When Myrtle spied Victor, she stumbled over to him. "Victor, help me! It's Olen! He's been stabbed! I think he might be dying!"

"Where…where did you leave him?" asked the young buck, trying not to panic. "Is Melinda with him?"

"No, she's gone!" cried Myrtle. "Rodney took her! Olen said he tried to stop him, but that's when Rodney pulled out a knife and stabbed him!"

"You mean Rodney kidnapped her?" asked Victor, stopping and holding the frenzied doe by both arms.

"Yes, he must have seen her coming and waited for her behind the saloon!" cried Myrtle, still on the verge of hysteria.

"I'll get Doctor Muskrat!" volunteered Georgie, moving north to the doctor's office next to the hotel.

"And I'll get Sheriff Lone Wolf and Deputy Eagle. I just saw them go into Harry Hawk's booth," added Billy, heading toward the courtyard square.

By the time Billy, Sheriff Lone Wolf, and Deputy Eagle reached the scene of the stabbing, Victor was sitting by the old stag, supporting his head and shoulders on his lap. Olen, for his part, was clutching a part of Myrtle's skirt that she had torn off to stop the bleeding.

Victor nodded to the sheriff and the deputy and then murmured to the stag, "The doctor should be right here, old friend. Just hold on!"

"Find her for me, Victor! Don't let him harm her!" whispered the older deer in return. "And one other thing—if something happens to me…"

"Now sir, you just take care of yourself. We'll find them," promised the young buck, as he looked up and saw Georgie arriving with Doctor Muskrat.

"All right, let me handle it from here!" said the muskrat, kneeling before the old stag.

"How does it look, doctor?" asked the wolf, crouching down on his haunches.

"It's a bad wound. I don't know," said the muskrat, shaking his head.

The sheriff glanced over at Victor, who had tears in his eyes. "Who did this?"

"It was Rodney, and he's kidnapped Melinda!"

CHAPTER TWENTY-SEVEN

THE SEARCH PARTIES

After the Spring Race, Winston Wise Owl had joined Thaddeus P. Turtle for lunch at the hotel across from City Hall. When he saw Georgie Beaver rush by the dining room window and return again with Doctor Muskrat, he hurried to the door and looked down the street.

"Something must have happened at the lower end of Main Street. There's a big crowd down there!" the owl called back to the turtle. "I don't have a good feeling about this. I think I'd better check it out. Please excuse me."

As the old owl neared the crowd, he could see Sheriff Walter Lone Wolf coming out of his office followed by Billy Bones, Georgie Beaver, and Sandy Antelope. Deputy Harold Eagle was standing just outside with Milton Brown Bear, Bison Bob, and some of Brother Fabian Lynx's lieutenants. The sheriff immediately addressed them.

"Deputy Bob, you take your group and search the barracks and the area around the New Meetinghouse. Ask anyone you come across if they've seen anything. Your lieutenants were closest to Rodney. Maybe you can figure out where he might have gone. Harold, why don't you check out all the routes that lead away from the crime scene? He can't have gone far, and you'll be able to see him better from the air."

As the wolf looked over the crowd, he spied Winston. "Mr. Wise Owl, I guess you've heard?"

"No, Walter, what's happened?" inquired the owl anxiously.

"It's Olen Buck. I'm afraid he's been stabbed. He's inside on a cot in one of my cells. Dr. Muskrat's with him. I'm afraid the wound is serious. It seems it was Rodney, and he's taken Melinda…" The sheriff hesitated for a moment. Winston could see that he was steeling himself. When he continued, he was again calm and professional. "Mr. Wise Owl, maybe you can give Deputy Eagle a hand. The two of you know this country better than anyone."

Sheriff Walter Lone Wolf finally turned his attention to Billy Bones, Georgie Beaver, and Sandy Antelope. "If you three don't mind, why don't you come along with Milton Brown Bear and me? We'll try Melinda's home and Rodney's old lean-to in the thicket. The area down by the river has the most places to hide." The wolf then turned and addressed all the searchers. "If you run across Rodney and Melinda, check with one of the deputies or myself. Don't try to play hero! He's got a knife with him! If you don't have any luck after a couple hours, come back here. All right, let's go!"

"How about me, sheriff?" said Victor, suddenly appearing in the doorway of the office. "What did you have in mind for me?"

"Maybe you'd better remain here with Myrtle and

Olen. I don't want you flyin' off the handle," said Walter Lone Wolf, putting a hand on the deer's shoulder.

"You know I can't just stay here and wait, sheriff!" returned the young buck.

"No, I suppose not," conceded the wolf. "Come with us then, but follow my lead. I don't want anyone else gettin' hurt."

As Winston Wise Owl made his way back to Main Street several hours later, he brought Lucinda Vulture's three sons, Felix, Festus, and Floyd, with him. He had stopped to talk to them outside their little hut in the Hill Country. They told him of a hiding place that Rodney might have chosen. As soon as the four birds landed, they learned that the sheriff's little posse had come back empty-handed after a fairly thorough search of the thicket on both sides of the river and the lean-tos belonging to Olen Buck and Rodney Deer. Bison Bob and his lieutenants and Harold Eagle had fared no better.

Before the owl could make it through the crowd that gathered around the searchers, he noticed that Billy Bones was just ahead of him. He was leading his old friend Whiskers over to where the good wolf was standing.

"Sheriff, Whiskers here told me that he saw Rodney take Melinda away. He'd been looking out of his second floor window at the boardinghouse," stated the dog, nudging his old friend forward.

"What can you tell us, Whiskers? Did you see which way they were heading?" inquired Walter, hoping for some kind of lead.

"Well, I know they turned west by the New Meetin' house. They seemed to be headin' toward the Old Wagon Trail," said the ancient cat, taking off his old felt hat.

"But we would've spotted them. There aren't many places to hide down there," interjected Deputy Harold Eagle. "Mr. Wise Owl and I covered that area pretty thoroughly."

The wolf put his hand to his jaw in a gesture of contemplation. "Deputy, look in the top drawer of my desk and bring out my map. Let's take another look at the terrain down there. There aren't too many places they could've gone."

"Unless they're in somebody's house," returned Milton Brown Bear.

After Harold Eagle returned with the map, the sheriff spread it out on the street so most of the searchers could see it. "You see, most of this area has no tall growth in it. I guess you're right, Milton, Rodney must be holdin' her captive in someone's house!"

"Unless they're here," interrupted Winston, as he moved into the center of the circle. He put the talons of his right claw on a place south of Dry Gulch called Castle Rock.

"But that's just bare rock. No one could hide there," insisted the sheriff.

"Not according to Felix Vulture here," said Winston, cocking his head to one side. "Felix, come over here and tell the sheriff what you know about Castle Rock."

The young vulture stepped cautiously forward. He

knew that he and his brothers were still considered outsiders here, and he felt out of place in his old patched shirt and soiled bandana.

"Go on, Felix, tell Sheriff Lone Wolf what you told me," urged the owl.

"Well, me and my brothers used to play in back of Castle Rock. There's an old cave up towards the top. You can't see it from the ground," remarked Felix, gaining confidence.

"And you can't see it very well from the air, neither," chimed in Festus.

"But that rock's a sheer drop-off and impossible to climb. How would they ever get up there?" asked Sheriff Lone Wolf.

"There's a way up the back side. It ain't too hard, but you gotta know where you're goin'!" said Floyd bravely, not wanting to be left out.

"Yeah, Momma told us that it was an old fortress at one time where the humans used to live. We even found some arrowheads up there," Felix proudly informed them.

"And you think Rodney might have gone there?" inquired the sheriff.

"We seen him up there a while back. It looked like he was cleanin' the cave out or somethin'," answered Festus, taking another step forward.

"Well, I'll take my group over there and do some exploring. Mr. Wise Owl, you and the vultures fly over to the foot of the rock and wait for us. Felix can lead us up to the cave once we arrive. Don't go around to the back though. If Rodney is there, we don't want him to know we're coming. Deputy Eagle, you go with Bison Bob and his crew and check out the different homes in the area and see if they're hidin' in any of them," ordered the wolf, circling a section of land to the south and southwest with his finger. "They must be somewhere in there, or you or Mr. Wise Owl would've spotted them."

CHAPTER TWENTY-EIGHT

CASTLE ROCK

Billy Bones agreed that the huge weathered rock formation did indeed resemble an old castle, especially viewed from the north. As he moved along the path to the formation, a strange anxiety was building up inside him. He glanced over at Victor, who seemed to be keeping a brave front. He thought back on how Melinda had hurt the deer's feelings after he had only tied in the Big Race during the Grand Fair, and how, afterwards, she had come for him outside of the shepherd dog's cottage. "How twisted and bizarre is this turn of events," he thought.

When the two groups got to the south side of the rock formation, Billy noticed that the slope of the structure was much more forgiving. Sheriff Walter Lone Wolf asked Milton Brown Bear to go up to the cave with him, but the big animal was too wide to get through the narrow crevice that led back to the hidden path. The sheriff decided instead to take Billy, Victor Running Deer and Sandy Antelope. Since the wolf knew that Rodney still had his knife, he gave each of them a club and made them temporary deputies. As promised, Felix Vulture led them along the right path. Winston, Milton, Georgie, and the other two vultures stayed down below in case something unforeseen happened and more help was needed.

The trail that the search party followed proved to be steep but passable. When they got to the ledge that led over to the cave, Billy noticed that the low opening faced outward in such a way that they could not be seen from where they were standing.

"If Rodney has Melinda inside, he probably doesn't know we're here," Walter whispered. "Our best bet is to surprise him so he doesn't have a chance to use her as a shield. I'll charge in first. Billy, you and Sandy follow me as quickly as you can. If possible, we'll capture Rodney right away. With luck, the element of surprise will be on our side." He then turned to the disappointed deer, who of course wanted to be in on the attack. "Victor, I think you'd better wait out here and guard our back. Felix, if anything goes wrong, fly directly to Deputy Brown Bear and Winston Wise Owl and tell them to get help."

Billy felt a chill pass through his body as he crept over to the ancient doorway behind Walter and Sandy. When he caught a glimpse of the wolf's face however, he was bolstered by its focus and determination. When they were just outside, the sheriff gave the sign to storm the cave. After madly rushing through the entrance, they found an empty room, well-supplied with food, a straw mattress, and an ancient stone cupboard.

"Well, it looks like we beat 'em to it!" concluded the wolf, as he started to leave.

"Wait, Melinda's scent is already here," said Billy, sniffing the air.

"Then they must have seen us comin' and are hiding outside," concluded the sheriff.

As Walter made his way out of the cave, he motioned for Victor and Felix to join them. "They've been in there, but they've escaped. They've probably gone to the top."

Victor Running Deer was the first to find the path that continued up the rocky incline. He immediately gestured to the others and scampered on ahead. As the young buck was about to climb over the top, Winston Wise Owl appeared seemingly out of nowhere and swooped down over him. "Watch out, Victor, he's just above you, and he's got a rock!"

The deer instantly ducked and slid backwards down the side of the cliff as a large rock just missed his left shoulder. Before he could recover, the sheriff and Billy rushed passed him and scrambled to the top. When the wolf and the dog peeked over the edge, they discovered that their worst fears had been realized. Melinda's hands had been bound, and she was standing close to the drop-off on the far side of the rock. Rodney was directly behind her with the blade of his knife dangerously close to her throat. The young doe had been silenced by her own scarf, wrapped tightly around her mouth. Walter instantly motioned for Billy to stay low as he pulled himself up and over the rim.

"Don't come any closer, sheriff, or I'll jump and take Melinda with me!" snarled the cornered deer, as soon as the sheriff's face appeared.

"Now Rodney, just put the knife down and walk over here. You need to stop this before someone else gets hurt!"

Out of the corner of his eye, Billy noticed that Victor, Sandy, and Felix had also attained the rocky plateau.

"I'm tellin' you again, sheriff, back off, or I'll take her over the cliff with me! I've got nothin' to lose. I've already killed her daddy."

"But he's still alive, Rodney. I'm tellin' you; give yourself up before you get into this thing any deeper! Besides, if you really loved Melinda, you wouldn't want to see her hurt!"

"But she won't have me, and I'll never let her go back to him!" cried the enraged deer, glaring in Victor's direction. "So what've I got to lose? If you don't want her killed, then take your ugly friends and get out of here!"

"Don't trust him, sheriff! He's a coward!" interrupted Victor, suddenly standing and taking a step toward Rodney.

"Sit down, Victor, there's no reason for you to get involved in this!" said Walter sternly.

"But you see, sheriff, I'm already involved. It's because of me he's behaving this way, and now he's too afraid to fight me for her!" The Rogue Deer looked at Victor with hate-filled eyes but did not answer. "That's what I thought...just a sniveling coward!"

"Listen, you jackass," screamed Rodney, moving forward for the first time, "if you didn't have your buddies backin' you up, you wouldn't dare say that to me! Send them away, and we'll see how much courage you really got!"

"Victor, I can't have you doing this! I want you to step back!" insisted Walter again.

"No, sheriff, I can't do that. Please, do what he asks. It's the only way!" pleaded Victor.

Although it went against the grain of his professional ethics, Sheriff Lone Wolf knew that Victor had succeeded in taking Rodney's attention away from Melinda. The deer's bold action also gave him some much-needed time to come up with an alternate plan for saving the doe.

"All right, Billy, Sandy, Felix, you heard Victor. Come on, we'll wait down by the cave," commanded Walter.

Billy Bones was the final animal to climb down off the top of the rock. As he started to lower himself, Rodney made one last demand. "And one more thing, Victor, get rid of that club tucked inside your britches, or the whole thing's off!"

"Fine!" shouted Victor, letting the sturdy piece of wood fly out of his hand and over the cliff.

"But Victor, you can't…" cried the dog, as he saw the odds drastically change in Rodney's favor.

"It's all right, Billy, I don't need anything against this piece of chicken liver!"

The last remark was too much for the irate rogue, who suddenly lunged forward, catching Victor off guard and cutting a gash across his chest deep enough to draw blood.

"I'll make short work of you, just as I did the last deer that tried to interfere with me and Melinda!" sneered Rodney, forcing Victor close to the edge of the drop-off.

"So, you admit you killed Terry Deer! I could have guessed as much!" countered Victor as he circled south, keeping just out of the reach of Rodney's blade.

Moving stealthily in several directions, Rodney finally forced Victor back to the north rim. After a wild slash that threw Rodney off balance, Victor was able to grab the rogue's wrist and bring it down hard against his knee. As the blade flew free, Winston Wise Owl suddenly swooped in from behind an outcropping of rocks just to the east of the smooth plateau and started untying the young doe.

"No! Get away from her!" screamed Rodney, as he broke free and slammed Victor against the north rim so hard that part of his torso hung off the edge. Immediately Rodney leaped back on top of Victor and grabbed him by both arms.

Still concerned about Melinda, Rodney twisted his head around to make sure that Winston had backed away. This break in concentration was what Victor needed. With all his might, he forced his legs straight up and flipped Rodney over the side of the cliff. Unfortunately, the all-out effort caused Victor to lose his balance, and he started sliding off the edge. With a Herculean effort, he caught hold of the rim with his hands while the rest of his body dangled helplessly over the cliff. Just as he was about to lose his grip, Billy and Sandy, who had regained the edge, dashed over from the rim of the plateau, grabbed the deer's wrists, and hoisted him slowly back to the top.

As for Melinda Doe, she stood for some time at the edge of the great rock and stared at the shattered body of Rodney Wild Deer as it lay on the rocks far below. Billy discerned that in spite of her previous animosity toward the Rogue Deer, she seemed full of remorse. "Perhaps her fascination for Rodney caused her to lead him on," he thought. "Well, if that's the case, his death will probably haunt her for many days to come."

Several hours after the searchers returned to Main Street with Rodney's body, Olen Deer also lost his battle for life. After a comforting word to Myrtle and Victor and Melinda, Billy walked slowly back to his cottage. He had come to the realization that the Prairie had a much more immediate problem. Olen had been the unexpected friend of the moderate position as far as *The Great Book of Rules* was concerned. Now Mayor Elmer Prairie Dog had to appoint a new chairman of the City Council, and this time his choice might not be so amicable.

CHAPTER TWENTY-NINE

THE NEW CHAIRMAN

One and a half weeks after Olen Buck's demise and the day before the regular meeting of the City Council, Mayor Elmer Prairie Dog called a special session to fill Olen's vacant seat. Rumors were rampant about who would get the nod. Winston Wise Owl believed that Calhoun Coyote or Doctor Muskrat were the most popular choices because of their prominence in the community and their personal integrity.

After the meeting Winston, George P. Beaver, and Thaddeus P. Turtle waited nervously in the good terrapin's office for Cornelius Van Mink to make the short trip from City Hall. When Cornelius arrived at the Old Meetinghouse, the owl knew by the mink's demeanor that something had gone terribly wrong.

"He picked Brother Fabian!" exclaimed Cornelius, as he sank deep into the old armchair in front of Thaddeus's desk.

"What do you mean he picked Brother Fabian?" asked Winston incredulously.

"Just what I said," repeated the mink. "Elmer chose his own spiritual counselor, Brother Fabian Lynx, to fill Olen's vacancy!"

"But choosing the leader of a meetinghouse has never been done!" rejoined Thaddeus. "Why, it isn't even ethical!"

"Apparently there's nothing in *The Great Book of Rules* that forbids it," answered Cornelius sullenly, "and to make things worse, they even made him chairman."

Winston walked over to the doorway and looked out into the warm spring afternoon. He could not help but notice the freshness of the air and the beauty of the leaves that had just attained their full growth. But now the mink's announcement threatened to tear apart the comfortable world he had come to love.

"It seems that Brother Fabian wants to begin work at tomorrow's session," the mink informed them, interrupting the owl's reflections, "which means we have to turn to our contingency plan. Winston, you speak to Billy Bones and Sandy Antelope this afternoon. George, you contact your brother and his son. My advice is to wait until midnight before we make the actual move so we can keep this thing under wraps."

"And how about Winston's books?" questioned Thaddeus suddenly, sitting up in his chair. "You know he'll go after them too!"

"Well, we can only move the furniture and George's rug and tapestry tonight. Technically the books weren't found by the original inhabitants and weren't addressed in *The Great Book of Rules*. I think I can fight their confiscation in the council."

"I can't believe Brother Fabian would go that far, although he did threaten to destroy them," recalled the owl.

"Well, we'll do what we can tonight," concluded Cornelius Van Mink, shaking his head. "Right now, we'd better be about our business."

The contingency plan was simple. The human artifacts belonging to Cornelius Van Mink, Winston Wise Owl, and George P. Beaver would be taken under cover of darkness to the Old Meetinghouse. Billy Bones and Sandy Antelope had agreed to help Winston Wise Owl move his tall case clock. Justin and Georgie Beaver had consented to help George P. Beaver transport his rug and tapestry. Then all four animals would haul Mary McMink's Irish pieces, now in the possession of Cornelius and Prudence Van Mink, back to the Old Meetinghouse. There they would remain under protection of sanctuary until a more favorable council was back in power.

By the time Winston Wise Owl got back to his tree house, he discovered that Billy Bones and Sandy Antelope had anticipated the proposed undertaking and were waiting by his spiral steps. Hester Groundhog had also gotten wind of the situation and had invited the two young animals for a late supper. Winston, as a matter of course, was welcome to join them.

Before sitting down at the groundhog's table however, Billy made an unusual request. "I think we need to get Mr. Wise Owl's clock out of his house as soon as possible. Perhaps we could hide it behind Hester's tree under the canvas where she keeps her garden tools."

Winston looked sadly at Billy for a moment but did not answer.

"I think perhaps you should listen to Billy, Mr. Wise Owl," said Sandy politely. "If he has a feeling, I'd go with it."

"So would I, Winston," said Hester, taking her pot pie back to the oven. "I'll keep this warm until you're finished."

When Winston got to the first landing where the grandfather clock stood, he carefully removed the cherry bonnet and said softly to Billy, "There's a gunny sack under the dry sink. Get it for me, and we'll haul the works, the pendulum, and the weights in it. They'll ride better that way, and we won't lose anything. Sandy, you're the strongest. Why don't you carry the case?"

Winston stood watch as the two young animals secured the clock under the canvas tarp behind Hester's tree. Before long, as Billy predicted, the owl spied Sheriff Lone Wolf and a couple of Brother Fabian's lieutenants coming toward Land's End. Quickly he motioned for the dog and the antelope to hide under the tarp while he distracted the sheriff and his helpers. "If they stick around, don't make your move until tonight," he warned. "And keep off the main paths as much as you can. I'll meet you at Georgie Beaver's!"

While Hester pocketed the extra spoons that had been laid out for the dog and the antelope, Winston walked nonchalantly over to the approaching sheriff. "Good evening, Walter. What brings you out here? Don't tell me you had a sudden yearning for Hester's pot pie?"

"I'm really sorry to tell you this, Mr. Wise Owl, but I have an injunction signed by the mayor. He's asked me and my deputies to guard the four places that still have old human artifacts. It seems he's afraid that some of them might be moved before the council has a chance to make a ruling tomorrow."

"I see! Well, it seems to me that flies in the face of one of our personal freedoms, don't you think, sheriff?"

"Now Mr. Wise Owl, you know I'm only following orders," said the wolf.

"Hmm…well, is there any reason why I have to remain here while you guard my place?"

"I have no right to detain you, sir."

"Well, thank goodness for that, Walter. I'm glad to hear that at least one of our freedoms is still intact," said the owl somewhat sardonically.

Winston could tell that Sheriff Walter Lone Wolf was extremely uncomfortable carrying out the controversial injunction, but he also knew that the wolf was a dutiful servant and would obey the City Council.

CHAPTER THIRTY

A PLACE OF SANCTUARY

Billy Bones and Sandy Antelope hid under Hester's canvas until twilight faded before sneaking back through her garden and across the open pasture leading to Jason Crow's cornfield. Only once did Billy fear discovery. Jason's son, Gerard, came cawing down the road near his home. Apparently he had spotted the sheriff heading toward Land's End and felt compelled to investigate.

After lying flat on the ground for at least a quarter of an hour, the two friends skirted wide around the crow's farmhouse by crossing the road and continuing through Charlie Pheasant's field. Billy was thankful that Deputy Harold Eagle had not been notified to do night patrol. Even though there was only a sliver of a moon, he could easily have spotted them from the air. It was almost midnight before the two animals hid the clock near Georgie's clearing and crossed the land bridge to his house on the pond.

Winston, Justin, and Georgie were waiting for Billy and Sandy just inside the beaver's snug little home. Sandy had to kneel under the low ceiling as the owl filled them in on the latest turn of events.

"Bison Bob, Milton Brown Bear, and several of

Brother Fabian's lieutenants are guarding George's castle and Cornelius's home," began Winston. "I hate to tell you this, Billy, but Victor Running Deer has been assigned to your home. Apparently, Sheriff Lone Wolf deputized him about a week ago. I guess he was impressed with the way Victor handled himself during Melinda's abduction."

At the news of Victor's assignment, Billy's head began spinning so violently that he had to sit down. As he tried to clear his mind, he had a vision of a herd of deer rushing through the two trees at Land's End. They were unchanged animals like those he used to chase in the old man's cornfield. He felt they were coming straight at him, and he had to duck to avoid them before the spinning stopped.

"What happened, Billy?" said Georgie, kneeling by the shepherd dog. "You've seen somethin', haven't you?"

"It's just that I never expected Victor…" Billy found he could not finish. He knew they were facing a more serious problem than having to analyze one of his visions.

"They're even guarding the other side of the dam. Apparently they think we might cross there. Fortunately, they've run out of deputies, and they had to enlist the Peccary Brothers for the job. We've already heard them arguing among themselves," said Justin, trying to return to the situation at hand.

"But what are we gonna to do?" said Sandy, who was already tired of carrying the clock's awkward case.

"Actually, Georgie came up with a plan," said Justin proudly. "He suggested that we go the rest of the way by water. We have several flatboats in our boathouse."

"I've already seen Cornelius and Prudence Van Mink. We were able to get Mary's furniture out to their boathouse in the nick of time. Milton Brown Bear and his crew arrived just as we were walking back into the main house," explained Winston, whose melancholy had been replaced with a new sense of adventure.

"In the meantime, Georgie here swam over to my brother's house and in through his underwater entrance," continued Justin. "They're going to pass the rug and the tapestry out their back window overlooking the water."

"But what about the peccaries?" wondered Billy. "Won't they see us?"

"Well, the moon's already set, and I think if we stay close to the east bank, we'll be OK," said Georgie excitedly. "Besides, Mom gave them some of her hot cross buns and her best elderberry wine. I don't think they'll be lookin' for us on the water!"

Billy and Sandy manned one flatboat with the precious tall case clock between them. Justin and Georgie went on ahead of them with the other boat. By the time the dog and the antelope caught up with them, they were catching the old tapestry that the former mayor and his wife were passing out the kitchen window. After what seemed like an eternity, they successfully retrieved the Oriental rug as well.

Unexpectedly Johnny Otter's head popped up between the two boats. "Doin' a little midnight movin' are we, Georgie? I just seen Bison Bob and his pals around the corner. They seem to be on guard as if somethin' was about to happen! You don't suppose…?"

Georgie Beaver was dumbfounded and could only stare wide-eyed at his old nemesis. Finally the playful otter chuckled and glanced back at Billy, who shook his head slowly back and forth.

"Well, I guess I owe you at least one favor! See ya' around!" exclaimed the unpredictable otter, disappearing into the darkness of the pond.

"Will he tell Bison Bob?" asked Sandy Antelope, leaning over to Billy Bones.

"No, I don't think so," replied the shepherd dog, trying to weigh the consequences.

"Well, I guess we have no choice but to trust him," called Justin softly, as he started to pull away toward the west bank. "Come on. We'll drop you and Sandy off on shore with the rest of the stuff. Georgie and I will continue on with the flatboats to the other side of the bridge."

"But you'll have to pass the yard where Bob and his lieutenants are!" exclaimed the concerned antelope in a loud whisper.

"That's why Georgie and I will have to go by ourselves. We'll swim alongside the boats. If we're lucky, they'll be too busy watchin' the island and the bridges to notice two flat pieces of board glidin' by."

After unloading the artifacts and hiding them in the bushes, Billy and Sandy hiked north and joined the two beavers, who had successfully maneuvered past the largest part of the island and under the west bridge. At that point all four animals climbed back into their boats, paddled silently around the north side of the island, and eventually docked at Cornelius's boathouse. Fortunately Milton Brown Bear and his crew were too engrossed in guarding the main house to think about the little shed on the water. With little disruption, the unlikely night raiders loaded the highboy on one boat and the four chairs on the other in quick order. On this last crucial journey, however, they all took to the water, since there was only room for Mary's priceless antiques aboard the little crafts.

By the time the four swimmers got back to the west bridge, it was nearly three o'clock in the morning. As they started removing the furniture from the flatboats, Thaddeus P. Turtle and Winston Wise Owl appeared out of the darkness and informed them that the Old Meetinghouse was also being watched.

"We better hide the artifacts in Thaddeus's house until the meetinghouse is left unguarded," suggested Winston.

The lovely little cottage with its thatched roof stood only a short way up the slope from the pond. By the time the ancient pieces were safely hidden inside the cozy home, there was little room left for the six friends. However, they eventually found comfortable niches in which to rest until they could safely finish their move.

Around eleven o'clock the next day, Billy watched Thaddeus casually venture over to the Old Meetinghouse. His mission was to find Cornelius Van Mink and find out what had transpired during the morning session of the City Council. When the turtle finally returned to the cottage around noon, all the brave companions except the dog were fast asleep. After much effort, Billy and Thaddeus managed to waken them with the news.

"The council has decided that all the human artifacts still in private hands shall be confiscated immediately and taken to City Hall. I'm afraid that includes your books, Winston," the turtle began. "I understand that Brother Fabian railroaded every ruling through concerning the artifacts in quick succession. In fact, he's already issued orders for Sheriff Lone Wolf and his deputies to begin rounding them up." The turtle stopped talking for a moment and sighed, "There is one positive note though. The meetinghouse is no longer being watched, so we can make our final move right now."

The shepherd dog noted that only a few woodland birds in the neighborhood witnessed the odd procession of furnishings that traveled from the turtle's cottage up to the Old Meetinghouse. The highboy and the tall case clock fit snugly into Thaddeus's office, and the tapestry, rug, and four chairs gave a new elegance to the main hall.

Afterwards Billy Bones pondered the bold move for some time. "Well at least it guarantees that some pieces will survive," he thought. "But I'm worried about Winston's books. They seem destined for destruction unless another miracle can be achieved!"

CHAPTER THIRTY-ONE

A PLAN OF ACTION

"Brother Fabian was furious when he discovered our human artifacts were moved right under the noses of the sheriff and his deputies," chuckled Cornelius Van Mink, as he cornered Winston Wise Owl on his way into the Old Meetinghouse on Sunday morning. "He was even angrier when he learned they were being stored inside our meetinghouse. After all, he and his friends had guarded the place all night!"

"How about Billy's corner cupboard? Did Brother Fabian ever find out it was a copy?" questioned Winston, when he saw Billy Bones approaching the two great doors.

"At first he thought it was Granny Muskrat's cupboard, but then Bison Bob told him that the peccaries saw Billy carting her cupboard out of the Prairie. He finally brought Doctor Muskrat in, and he assured him it was not his mother's."

"What happened after that? Did Billy get his new cupboard back?" inquired the owl.

"I understand that Victor Running Deer insisted that it be returned right away. I guess Victor felt bad about taking it, since he and Billy are good friends."

"Well, I'm afraid Brother Fabian's doubled the guard

around my tree and ordered Sheriff Lone Wolf to stay inside my library until all the books can be moved into some sort of wagon," sighed Winston. "Fortunately, by the time the order reached Walter, it was late Saturday evening. Since government transactions can't be carried out on Sunday, they have to wait until Monday morning. After Thaddeus's meditation this morning we're going to meet and discuss the issue. I understand Billy Bones has a plan!"

Every member of the Old Meetinghouse had been touched in some way by Winston Wise Owl's books. The meetinghouse itself was described in a book about eighteenth century New England. Winston had been generous in loaning the books, and most of the members had grown up with the old legends and fairy tales of the ancient humans.

The many woodland birds and songbirds that lived around the perimeter of the pond were especially close to the owl. Like Winston, they valued the vast quantity of knowledge stored in the books. They also knew that the complete body of works was a gift from the ancient human, W. N. Stone, who was buried north of the owl's great tree at Land's End. Winston was aware that many of them had fond memories of the humans in the outside world and had lived in harmony with them.

After Counselor Thaddeus P. Turtle's meditation, Winston explained the possible fate of his books to the members who wanted to stay. Almost the entire small-bird population gathered around the owl and begged to know what they could do to help. The owl was greatly moved and addressed them warmly. "My good friends, Billy Bones is in the Hill Country this morning working on a proposal that might work. George Beaver has offered us the use of his home as a gathering place later on. I'm afraid this meetinghouse will be watched too carefully."

"When would you like us there?" inquired Hosea Brown Thrasher, who wanted to be counted first among his winged brothers.

"Yes, when do you want us? You can count on me too!" interjected Melba Thrush, not wanting to be outdone.

"And me, and me!" warbled a number of other woodland creatures.

"Very fine!" said Winston sincerely. "Billy Bones will meet you on Monday evening around six o'clock in the castle courtyard. Follow him as you would me. Of course, I'll be at Land's End overseeing the dismantling of my library."

The owl suddenly turned away from his avian friends. He had started to choke on his words, and he did not want to lose his composure in front of them.

"Winston, have you any last-minute instructions for us? Is there anything we need to bring?" asked a tiny wren, who always had a cheery word for the wise old bird.

"Yes, thank you for reminding me. I have two requests. The first is to bring a satchel that will hold at least one book." The owl stopped and smiled at the little wren. "And the second is to tell no one who might jeopardize our cause, because if you do, we're surely lost!"

On Sunday evening Billy Bones and Sandy Antelope met with Winston Wise Owl and Justin and Georgie Beaver at the beavers' house. Billy had been successful on his trip to the Hill Country and was anxious to pass on the good news.

"Maurice Rabbit is willing to store the books if the Old Meetinghouse is guarded on Monday night. And he got permission to enter the Hill Country from Omar Mountain Goat. Lucinda Vulture also offered to help, and she volunteered to bring her three sons. They'll meet us tomorrow evening at the castle, and they'll even lead the way into Echo Canyon so our birds can enter safely."

"How about Deputy Eagle? Will he be a problem? He'll surely catch on to the plan if he's on patrol," declared Justin, trying to foresee complications.

"Apparently he refuses to have anything to do with confiscating someone else's property," explained Sandy, "'specially if it involves Mr. Wise Owl."

"Now if we can just get the rest of the plan to work," said Winston, still a little uneasy about taking the books into Lucinda's jurisdiction.

"The sheriff plans to haul the books in Deputy Brown Bear's lumber wagon," the older beaver informed them. "It's the only one large enough to hold all the books. I made that vehicle, and I can rig two of the wheels so they'll fall apart—if I can just get my hands on it for a couple hours!"

"Knowing Milton, he's probably taken it out and greased the wheels already. I understand he's on guard from midnight to dawn at Land's End. I'm sure we can make the change in that time," said Sandy, who was pleased that he could be of use.

"Well, I hope he's already greased them and doesn't look at the wheels I'm installing too closely," exclaimed Justin, "because if he does, our whole plan is for nothing."

"Exactly how does it work?" questioned Winston. "Will it take much effort to set it off?"

"Nah, it's real easy," interjected Georgie. "All you do is pull two pins on each front axle, and when the wagon starts to move, the front wheels fall apart."

"And that'll buy us the time we need, because they'll have to wait till Tuesday to get Justin to repair the wagon." smiled the shepherd dog.

"That is, if everything else works," answered the old owl.

"But who'll pull the pins? Won't they be suspicious if one of us goes near the wagon?" asked the youthful beaver.

"Well, that's the catch, Georgie. We'll have to rely on an insider," confessed Billy.

"But who?" said Justin. "Winston would be too obvious, and Hester isn't strong enough."

"Victor!" yelled Georgie suddenly. "It's Victor. But will he do it?"

"Yes, I think he will," said Billy softly, hoping the deer would finally remember his pact with Olen—even though he had broken it once with Billy's cupboard. "Anyway, he's our only hope."

"And he goes on guard duty on Monday afternoon," continued the antelope. "He'll have to find a time when the others are at lunch or bringing books down from the tree house."

"So you've already spoken to Victor?" questioned Justin, who was still uncomfortable with the choice.

"Yes," said Billy, "both Sandy and I did. We tried to explain how important it was to the community and to Mr. Wise Owl."

"This will be Victor's moment," stated Winston solemnly, not knowing about the secret pact. "He'll have to decide where he stands. It all comes down to that. Well anyway, I better be on my way. I have to organize my lists. I want to document each book as it leaves the library. Elmer Prairie Dog has allowed me that much consideration." The old owl scratched his head and looked sadly over at his comrades. "It'll buy us some time. That way the actual loading process will last most of the day. If Billy's plan is going to work, the wagon can't leave the vicinity of Land's End until late Monday afternoon."

Billy and Sandy spent the evening securing the props they would need on Monday while Justin and Georgie worked on the trick wheels. Shortly before midnight all four animals took turns rolling the two wheels over to Deputy Brown Bear's home. As Sandy had correctly assumed, the wagon sat in front of the bear's cave with the wheels already greased, and Milton had already left for guard duty. Since he lived alone, there was no one to keep them from accomplishing their task.

On Monday morning Winston Wise Owl watched from his tree house window as Sheriff Walter Lone Wolf relieved Milton Brown Bear and asked him to fetch the all-important wagon. After that he issued the order to confiscate Winston's books. From the sheriff's demeanor, Winston surmised it was the hardest thing the wolf had ever been required to do.

CHAPTER THIRTY-TWO

THE FLIGHT OF THE BIRDS

Around midmorning the wagon arrived, and to Winston's relief, nothing about it seemed suspicious. The cataloguing of each book took a lot of time and patience, but the owl stuck to his guns and listed every critical element of each book. As the process dragged on into the afternoon, the deputies became increasingly edgy and short tempered. By suppertime the last books was finally stacked on the wagon. Winston had no way of knowing whether Victor Running Deer had been able to carry out his assignment. He watched with bated breath as Milton Brown Bear and nine of his deputies picked up the tongue and took up positions around the wagon in preparation for the big push. Winston's heart sank as the wagon lurched slowly forward and started gathering momentum. He feared that the young buck had decided not to cooperate. Suddenly, however, the cart shook violently, the vehicle collapsed, and the carefully-stacked books flew helter-skelter around the yard. "I was afraid of something like this!" barked Sheriff Lone Wolf in disgust, as he turned to Milton Brown Bear, who was picking himself off the ground. "There was too much weight for those blasted wheels! You probably haven't checked them in years!"

"Well, they seemed all right last night when I greased them," answered the brown bear apologetically.

"Well damn, now we'll have to stack the books and wait till morning," concluded the wolf. "I can't ask Justin to come at this time of day. It would take him most of the night to fix the stupid thing!" Winston Wise Owl felt enormous relief. Not only had Victor remained above suspicion; the sheriff had not suspected sabotage.

Sheriff Lone Wolf immediately sent Victor, Bison Bob and the three Coyote Brothers back to City Hall to inform Brother Fabian of the accident. Later that evening, Victor returned alone. Winston climbed quickly down from his tree house. He wanted to hear what the deer had to say.

"Brother Fabian wants us to guard the books all night, and no one is to be relieved until they reach City Hall," the deer reported.

"But how about Bison Bob and the coyotes?" snarled the sheriff. "What happened to them?"

"Brother Fabian kept them. He wants them to guard the Old Meetinghouse in case some books make their way over there," returned Victor.

"Damn," said the sheriff under his breath. "That only leaves me with you, Milton, Wiley Weasel, Rattlesnake Pete, and the Peccary Brothers. How can I keep everyone awake? Milton and the peccaries haven't slept since Sunday afternoon." The wolf hesitated a moment and then made his decision. "Victor: you, Wiley, and Pete take the early shift. Milton: you and the Peccary Brothers take the second. That's the best I can do."

Winston excused himself and returned to his tree house. Once inside, he moved his comfortable old armchair by the window. He wanted to watch all the proceedings.

To keep themselves occupied, Victor and his party stacked the books that were still on the wagon in a large pile on the ground so the broken vehicle could be repaired in the morning. After that they picked up the books that had been strewn about during the accident and placed them on top of the others. When the long spring twilight finally faded, a lantern was lit and hung on the collapsed lumber wagon nearby. At midnight they were relieved by Deputy Brown Bear and his crew of swine.

Around one a.m. sleep-deprived Sheriff Lone Wolf finally succumbed to his own sleep deprivation and laid down for a much-needed nap. Up in his room Winston also dozed off. A half hour later, he was jarred awake by the Peccary Brothers, who were arguing among themselves. When the owl peeked out the window, he saw two hooded animals creeping cautiously up to the makeshift pile and removing several of its contents. As they turned to escape, Milton Brown Bear saw them and shouted to the pigs, "Hey! They're stealing the books! After them, you fools! Don't let them get away!" The peccaries immediately took up the chase, followed by the huge bear. The thieves ran blatantly down the middle of the path in the direction of the beaver pond, staying just ahead of their pursuers.

Back at the book pile Winston watched in amazement as a sudden hum and whir of many feathers filled the air. Soon a host of small winged creatures swooped down and began collecting books, some taking five or six, others one or two, until the pile was almost gone. By the time Sheriff Lone Wolf was able to rouse, there was only swirling dust and the flapping of many wings. As the wolf bolted upright, the shadowy outlines of four larger birds dove quickly down and scooped up the remaining books.

As soon as he could, the sheriff stood and crossed to the broken cart. At the same time, the bear and the four exhausted pigs came running up the road toward Land's End.

"We tried to catch them, sir," grunted Milton, as he approached his commander, "but they were too fast for us!"

"Who in the name of The Great Spirit are you talking about?" inquired the exasperated wolf.

"The thieves, of course," returned one of the pigs. "They stole some of our books!"

It was only then that Milton and the peccaries noticed that the whole pile of books was gone. "You left your post because a couple of books were stolen? All of you?" growled Walter. "You idiots, can't you see that the real thieves came while you were gone! And they didn't run away either. They flew away—and there weren't just a few. There were hordes of them!"

Winston Wise Owl turned away from the library window and trudged up the stairs to his bedchamber. Although the episode had been a success, his eyes clouded with unrestrained tears as he glanced around at empty shelves and the spot on his landing where the ancient timepiece once stood. He knew he would be interrogated tomorrow, but for tonight, he was going to his bed, and for a few grateful moments, forget.

CHAPTER THIRTY-THREE

THE OWL'S ARREST

Two days after the daring early morning raid that removed Winston Wise Owl's entire library, the owl was arrested and called before the City Council for questioning. Sheriff Walter Lone Wolf and Deputy Milton Brown Bear were also asked to attend. Elmer Prairie Dog had been reluctant to call a special session to discuss the unprecedented occurrence, since most of the community's small-bird population was probably involved, not to mention four of the larger ones.

"Sheriff, are you telling us that you were unable to identify any of the birds that absconded with Mr. Wise Owl's books?" queried Brother Fabian Lynx.

"No sir, I was just wakin' up from an hour's sleep after being on guard duty for two days. I only remember hearin' a rustling noise, and when I glanced up, I saw a horde of birds flying away. Four large birds were still on the scene, but because of the location of my bedroll, I was too far away to make a positive identification."

"And Deputy Brown Bear, where were you at this time? You and your crew were supposed to be guarding the books, I understand," pursued Brother Fabian impatiently.

"We were just returnin' to the area," stated the Brown

Bear, looking down at the floor.

"And why was that again?" asked Phineas T. Fox, who was anxious to side with the lynx.

"We were chasin' a couple of thieves who had stolen some books off the pile we'd made in the yard," continued Milton. "Unfortunately, we couldn't catch 'em."

"I see," continued the fox, "and were you able to recognize these thieves?"

"No sir, it was too dark."

"But I understood there was a lamp hangin' from the wagon," interrupted Charlie Pheasant, wanting to be part of the interrogation.

"Both of them had on hoods and capes. Besides, the light wasn't very strong, and they ran away as soon as we hollered," responded the deputy.

"Deputy Brown Bear, did it ever occur to you that these creatures might be decoys?" questioned Brother Fabian again. "Surely that must have been obvious to you!"

"Only afterwards, sir," responded the bear, becoming more and more uncomfortable.

It was at this crucial time that Brother Fabian Lynx asked Mayor Elmer Prairie Dog to announce his latest appointment. The little rodent stood and read from a prepared text. "Because of a number of failures by our sheriff's department, I have appointed Phineas T. Fox to be Head of Law Enforcement here in the Prairie. From now on, Sheriff Lone Wolf and his deputies will report directly to him."

"I protest!" yelled Cornelius Van Mink, shooting up from his chair. "This appointment is preposterous as well as unprecedented—having a councilman head of the sheriff's department!"

"There's nothing in *The Great Book of Rules* that prevents it," said Brother Fabian evenly. "And besides, someone has to see that our laws are carried out."

"Your laws, you mean!" rebuffed Cornelius.

"I think maybe we should adjourn now," declared the shaken prairie dog. "We'll continue this afternoon at two o'clock with the questioning of Mr. Wise Owl."

"Yes, maybe you'd better do that!" exclaimed Cornelius Van Mink, as he stormed out of the meeting followed by Wendell Red Breast. An angry sheriff and deputy waited with Winston Wise Owl so he could address the new chairman, the mayor, and the other strict constructionists.

"One day you'll dig a hole you can't get out of, Brother Fabian Lynx! At least half of our population disagrees with your little cleansing process, and you can push them only so far. As for you, mayor, you were once an upstanding citizen. I'm ashamed to say that you and these two cowards beside you are now just puppets of this tyrant."

"Dig a hole, will I?" shouted Brother Fabian, "Well, we'll see who digs a hole for himself, Winston Wise Owl! I'm not finished yet!"

That afternoon when the council met again, Bison Bob was an added witness.

"Mr. Wise Owl, were you given a written decree by Sheriff Lone Wolf that your entire library was to be removed and taken to City Hall?" asked Phineas T. Fox, the new head of law enforcement.

"You know that I did," returned the owl.

"And did you comply with that request?" continued the fox.

"Yes, I did," answered Winston.

"Every book that you owned…?"

"My library was completely displaced, if that's what you mean."

"Deputy Bob, did you carry out the order I gave you this morning?" asked Phineas, suddenly opening a new line of questioning.

"Yes sir, I did!" answered the buffalo.

"And could you explain to the council what that was?" continued the fox.

"You asked me to search Mr. Wise Owl's tree house."

"And did you find anything the council might be interested in?"

"Yes sir, I did. I found this book. It was hidden in the trunk at the foot of Mr. Wise Owl's bed." The deputy held up the copy of *Grimm's Fairy Tales* that had been given to Jimmy Stone by his grandfather. The owl had forgotten about the book, but it was the one book he never would have allowed out of his possession.

"You mean you went through Mr. Wise Owl's things without his knowledge?" queried Cornelius Van Mink, standing and showing his disgust.

"It's all right, Cornelius. I gave them permission this morning," responded the owl, shaking his head. "I'm afraid I forgot about that book."

"Well, I think it's unconscionable!" stated the mink, sitting back in his chair.

"Mr. Wise Owl, were you aware that the books we removed from your tree house were going to be stolen?" asked the fox, trying to get to the crux of the matter.

"You mean stolen or taken to a safe haven?" answered the owl sarcastically. "After all, if anyone was stealing my books, it was the City Council!"

"I see. Then you apparently knew the raid was going to take place?"

"I was certainly hoping it would—if that's what you're asking me."

"Mr. Wise Owl, did you or did you not instigate the removal of your books once they were sitting outside your house?"

"No, I didn't, but I'm certainly glad someone did!" smiled the owl, starting to enjoy the conversation.

"And do you know the culprit or culprits who organized this travesty?" questioned Brother Fabian Lynx, interrupting the procedure.

"Well, Brother Fabian, if I knew that, I certainly wouldn't tell you now, would I?" hooted the owl with much satisfaction.

"Can you also tell us who took the grandfather clock out of your house and the other artifacts belonging to Mr. Van Mink and Mr. Beaver?" inquired Phineas, trying to prove his fitness for his new position.

"I protest again!" broke in the mink. "Those articles were removed before any order to confiscate them was sent out. They cannot be considered here!"

"Very well, Councilor Van Mink, we'll stick to the subject at hand. I hereby charge Winston Wise Owl for conspiring to steal the books that once belonged to W. N. Stone and that now belong to the state. I also charge him for being the guiding force behind a rebellion against that state!" yelled Brother Fabian, pointing an accusing finger at Winston.

"But you can't!" cried Cornelius. "They were his own books! This is outrageous!"

"And I also accuse him of deliberately withholding one of the said books," continued the lynx, unabated.

"But he explained that!" interjected Wendell Red Breast. "He simply forgot about the book in his trunk!"

"Hah, a likely story!" snarled the lynx. "I say we put it to a vote right now!"

The stunned moderate members could only sit by and watch as Winston was convicted and sentenced to banishment through the magic portal at the time of the summer solstice—a sentence accorded to only the worst criminals for crimes against the state.

The arrest and conviction of Winston Wise Owl was not the only business enacted by the new City Council. Winston stood by in horror as Brother Fabian pushed through a decree that called for the destruction of Mary McMink's furniture that was now being held inside the New Meetinghouse.

"On Saturday following," gloated the lynx loudly, "the Irish dining table and four chairs that once belonged to Mary McMink will be stacked in front of City Hall and destroyed by fire. As for the evil book called *Grimm's Fairy Tales*, it will be placed on top of the pile like frosting on a cake and burned to a royal crisp!"

CHAPTER THIRTY-FOUR

VIVIAN'S COMMAND

Billy Bones learned from his neighbor Gloria Meadowlark that nearly the entire community of birds that attended the Old Meetinghouse had participated in the daring raid at Land's End. Afterwards Lucinda Vulture and her sons had led them safely to Maurice Rabbit's dugout in Echo Canyon, where the books were deposited in a great heap in the middle of the rabbit's studio.

As promised, Billy Bones and Georgie Beaver arrived the next morning to construct temporary bookcases. The ambitious project lasted four days, during which time the three animals isolated themselves in order to complete the job. Consequently, they knew nothing of the arrest of Winston Wise Owl and the City Council's plan to burn the artifacts in their possession.

On the last day of the project, Lucinda Vulture thrust herself upon the scene with the dreaded news. Without ceremony, she threw open Maurice's door and flapped into the center of the room. "Brother Fabian Lynx has finally done it! Just as we feared, he's passed a decree calling for the destruction of Mary McMink's furniture by fire!" she screamed, as she passed back and forth in front of the newly formed library, jealously eyeing a number of the books. "They have also placed Winston Wise Owl under house arrest until the day of the summer solstice, at which time they plan to expel him from The Enchantment! As soon as they passed sentence, Brother Fabian had Winston's wings clipped so he can't fly for another three months!"

"But doesn't that ensure his death in the outside world? A bird that's unable to fly would be easy prey for any predatory animal!" cried Billy, recognizing the extreme danger to his old mentor.

"Yes, that's true. Like a dog, for instance!" declared Lucinda, permitting a rare glimpse of her sarcastic wit. "Therefore, Billy, you must act quickly. The burning takes place tomorrow morning. You must get the crowd to rebel against it. I'll be there myself to give you support. Unfortunately, they are unlikely to listen to me!"

"Or to me for that matter, especially after Mr. Wise Owl's arrest," answered Billy. "My guess is they'll be too afraid to do anything!"

"Nevertheless, we must do what we can. Now off with you! You too, Georgie. See what kind of support you can drum up tonight."

"The trouble is that most of them don't believe that anything will really happen when the artifacts are destroyed. It will be difficult to ask them to act on my dreams alone! It seems preposterous, even to me," said Billy, suddenly doubting himself.

"No, you must have faith! We already know what *The Vulture's Appendix* says! We can't take a chance!" screamed Lucinda again. "Now off with you! Do whatever's in your power to stop this thing!"

CHAPTER THIRTY-FIVE

THE FATAL BURNING

Saturday morning dawned bright and sunny with little suggestion of a storm. "At least, maybe that part of the dream won't come to pass!" Billy said aloud, as he quickly dressed.

On Friday evening, the dog had gone to visit Victor Running Deer. He knew that the young buck would be asked to be one of the guards at the burning. "Just position yourself away from the side where Brother Fabian Lynx and the council will be watching! Let Nosey do the rest!" the dog pleaded before he left the deer's newly refurbished lean-to.

When Billy Bones arrived at City Hall with Nosey Coon, he noticed that the endangered furniture was neatly stacked just south of the old building. Underneath and around the edges of the antiques were piles of sticks and brush that could easily catch fire. The ancient book of fairy tales had been placed on top of a chair that sat on the center of the table. The three deputies Bison Bob, Milton Brown Bear, and Victor Running Deer stood guard around the pile. As promised, Victor covered the section away from Court Street.

A large crowd of animals had already gathered. As Billy feared, most of the birds from the Old Meetinghouse were absent. Only Wendell Red Breast had braved the exposure, standing with Cornelius and Prudence Van Mink and their grandchildren, Priscilla and Conrad; George P. and Constance Beaver; Justin, Gladys, and Georgie Beaver; and Counselor Thaddeus P. Turtle. The little conclave stood apart from the others and to the left of City Hall.

Mayor Elmer Prairie Dog and his extended family, including his grandfather, who was a son of one of the first inhabitants, positioned themselves directly in front of the steps. Brother Fabian Lynx, Phineas T. Fox, Charlie Pheasant and his family, and Farmer Jason Crow and his family positioned themselves to the right of the mayor. Billy was sad to see that the crow had also seated his grandfather in front of his entourage in direct defiance of *The Vulture's Appendix* and the dog's premonition.

Before Billy joined Georgie's family, he whispered a few instructions to Nosey, and the raccoon darted off around the crowd and to the back of the furniture. As the shepherd dog reached the beavers, Georgie pulled him aside. "Billy, I thought you'd never get here. Phineas T. Fox is already trying to get the crowd's attention. What do you plan to do?"

"Let Phineas talk first. Then I'll see if they'll listen to me. I think I've got a better chance once he gets their attention, especially since so many of them support Brother Fabian," explained the young dog, as he noticed the sky turning dark and ominous.

"May I have your attention, please," shouted the fox, enjoying his new role as Head of Law Enforcement. "The majority members of the City Council have asked me to read the following phrase from *The Great Book of Rules*. It's from *The Prairie Dog's Appendix*: 'The hoarding of articles left by human pioneers should be strictly forbidden. These items are highly dangerous and should be kept away from the general population.'"

The fox lowered the book. "As you can see, the majority members of the council have acted quickly to protect the general welfare of the public!"

At this point, Billy Bones stepped forward. "I also have a quote from *The Mink's Appendix* of *The Great Book of Rules*," and without hesitation, he continued in an equally loud voice. "'Artifacts found along the old wagon trail are of the highest quality and must be safeguarded at all cost.'" He then turned back to Phineas. "I beg the council to reconsider before a great wrong is unleashed!"

An instant roar broke out among the prairie dog's extended family and among those standing on the mayor's right, making it difficult for the dog to continue. Almost at the same moment, a great screech was heard as Lucinda Vulture and her sons flew in over the crowd and landed on the roof of the City Hall.

"Listen to him, creatures of the Prairie!" squawked Lucinda. "*The Vulture's Appendix* warns of great disaster if any of the artifacts are destroyed! And Billy Bones has had prophetic visions warning of catastrophe! Listen to him! Do not let this burning take place!"

Immediately onlookers from all sides began to cry out to Mayor Prairie Dog and Councilor Fox to heed Lucinda's warning. Many of them were in awe of the vulture, and her spiritual prowess was legendary. The darkening sky all around them added to their fear.

Phineas T. Fox quickly motioned to Bison Bob to light the brush around the furniture. Billy saw the deputy and made a desperate rush to stop him.

"No, no, you can't!" the dog hollered but was restrained by Milton Brown Bear and the three Coyote Brothers standing nearby. Billy could only watch in horror as the brush and sticks began to crackle and burn brightly.

A sudden gust of wind helped fuel the fire, and before long flames licked at the table and four chairs. When a thick smoke finally started to rise and blanket most of the furniture, Billy saw a little hand reach up and snatch the book of *Grimm's Fairy Tales*. None of the dignitaries in the front noticed nor did Bison Bob or Milton Brown Bear.

As the heat from the bonfire became more intense, the crowd began backing away on all sides. With wide eyes and morbid fascination, they watched the total destruction of the human artifacts in absolute silence. An unnatural draft had suddenly risen and was carrying the smoke upwards as if it were funneling the remains of Mary's furniture into the heavens. Accompanying this was the sound of far-off moaning that could just be heard above the roar of the fire.

To offset this phenomenon, Mayor Prairie Dog and Brother Fabian Lynx gathered at the chair of the oldest prairie dog and were laughing and pointing at the good health of the old rodent, as well as that of Grandfather Crow. Their mirth was interrupted by a terrifying cry. When Billy discovered its source, he was startled to find that it came from the mayor's own wife, Edwina. Their daughter Patsy was being bathed in yellow light and was shrinking to the size of prairie dogs in the outside world, just as he'd seen in his visions during the Grand Fair. When Edwina reached for her, the little animal scurried toward Prairie Dog Town and the nearest hole she could find.

Edwina's scream was followed by an even more dismayed shout from Farmer Jason Crow. His eldest son, Gerard was also enveloped in a yellowish light and had shrunk to the size of an ordinary crow. He quickly flew away to the nearest tree.

Soon afterwards Prudence Van Mink cried out in a like manner, as her granddaughter Priscilla, covered in a similar light, wilted, slithered out of her clothes, and headed for the safety of the beaver pond. In desperation Prudence called after her, but the little mink only cried back a disturbing scream of her own.

Gladys and Justin noticed Georgie's transformation at the same time. Fortunately Justin bent down and picked up the little creature before he could scamper away, just as Gladys let out a great moan that could be felt as well as heard by the whole circle of spectators.

The final and fifth mutation was heralded by Lucinda herself. Her first son, Felix, was changing to a simple scavenger and was flying away toward the foothills. Lucinda quickly sent her other sons in pursuit as she circled swiftly over the crowd and then over Mayor Elmer Prairie Dog and Brother Fabian Lynx, now huddled about the mayor's distraught wife.

"I told you a disaster would follow, but no, you wouldn't listen!" the vulture shrieked. "Now see what you've done! You've killed part of the old memory for all time, you fools—you blind, ignorant fools!" And with those distressed words, Lucinda flew off in the direction of the Hill Country as rain began pelting her black-robed body.

Utter chaos erupted as Billy Bones watched the remaining creatures grab their offspring and rush for the safety of their homes. Four of their own and one of the Hill Country's youngest generation had fallen victim to the aftermath of the dreadful burning. Gradually it dawned on the dog that all five changelings—Patsy Prairie Dog, Gerard Crow, Priscilla Van Mink, Georgie Beaver, and Felix Vulture—were direct descendants of the original inhabitants after the first great rift. As *The Vulture's Appendix* had predicted, the old memories associated with the five destroyed human artifacts had been lost forever, and with them the gifts of speech and awareness to five of The Enchantment's youngest citizens.

CHAPTER THIRTY-SIX

THE AFTERMATH

During the wind and rain and the dazzling display of lightning and thunder that followed the burning, Billy Bones found himself alone and forgotten. He quickly headed for the security of his own little cottage. When he arrived, he found a candle burning on the table and the leather book that Nosey Coon was able to save lying nearby. The faithful raccoon had crawled into the bunk above the dog's cot and was staring down at him with round expectant eyes. Needles Porcupine was nestled on the floor near the reproduction corner cupboard. The young dog picked up the book of *Grimm's Fairy Tales* and held it to his chest. "Thank you, Nosey. I'm happy you were able to save it. I know Mr. Wise Owl will be eternally grateful."

"Is it over?" asked the raccoon, poking his head over the railing.

"What…oh, you mean the changing? Yes, I believe so. I guess the old memories needed five for five. Well, what's done is done. I just wish it hadn't happened to Georgie."

Billy blew out the candle and crawled into his own bed. Warm tears started to well up in his eyes as he pondered the transformation that had befallen Georgie Beaver. Finally he fell into a fitful sleep that blotted out, for a time, his desolate feelings.

Sometime later Billy was awakened by an urgent scratching at the Dutch doors. Feeling some trepidation, he got up and relit the candle. With Nosey and Needles huddled close behind him, he crossed to the entrance and opened the top door but saw no one. Finally, after another round of scratching, he opened the bottom door. Immediately a chubby little animal scurried in and began rubbing its nose against the dog's leg. Tenderly Billy reached down to pet it. "Ah Georgie, it's you. Came down to spend the night, eh? Well, come on over and lie down by the bed. I'll take you home in the morning."

Georgie Beaver did not understand the words that Billy Bones spoke, but he was happy to be with the dog he loved.

For two weeks following the catastrophic fire, Billy Bones did not stray far from the safety of his home, nor did most residents of the Prairie. The dog had fallen into a deep depression that he could not seem to shake. Even Nosey Coon and Needles Porcupine and their occasional antics could not break through his melancholy. As a last-ditch effort, the raccoon finally confronted him directly.

"How about Mr. Wise Owl? Ain't ya' got any plans for him?"

"Well, what is everybody else doing? Surely they're not waitin' for me?"

"Course they are," said Needles. "You're the one they look up to, and time is growin' short, Billy."

Billy Bones felt ashamed that he had allowed himself to wallow in self-pity. The situation changed by the end of the third week when Gloria Meadowlark dropped by to tell him that a petition was being circulated at the Old Meetinghouse on the following Sunday. The petition expressed a vote of no confidence in Mayor Elmer Prairie Dog and the City Council and called for a special election one month from their next regular meeting. By law, the petition needed to be signed by a majority of the Prairie citizens.

On Sunday morning Billy attended the Old Meetinghouse for the first time in three weeks. To his delight, the place was filled to the rafters, and a line of citizens had gathered outside its double doors and partway around the block. After a short meditation by Thaddeus P. Turtle, both Cornelius Van Mink and Wendell Red Breast gave impassioned pleas on behalf of the petition. Billy was surprised to see that the next speaker was Farmer Jason Crow.

"I want to be the first one to sign this here petition! I do not have the words to express to you the heartache these scoundrels have caused me and my family!" cawed the crow in a loud voice. "I admit I stubbornly stood by and allowed Brother Fabian to think for me, believin' his interpretation of *The Great Book of Rules* was the correct one! Well, apparently I had to be hit over the head before

I could see the light! I know there probably ain't nothin' I can do to change my son back to the way he was, but at least me and my family can try to do the right thing now before any more calamity befalls this community!"

As it turned out, the signatures of the good crow and his extended family and friends were enough to give Councilor Van Mink and Councilor Red Breast the majority of names they needed. Billy learned that morning that although Farmer Crow was a stubborn old bird, once he changed his allegiance, he was a staunch ally.

Unfortunately, Billy's hopes for the Prairie and Winston Wise Owl took a disastrous turn on Wednesday morning when Bison Bill and Milton Brown Bear showed up at his door. Billy just had time to pull on his trousers.

"We arrest you in the name of the City Council for entering the mists unlawfully on your second day inside The Enchantment," bellowed the buffalo.

"But why?" answered the bewildered dog. "I thought that was settled. The City Council didn't make their ruling retroactive."

"Well, they changed their mind. So put your shirt on and come with us. You have to appear before them this morning."

When Billy arrived at City Hall under the watchful eyes of the two deputies, he discovered that the mayor and his council were meeting at the long table located in the large Entrance Hall. The only other citizens present were Thaddeus P. Turtle and Justin Beaver, who were sitting along the wall. Justin had Georgie with him on a short leash. Billy guessed they were there on his behalf.

As the dog seated himself between the bear and the buffalo, he noticed that Cornelius Van Mink and Wendell Red Breast were just introducing the petition signed by over half of the Prairie citizens. At the end of their presentation they requested that Winston Wise Owl's expulsion be delayed until after the special election. Brother Fabian Lynx, Phineas T. Fox, and Charlie Pheasant refused to consider the owl's plight even after Mayor Elmer Prairie Dog voiced his objections. When Brother Fabian deliberately ignored the prairie dog's plea, Billy knew that the lynx was no longer making any pretense about who was really in charge.

After Winston's fate was sealed, Phineas T. Fox ordered Billy to stand before the council. To the dog's surprise, Bison Bob and Milton Brown Bear got up with him. Feeling the presence of the two deputies on either side of him and seeing the smug countenances of the three majority members, the dog intuitively knew that the outcome had already been decided.

"It's been brought to our attention numerous times that Mr. Billy Bones here unlawfully entered the mist on the second day of his arrival into our fair land," the fox began. "Unfortunately, that's a violation that the old council refused to deal with. Therefore, I propose that we clean house and handle this matter immediately!"

"I second the motion!" assented Charlie Pheasant, fairly flying out of his chair.

After allowing the objections of Thaddeus and Justin to be heard, Brother Fabian rose to speak. Billy could tell by the glint in the lynx's eye that he was relishing the moment.

"As you are all aware, Mr. Bones here spent a good part of his second day inside the great mist that surrounds us. We all know that *The Great Book of Rules* clearly warns that we should never enter this area for any reason. It also says that we could face injury or possible death. In fact, it even goes so far as to say that we could become disoriented or even lose our mental faculties altogether. You might ask yourself, 'Why then was Mr. Bones not affected? And why did the blasphemous Lucinda Vulture make such a fuss over him in front of her own Tribal Council if they did not have something in common?' We all know she is infamous for breaking the rules of *The Great Book* and that she hides inside the Hill Country where she is free to do as she pleases!" Brother Fabian stopped and stared at Billy for a long moment and then continued in a soft soothing voice. "It's becoming clear to me, as it should to you, that something abnormal is going on here—something strangely diabolical—something that smacks of…should I say the word…sorcery!"

As the lynx finished, there was an audible gasp from Thaddeus P. Turtle, who jumped to his feet. "Brother Fabian, as a fellow counselor, I must say that I'm appalled! How dare you say such a thing! Why, that's unfounded superstition at its worst!"

"Counselor Turtle, will you please not interrupt me, or I'll have to ask you to leave," purred the lynx with a sardonic smile. "May I remind you that you're only a guest here. You and your petition will have a chance to change things in another month. In the meantime, take your seat and be quiet!"

After the turtle's outburst, Cornelius Van Mink finally found his voice. "I think perhaps we should hear from Mr. Bones now, before this charade goes on any further!"

"Yes, of course, Cornelius," agreed Brother Fabian in a condescending tone. "Well, Mr. Bones, what do you have to say for yourself?"

At first the shepherd dog could only gaze quietly over the heads of the mayor and the City Councilors. During Brother Fabian's accusations against him and Lucinda Vulture, all feelings of inadequacy in the presence of the charismatic lynx had strangely vanished, but he still wanted to say something that would help his mentor, Winston Wise Owl.

"Well, Mr. Bones, we're waiting," growled Phineas. "We haven't got all day."

"I think you're all familiar with my circumstances," began Billy flatly. "And I think you all know that I went innocently into the mist. If you want to find me guilty, I'm afraid there's nothing I can say to change your mind." The dog hesitated again and then looked directly at Brother Fabian. "However, as far as Mr. Wise Owl is concerned, what you've done to him is paramount to murder. I'm sure you're all well aware of that!"

"I think that's quite enough, Mr. Bones!" spat the lynx angrily. "I'd feel grateful if I were you that you're not facing the same fate!"

"Why?" barked the dog fearlessly, "because I'm telling you the truth? Maybe you've got some of these councilors wrapped around your little finger, but don't count me among your patsies!"

"Enough, I say!" screamed Brother Fabian in return. "Phineas, do your duty. Charge this dog before I really lose my patience!"

The fox quickly accused the dog a second time with illegally entering the mist at Land's End, and the lynx called for a vote. When the vote was taken, the dog was found guilty by a majority of three to two and sentenced to six months in the local jail. To make matters worse, the incarceration was to take effect as soon as the trial was over.

Billy Bones was stunned. He hadn't considered immediate imprisonment. He instantly realized that if he stayed where he was and did nothing, he would have no chance of saving Winston Wise Owl, who was scheduled to be expelled from The Enchantment in only a couple of days.

At that precise moment, Billy heard a male voice inside his head screaming, "Go, Billy! Break free! Do it now!" Without hesitating, the dog broke free from his captors and with a great cry of, "No!" jumped onto the table around which the mayor and his councilors were sitting. Instinctively he turned and saw that the east window had been left open to let in the morning air. Using Phineas T. Fox's left shoulder as a springboard, the dog dove through the window, landed in the courtyard below, and somersaulted back onto his feet.

As the dog rushed off, he could hear pandemonium break out as Brother Fabian Lynx shouted orders to Phineas T. Fox, who in turn shouted orders to Sheriff Lone Wolf, who shouted orders to Milton Brown Bear and Bison Bob. By the time anyone made it outside and around to the escape route, Billy Bones was nowhere to be seen.

CHAPTER THIRTY-SEVEN

ESCAPE TO THE HILL COUNTRY

Although Winding Walk was sheltered on both sides with a thick cover of pine trees, Billy Bones was careful to stay off the main path. As he zigzagged back and forth through the trees, he remembered his earlier trip after the autumn equinox. At that time however, he was coming away from the Hill Country, not rushing toward it, and his race through the sweet-smelling conifers had been free and uninhibited. He had even given himself the luxury of lying on his back on the soft needles and daydreaming of his experiences in the outside world with Billy Stuart. Although three-quarters of a year had passed since then, his love for the boy had never faltered.

By noon the dog reached the border, but once again he stayed off the main road and climbed the rocky plateau just south of the crossing. Several times during the late morning, he had seen Deputy Harold Eagle and Chester Hawk soaring overhead. He was sure they were looking for him.

Partway up the steep incline, he came upon a breath-taking view of Rainbow Falls. This time he found his mind racing back to Georgie Beaver. He recollected how the good-natured rodent had insisted that he take time to see the 'Enchantment's most glorious natural wonder' just as the sun was rising. Despite his need to keep moving, he felt a painful lump in his throat as he thought of the devastating conversion that had taken away his friend's awareness.

At that moment he saw the two great birds again, speeding in his direction. He threw himself beneath a small bush that was clinging to the side of the hill just in time to escape detection. Strangely, the eagle and the hawk seemed to be riveted on something beneath him and closer to the path. They circled several times above the object of their attention and then turned and flew east in the direction of Main Street.

Billy Bones finally reached the rim of the plateau and headed cross-country in the direction of Maurice Rabbit's home. Now that he was inside the Hill Country he felt safer, although the flying deputies somewhat unnerved him. He surmised that the two birds had search warrants from the City Council tucked securely in their belts. He remembered from his experiences on the Tribal Council that sheriffs and their deputies were allowed to follow escaped prisoners across the border.

When the tired dog reached Maurice's house built into the side of the canyon, he found to his surprise that the door was closed and locked. For a second he panicked, until he spied a small cloth sack wedged into a corner of the doorway. Upon opening it, he discovered a sandwich of fresh bread and honey, a ripe tomato, and a sticky note that read, "Had to go to Tribal Council Meeting. Try second option! P.S. Sorry about the books!"

With some trepidation, the young shepherd put his

hand to his forehead and peered inside the studio window. He had to allow a few moments for his eyes to adjust to the darker space. After a couple seconds, he pulled his head back from the glass, blinked his eyes slowly, and then repeated the process. Although his corner cupboard was still against the northeast wall, the bookshelves that he and Georgie had so carefully fashioned had vanished, as had all of Winston Wise Owl's irreplaceable books.

Billy turned away from the window and slumped slowly to the ground. His head was starting to ache, and he felt alone and dejected. He finally forced himself to speak aloud, willing his mind to make some sense of the rabbit's note and what he had just seen.

"What does he mean—second option? And where are all the books?" Suddenly the dog looked up at the sky. "They're running scared! They think Brother Fabian Lynx will find a way to take the books back to the Prairie and destroy them!" Then he put his hand to his jaw. "Lucinda's behind this! She's taken them to their sacred lodge so they can claim sanctuary. That's it!" The dog glanced back toward the old stone bridge that led to the other side of Echo Canyon. "Even if Winston makes it through this mess, it'll be years before he gets those precious books back! Oh, well—we'll save that mess for another day."

As his head began to clear, Billy Bones realized that he would have to keep the Tribal Council out of his escape plans. If there was to be a semblance of cooperation between the two states, the Hill Country's governing body could not be privy to his whereabouts, no matter how unjust his conviction.

Having concluded that he should not go to the Tribal Council and having guessed the fate of his mentor's books, he still pondered the meaning of Maurice's note. "What did he mean—try the second option?"

Once again his attention was drawn skyward. Just to the east, Harold Eagle and Chester Hawk were circling over a section of the woods where he had just traveled.

"Did I leave something behind? Was I that careless?" he thought.

Quickly Billy pulled himself up off the ground, picked up the cloth sack, and scampered around to the side of the building that protruded out just far enough to offer him a hiding place. Once out of sight of the two deputies, he wolfed down the tomato and the sandwich and then scurried further up the hillside to get a better view.

About halfway up the slope, Billy climbed a sturdy evergreen that allowed him to see the entire canyon floor. Less than a mile to the east, he detected movement in the pines directly below the circling birds. After closer inspection, he recognized the large frame of Bison Bob moving directly toward the dugout. Soon afterwards he spotted Milton Brown Bear and one of the three coyote brothers. Finally, it seemed as if the entire forest was coming alive.

"It's a whole posse!" the shepherd mumbled under his breath, "but how did I leave such a clear trail?"

Presently Billy noticed that the flying deputies had changed their course and were inspecting the bridge that spanned the river called Spirit Moves. In the next instant they were rushing down the path directly toward Maurice's home. Billy quickly jumped to the ground and hid under the thick boughs at the bottom of the pine tree he had recently climbed. He glanced up just in time to see the eagle swoop over the dugout and up the canyon wall within fifty feet of his hiding place. Shortly afterward, the hawk followed a similar path slightly to the west of him. After a number of attempts, the two birds returned to the bridge and began searching both sides of the river.

While observing the birds along the banks of Spirit Moves, Billy Bones finally recalled what Maurice Rabbit referred to as "the other option." Omar Mountain Goat had stopped him after the last ceremony during the spring equinox and cautioned him, "Your first contact should be Maurice, of course, but if there isn't time, come straight to my cave."

"Omar's cave. That's it! But how do I get across that river without being seen? I can't swim the blasted thing because my head will keep poppin' up!" The dog's mind was racing wildly again. He knew that he had to get to the temporary safety of the goat's cave before the sheriff's posse caught up to him.

Quickly he scanned the river bank again for any possibility of bridging the span. Before long, his gaze fell on the spot where the water came crashing out of the mountain. Just at that point it seemed that the river and the mist merged together, causing the area above it to vanish into the murky gold of the mist surrounding The Enchantment.

"If I could just get to that spot without being seen,

maybe I could find a way to cross above it!"

As quickly as he could, the shepherd dog made his way over to the river's turbulent entrance by slipping from tree to tree. From his new vantage point near the water, he noticed that his pursuers had already searched the rabbit's dwelling and the hillside directly above it.

Just behind and above the steaming gap in the mountain that marked the river's entry into the Hill Country, Billy observed a large boulder that disappeared into the mist. On the other side, the end of what seemed to be the same boulder jutted back out just above the stream. He felt a rush of excitement. If he could make it to the boulder without being seen, maybe he could feel his way around the backside of the huge rock. The constant rising vapor was some help to him, but he also had to wait until both birds were flying away from the entrance. When everything was finally in order, the dog rushed to the boulder and stepped inside the mist.

Billy tried to keep in constant contact with the stone wall. However, another larger boulder part way around the first boulder forced him further inside the mist, and after that, another. Soon he heard the distant wailing and fluttering of wings that he had encountered during his last journey inside the forbidden border. No matter how hard he tried to concentrate, the ancient sounds kept drawing him in like a magnet until he lost contact with the stone wall altogether. By the time he was able to restrain himself and return to the safety of the boulder, he had already become disoriented. It was the thing he feared most.

"Keep the wall to your left, dummy," the dog finally uttered in disgust. "But is this the same boulder? And why is it so dark? I should be close to the other side!"

Summoning all his willpower, he blocked out the sounds of the old memories and felt his way along the damp stone, keeping it always on his left. After several nervous moments, it started to get lighter just ahead of him. His pace picked up considerably, and his heart began to pound more rapidly as he approached the reentry point. He prayed that he had crossed the river and had not returned back to his starting position.

When he got to the mist's edge, he knelt down and carefully stuck his head out into the fresh air. Instantly he gave a huge sigh of relief. Just behind him and to his left, the river roared out of its hidden portal. Ten feet in front of him the trees became thick again, and below he could see the Hill Country's Sacred Lodge.

Lying flat on his stomach, Billy noticed that all six of the Tribal Councilors were standing in front of the sacred building. Facing them was the new Head of Law Enforcement, Phineas T. Fox, with Sheriff Walter Lone Wolf and Deputy Harold Eagle. Behind them stood Lester Coyote and the rest of the posse and the answer to why Billy had been so easily followed. In the coyote's hand, he held a leash, and tugging at the end of that leash was Georgie Beaver. The poor little rodent had apparently pulled free from his leash and inadvertently led the deputized birds and the entire posse all the way to Maurice's dugout. Once the eagle and the hawk spotted him, the rest was easy.

CHAPTER THIRTY-EIGHT

THE FOX'S BLUNDER

Billy Bones crawled along the mist's edge, staying partly inside its thick veil until he reached the safety of the trees behind the lodge. From there he managed to make his way up the hill to the mountain goat's retreat.

A small clearing stretched out in front of the cavern. To Billy's great relief, he noticed that the door was slightly ajar. Before crossing the space, he looked in the direction of the lodge and saw Omar Mountain Goat leading Phineas T. Fox and his entourage up the path toward the cave.

When the odd procession reached a bend in the path where they were momentarily out of sight, Billy rushed across the clearing and dove through the partially opened door. From the silence that followed, he concluded he had still eluded his captors.

Once inside, Billy glanced quickly around. On the wooden table was a cloth sack similar to one he had found in Maurice's doorway. He knew intuitively that it must be for him. Rolled up alongside the opening of the inner cave was the same rope that he had used on his previous visit. Carefully he fastened one end to the lowest board in the most distant corner and covered it with dirt. Then he tied the other end around his waist, grabbed the sack on the table, and crawled under the boarded-up opening that led inside the forbidden mountain. Just as he heard Omar's voice inviting his visitors to step inside his cave, Billy Bones slid down to a spot up against the wall where he could hear what was happening on the other side of the opening.

"I think he's been in here!" Billy heard Sheriff Walter Lone Wolf declare. "I could swear that's his scent."

"Well, if the poor hound stepped in there, I feel sorry for him. I don't know of anyone who's been able to find their way back!" responded Deputy Harold Eagle. "Unless…?" Billy could detect movement toward the corner where the rope was tied. He realized that the eagle had an equally potent sense of his own, his eyesight. "Ah, there it is, over in the corner, where the earth's been disturbed." After a slight pause, the large bird asked, "Is he in there, sir?"

Billy knew at once that Deputy Eagle was talking to Omar. He moved a little closer to the light to hear the mountain goat's response.

"I can swear to you that I have not seen Mr. Bones since the autumn equinox," returned Omar. "If he's gone inside the mountain, then he's done it on his own."

Billy could detect more shuffling on the other side as the voice of Phineas T. Fox exclaimed, "Then you won't mind if I do this!" All of a sudden Billy could just make out the other end of the rope that he was connected to. Apparently, Phineas had untied it and tossed it inside the cave just beyond the barricade. "There! That should take care of Mr. Billy Bones!" the fox jeered.

"No, he'll die in there!" cried the good sheriff. The shepherd moved quickly back against the wall as the wolf dove under the barricade into the partial darkness. Fortunately, by the time the wolf reached the spot where the rope should have been, Billy had pulled it even further inside the cavern.

Before Sheriff Lone Wolf got all the way under the bottom board, Deputy Eagle shouted, "Sorry Walter, you can't go in there! You'll be lost in a matter of seconds!"

While the strange saga between the fox, the wolf and the eagle was unfolding, Billy noted another voice. It came from one of the coyote brothers. "Watch out! He's gettin' away! Grab his leash!" And without warning, something rushed by the dog and scampered into the darkness of the cavern.

"Ah, the poor little fellow!" cried Harold Eagle. "Now I really hope Billy's in there! Georgie doesn't stand a chance of survivin' by himself, 'specially the way he is now."

"What do you plan to tell Georgie's parents?" asked Omar almost immediately. "And you, Phineas T. Fox, with your trumped-up charges, how will you ever explain this to the citizens of the Prairie?"

"What we do is none of your business, Omar Mountain Goat! Now if you'll excuse me," snapped the fox, whose voice was suddenly more distant. "Lester, I'm sending Bison Bob back here to help you guard the entrance to this cave. I don't want either of you leaving your position until the solstice is over. Do I make myself clear?"

"But Phineas, that's not until Friday! I...I don't want to miss..." the coyote was sputtering.

"Do I make myself clear? I don't trust that sneaky dog. I wouldn't put it past him to find a way out of here."

CHAPTER THIRTY-NINE

RETURN TO THE SACRED MOUNTAIN

Billy Bones could wait no longer. He had heard what he needed to know. Now he had to go deeper inside Spirit Dwells and find Georgie before he too was lost. In his rush to find his friend, he forgot about the rope that had once been tied securely to the barricade. Now it dragged behind him like a lifeless snake.

As Billy Bones climbed further down into Spirit Dwells, he kept close to the left wall until he reached the first big corner. He knew from his previous experience that the cavern opened up into a much larger room at this point. When he remembered that the rope around his waist was useless, he reasoned that he could always find his way back by keeping the wall to his right. Since Phineas T. Fox was the one who untied the rope, he was fairly certain that no one would be coming in after him or Georgie Beaver.

Georgie's escape into the cave had taken Billy by surprise. Before he realized who it was, the little rodent had shot past him into the larger room. While crouching close to the stone wall, he listened for any sound at all. Finally, it came. The dragging of a leash and the padding of four little feet were just audible somewhere in front of him.

"Georgie, is that you? Come here, fella! I'm over here!" called Billy in a loud whisper. The dog almost risked leaving the wall when he heard the rattle of the beaver's leash once again. Somehow the rodent had heard the shepherd dog and was pacing back and forth. "Georgie, over here…Come on, fella…!"

In the next few seconds the pudgy little animal jumped all over the dog and knocked him over in his exuberance at finally being reunited. To calm the young beaver, Billy picked up the sack that Omar had left on his table and shared its contents. "Help yourself! It looks like we're in for a long wait, and there's no reason we have to do it on empty stomachs."

After eating his part of the lunch, Georgie curled up by his old friend and went to sleep. For his part, Billy decided to play a waiting game. The summer solstice and Winston Wise Owl's expulsion were not for another day and a half. He hoped that whoever was guarding the entrance to the inner cave would eventually give up or at least get careless after a number of hours. From Lester Coyote's remarks, Billy was sure they did not want to miss the drumming-out ceremony that Brother Fabian had planned for Winston.

While waiting next to the wall, Billy thought back of all the happy times he had spent in the beaver's company. He also reminisced about all his other friends in the Prairie and the Hill Country who had been so loyal and kind to him.

After an hour or so Billy finally succumbed to the rigors of the escape and dozed off. In a few moments, he was jolted back into full consciousness by a vision of over-whelming power. He was back at Land's End, standing between Winston's tree house and Hester's little cottage. When he looked up, a herd of deer crashed through an opening in the mist and headed straight for him, causing him to cry out and scramble out of the way. He remembered instantly that it was the same vision he had experienced when he found out that Victor Running Deer had been deputized. This time, however, the illusion lasted longer, and there was a pack of wild dogs chasing the deer. One of the dogs, in fact, stumbled over to him and looked up at him with sad longing eyes.

Billy sat up and leaned back against the cool damp wall. He realized he must have screamed during the vision because Georgie was thumping his flat tail and nudging his arm. Billy reassured him, "Now, now, it's OK, my friend. I just had another of my wild dreams."

As Billy sat in the dark cave quietly comforting the beaver, a plan gradually formulated in his mind. It was becoming obvious to him that his visions of deer herds and wild dogs were harbingers of things to come. If he could get back to Winston's home, perhaps he could use this knowledge to save the old bird. Maybe in a couple of hours he could reenter the shaft leading to the goat's room and find a way past any guards who might still be watching.

As Billy continued to contemplate various aspects of his plan for Winston's release, he became increasingly melancholy. He wondered how he could possibly measure the joy of his newfound awareness in this world against the love and affection he felt for the boy in the old world. From his conversations with Winston, he knew that if he ever did find his way back to Billy Stuart, he would have to revert to being the animal he once was before entering The Enchantment. No matter how he tried, he never would have the clarity he now enjoyed.

"And what about the old memory that attached itself to me?" the dog pondered. "Would it die if I left it here, or would it linger in some sort of limbo—not to mention the mystery of Jimmy Stone. And what about Georgie's old memory? Did it pass on forever with the smoke that rose above Mary's burning furniture?"

To complicate matters further, there was the memory of the young dog who had looked at Billy so longingly during the vision he had just witnessed. There was something in the depth of her gaze—something that promised a whole new beginning.

Still exhausted, the dog closed his eyes and fell into a deep sleep that lasted many hours.

Lucinda Vulture's predictions about the preternatural elements inside the great mountain came true for Billy Bones on the long night that followed. Sometime toward morning he thought he was awakened by a mysterious cry. When he tried to peer through the absolute darkness, a familiar face and form took shape in the distance. He immediately recognized it as the well-dressed mink he had seen on his last visit to the cave. It was beckoning him to come closer. With leaden feet the young dog struggled over to where the mink was standing. Before he could get too close, the mink pointed down into a deep crevice that was being lit with a pale-green light. "There, you see? Way down there! That's me. That's my body."

"Ernest," muttered Billy with some difficulty, "Ernest, I've seen Mary. I showed her the emerald tiepin, and she believed what I told her!"

"Does she still love me?" inquired the mink anxiously, as the bones in the deep pit slowly vanished.

Just as Ernest finished his question, another light began radiating off in the distance. As it floated toward them, Billy could see that it was taking the form of Mary McMink.

"Ernest, it's me, Mary, I've come for you. You're free to leave now!"

"Mary, you know that I've always loved you," said the well-dressed mink, as he reached out to his wife.

"Yes, my dear, I know that now." Calmly the spirit of Mary McMink turned her attention to Billy. Her eyes were shining, and she had a youthfulness about her that the shepherd dog had never seen. "Thank you, Billy Bones. Thank you for giving my husband back to me."

Billy watched in wonder as Mary took Ernest by the hand and gently led him away.

Just before they faded completely from view, Ernest turned back to Billy one last time and called, "Use your sense of hearing, Billy. Listen for the water."

A tugging at Billy's pant leg quickly brought him back to full consciousness. When he looked down, he could see nothing but knew it had to be Georgie. As the dog started to take a step forward, the little beaver yanked him so hard that he toppled backwards instead.

"Georgie, what…?" When the dog touched the ground around him, he soon realized that he was no longer near the stone wall. In fact, when he knelt down and felt the space ahead of him, he discovered that he was standing on the edge of a precipice. Georgie had managed to save him from falling into the same pit that he had been trapped in after the autumn equinox. Carefully Billy backed away on his hands and knees until he came to a solid wall. He no longer knew in which direction the old goat's domain lay. He only hoped he had not walked too far in his sleep and that the shaft leading to the entrance was still on his right.

For the next two hours, Billy Bones and Georgie crept along the edge of the wall. Several times Billy discovered deep depressions, but none of them led back to Omar's home. Until that moment he had resisted moving away from the rock wall or even retracing his steps, even though the eerie songs of the old memories were irresistible at times.

At long last the dog could go no further. "I think I'm too late, Georgie! I can't even tell you if it's night or day. Perhaps the solstice has already happened!"

Feeling worthless and dejected, Billy sat down on a cold damp rock. Georgie tried to keep him moving, but eventually he stopped too and just waited quietly alongside the dog. Billy wondered again about The Great Spirit.

Was it really stronger inside the mountain as Lucinda had intimated? Finally he stopped wondering and allowed himself to fall into a fitful sleep.

This time the dream that occurred was as disturbing as his slumber. Winston Wise Owl had reverted back to the size of owls in the outside world. Several coyotes had surrounded the bird and were tearing at his clipped wings and unprotected back. The owl could only make a sort of whooping gesture along the ground. He did not stand a chance. Ultimately the coyotes moved in for the kill.

Billy awakened with a start. "How could I let this happen?" he thought. "Is this how it ends for Mr. Wise Owl in the outside world? And why is The Great Spirit giving me this dream now when I'm so hopelessly lost… or has it already happened…or is it happening right now?"

Inexplicably, the vision of Mary and Ernest McMink popped back into Billy's conscious mind. He smiled in spite of his dejection. "Well, at least they found a way out!" he mused. Suddenly the same voice that had urged him to escape from the City Council spoke though his hopelessness. "Remember what Ernest McMink told you, Billy. Use your sense of hearing. Listen for the water!'"

"The water…?'" Billy whispered to himself. "What in the name of The Great Spirit does that mean?"

Then the dog heard it—the faint sound of running water. It was coming from somewhere ahead of him. "Come on, Georgie, we're going to do just what Ernest McMink told us to do! We're going to find water! Maybe it's not too late!"

Before long the two companions saw a tiny spot of light and the rushing sounds of water got louder and louder. As they got closer to it, the murky atmosphere got bright enough for Billy to make out the shadowy figure of the beaver moving just behind him. "Of course, why am I so dumb? It's the underground river, Spirit Moves. Perhaps there's still a chance, old friend!"

When Billy and Georgie got within ten feet of the rushing water, the rocks became so slippery that both animals fell and slid headlong into the water.

As usual, the shepherd dog found himself bobbing immediately to the top. At first, he was all right because the height of the cave allowed for some headroom above the water line. Just ahead of him though, he discerned that the water went all the way to the ceiling. He quickly gulped in as much air as his lungs could hold and tried to dive. Once again, his head popped back up and hit the ceiling, making progress difficult as well as painful.

Just as Billy thought he would surely drown, Georgie's chubby form swam up next to him. In desperation, the dog grabbed the beaver's shoulders just as the little animal dove as deeply as he could. For the next few moments, Billy could barely hold on as the strain on his lungs became unendurable. Georgie, on the other hand, was in his element and swam for both of them. Suddenly a beam of sunlight shattered the space just ahead of them. As soon as they reached it, Billy Bones let go of the beaver and exploded to the surface where he joyfully inhaled the glorious air of The Enchantment.

CHAPTER FORTY

A STATE OF EMERGENCY

"Hey, Georgie, come on, before someone sees us," called Billy Bones, as he clambered up Spirit Move's steep embankment. Even though the little beaver was enjoying the water, he followed as quickly as he could. He did not want to lose the shepherd dog again.

Cautiously Billy and Georgie made their way north through the thick pines until they came to a little clearing in front of Maurice Rabbit's dugout. As they started to cross the clearing, the door of the dugout was flung open and a joyful rabbit bounded toward them.

"Billy Bones! I can't believe it! And Georgie, you're soaked to the bone…both of you! Come inside before someone sees you! They told me you were lost inside the mountain! How did you ever manage?" he asked, sputtering one question on top of the next. "We were planning to organize a rescue party, but we had to wait until after the guards were gone. They told us our chances of finding you were slim at best!"

As Maurice helped Billy pull off his wet clothes and lay them in front of the large windows, the dog related his incredible story. Just as he was describing his near-drowning experience and the beaver's rescue, a black

shadow darkened the window and landed in front of the doorway. Both Maurice and Billy immediately realized how careless they had been, but it was too late to hide.

Lucinda Vulture made her usual dramatic entrance as she threw open the door, locked it behind her, and began berating Maurice. "What's the use of hiding someone if you don't lock your front door?"

"Lucinda, it's good to see you too," smiled Maurice, who was used to the old vulture's sharp tongue.

"But how did you know?" muttered Billy, who was still shocked at the big bird's opportune arrival. Georgie, for his part, had backed away into a corner. As his former self, he had been very leery of the vulture. In his present circumstance, he was downright fearful of her.

"You surely didn't think your escape from Spirit Dwells would go undetected? I knew immediately when you burst out of that cave. We're connected, Mr. Billy Bones! There's no way around it! And what's more, I know that The Great Spirit spoke to you."

"Well, it was more like a dream."

"Mr. Bones, surely you knew it was The Great Spirit. Now tell me. What did you see?"

Billy sat down at the table. He began with the dream that concerned Winston Wise Owl in the outside world.

"I see. And what are you planning to do about it?" questioned Lucinda. Billy could feel her steely black eyes penetrating the very depths of his soul.

"Well, I did have a plan…" the dog began again. Then he hesitated. He was starting to rethink the whole idea. The sacrifice it called for was too all-encompassing, too irreversible. "But…perhaps there is another way. Perhaps…"

"No, Mr. Bones, if you decide to free Winston Wise Owl, I'm afraid there's only one way!" insisted the vulture. Unexpectedly she softened her tone as she glanced over at the disheveled shepherd. "Mind you, I'll understand if you choose not to go through with it. You can hide here in the

Hill Country until after the elections. I'm sure George P. Beaver will win, and I'm also sure he'll be glad to grant you a pardon."

"But what are the citizens of the Prairie doing to free Mr. Wise Owl? Do they have something in mind?" inquired the dog, hoping an alternative plan was being considered.

"No, you don't understand, Billy. Brother Fabian Lynx has declared a state of emergency until after the summer solstice. The inhabitants of the Prairie have been asked to remain in their homes, and that's exactly what they will do," explained Lucinda.

"But surely they'll rise up! Surely they know that Brother Fabian must be stopped!" cried the dog, continuing to protest.

"They'll rise up, yes, but at the ballot box. Unfortunately, Brother Fabian's the law now. They'll allow fate to take its course, no matter how unjust."

"But the birds, look how they rebelled!"

"Yes, but you were there to lead them, and you weren't an escaped prisoner then!" exclaimed the vulture, closing down all avenues of discussion. "I'm afraid if Winston is to be saved, it's up to you."

Billy lowered his head. The realization of the awful truth was almost unbearable to him. He remembered the voice that had urged him to escape after his trial and then had assisted him in finding the river that ran out of the mountain. He was sure now that it was the young Jimmy Stone. "But why is this ancient human speaking to me?" he pondered to himself. "And what does he want?"

At that moment Billy Bones finally understood. Jimmy Stone was reaching out to him to save Winston and ultimately his grandfather's books. The dog wanted to cry out his resentment, but when he turned to Lucinda, all he could mumble was, "I'll need your help…"

"That, my friend, I cannot give you, nor can Maurice. The councilors in the Hill Country need to honor this state of emergency. We have an ancient agreement with the Prairie that we dare not break," said the old vulture solemnly. "However, there's no law restricting my sons. They'll be at your disposal."

"Thank you. I'll need a diversion to get close to Mr. Wise Owl's eviction ceremony."

"That I can give you…" For the first time, Billy detected a note of genuine sorrow in the old vulture's voice. "I have the very thing for you. My son Felix is no longer fit for living inside The Enchantment. I'm sure now that he can only find happiness in the other world. I'll send him with Festus and Floyd to Land's End with a plea to release him when the great rift occurs. I'll instruct them to make as much racket as they can, but you must tell me the proper time."

"I would guess about an hour before sunrise, when everyone is very sleepy and not on their guard," decided Billy, trying to visualize the situation.

"That's fine, but I must warn you to be extremely careful. The area around Winston's tree house has become an armed camp. Phineas T. Fox has deputized almost every young male large enough to show some authority. Unfortunately, that happened when they were hunting for you. I'm afraid many of your friends are now among Brother Fabian's lieutenants. If they're not at the camp, they're patrolling the streets, making sure everyone stays in their houses."

"Only Deputy Eagle refuses to help," interrupted Maurice. "He uses the excuse that he's needed here in the Hill Country in case you escape. Of course, he's really saying that he'll have nothing to do with Winston Wise Owl's expulsion."

"Well, I'm relieved to hear that. At least I won't have his eagle eyes to worry about!" exclaimed the shepherd dog. "But how about Sandy…Sandy Antelope…? He was taking care of Mary McMink the last I heard. Surely they won't draft him?" inquired Billy, trying to get a firm grasp of the situation.

"Mary McMink died, Billy, the day you escaped from City Hall," said Lucinda. "I know nothing more than that."

Billy gazed over at the old bird with a look of utter disbelief. Once again, the mountain had amazed him. "Perhaps Mary really did come for Ernest then," he thought to himself.

"You saw Mary there too, didn't you, Mr. Bones? There inside the mountain!" declared the vulture. "She came for her husband, didn't she?"

The dog nodded in agreement. Now he was even more positive that his earlier vision concerning the herd of deer and the wild dogs was going to happen. "I still need someone else, someone inside the encampment."

"But you already have someone, don't you—someone

who's very close to you."

"Yes…yes, there is one animal I think I can trust." At the thought of Victor Running Deer, Billy's recent melancholia resurfaced once again, as he gazed out the window at the beauty of Echo Canyon with its vivid colors and wonderful golden light.

"Don't say his name!" Lucinda interjected quickly. "It's better that we don't hear it. If it helps, I think your choice is correct." Lucinda turned abruptly and began pacing across the studio floor. "One more thing, Billy: don't ask your friends to do anything that can later be construed as breaking the law. You cannot put their lives in jeopardy, especially if your plan doesn't work." Without missing a beat, the vulture turned to the rabbit as if she had never spoken anything unpleasant. "Now Maurice, get these animals something to eat and let them wait here until after dark. That is, if you have anything besides rabbit food? A good piece of chicken, perhaps…!"

Before either the rabbit or the dog could respond, the vulture gave Billy a long parting glance, turned away awkwardly, unlocked the door, and vanished as quickly as she had appeared.

CHAPTER FORTY-ONE

THE FINAL PREPARATION

The first stop on Billy Bones' list was Sandy Antelope's dugout. When he discovered the buck wasn't there, he tried Mary McMink's stone house just down the road. He wanted to make sure that the antelope was alone so he peered through one of the side windows. The buck was in the great room, resting on an easy chair that Percival Gander had given Mary.

"Psst, Sandy…Sandy, are you by yourself?" Billy called softly through the window.

"What? Who's there?" the antelope responded, bouncing out of the chair. When he saw Billy standing outside the window, he grinned and leaned out into the night. "In the name of The Great Spirit, Billy, they told me you were lost in Omar Mountain Goat's cave. And Georgie, I see you got him with you. Am I ever relieved to see you! Everything's gone crazy since you escaped!"

"What's going on, Sandy? I'm hearing some terrible things!"

"It's hard to explain, Billy. They even got me involved. I'm supposed to go to Winston's tree house tonight around midnight. They tell me I have to patrol the streets until dawn. Sarah Mourning Dove's comin' over here to sit with

Mary's body."

"How'd you get mixed up in this, Sandy? You of all animals!" inquired Billy, coming straight to the point.

The young antelope turned his head away from Billy. "Sheriff Lone Wolf deputized me after you left. I told him that Mrs. McMink just died and that I needed to take care of things, so he excused me from the posse. Later that same day, though, Brother Fabian declared this state of emergency, and Deputy Brown Bear came by and told me I had to report tonight. He said that in a state of emergency, the law can draft whomever it pleases."

"And you went along with that?" the dog continued.

"Should I have refused, Billy? If you tell me to, I will. I swear I will!" responded the gentle buck. Billy could see tears welling up in the antelope's eyes. For all his size, he was having difficulty in knowing how to respond.

"No, Sandy, I think you'd better do what they ask," conceded Billy, remembering Lucinda Vulture's earlier admonition about putting lives in jeopardy. "But tell me, where's Victor? Is he at the camp, or is he walking the streets?"

"He's been guardin' Winston's tree house all the time you were away. He even has his bed roll over there. Arnold says he'll be stayin' there until after the solstice."

"And where's Arnold?"

"He's with the posse, and so are Alvin Muskrat and Lenny Coyote and Johnny Otter and Phillip Fox. I'm afraid Brother Fabian's got 'em all walkin' the streets. I guess that way there'll be no one to rise up against him, at least none of the younger ones."

Billy felt his body start to shake in spite of the warm evening. "Then what Lucinda said is true. Brother Fabian's got you all in his army!" With those final words, the dog turned and trudged up the hill with the beaver close at his heels. For a moment he forgot why he needed to see the young antelope.

Swiftly Sandy leapt over the windowsill and caught up with the young dog. "Wait, Billy, there must be somethin' we can do. Sarah will relieve me soon."

Billy Bones stopped walking and turned around. "It's not your fault, Sandy. I know that. And there is something you can do," added the dog, looking straight into the young buck's eyes. "I want you to give Victor Running Deer a message for me. Tell him that I need him to do two things. Tell him that Mr. Wise Owl's life depends on it!"

The dog not only went through Victor's instructions but took time to tell Sandy about Mary and Ernest McMink. After their farewells, Billy and Georgie headed toward the dog's cottage. Sandy had mentioned that Nosey Coon and Needles Porcupine had gone into hiding, but Billy thought he knew exactly where they would be.

"OK, I know you're in here," said Billy, lighting the candle on the pine table. After it was burning, he raised it high enough to see into the top bunk. He immediately noticed a lump under the covers. He gave them a quick flip and out rolled a frightened Nosey Coon.

"Billy! Is that you? Is it really, really you?" asked the raccoon, putting his masked face close to the dog's. "They've been lookin' for us, Billy. They wanted us to join the posse, so we hid!" The raccoon quickly hopped down and opened the bottom doors of the corner cupboard. The porcupine was curled up in the back with his hands over his eyes. "It's OK, Needles; it's only Billy. He's come back, and he's got Georgie with him. They ain't lost like everyone said they was!"

Billy spent the next few minutes explaining how he avoided being taken into custody and how he and Georgie escaped from Spirit Dwells. Then he made them promise to look after the beaver until the state of emergency was lifted. After that they were to restore him to his parents. Finally he asked them to watch over his home until he returned. When it was time to leave, Georgie proved to be the hardest good-bye, and Billy could hear him scratching on the Dutch doors long after he started down the path toward Percy's shop.

Percival Gander's shop was dark inside when Billy reached it. He glanced around the road and found several small pebbles. Cautiously he threw one against Percy's office window where the gander slept, and after a few moments, a second and then a third. Before long, Percival poked his head and neck out into the warm night air.

"Hey Percy, it's me, Billy. Open up, will you? I need your help!"

"Oh my, Billy, oh my, yes; I'll be right with you! Yes, right with you!"

With surprising quickness Percival threw open the door and waddled down the ramp.

"Billy, it is you! Oh my, oh my! I knew you'd find a

way out! I knew it!" the gander squawked, as he shook the dog's hand vigorously up and down and up and down.

"Percy, I'm here to get your help. I have to get close to Hester's tree house at Land's End before dawn, and I need a disguise."

"You don't need me, Billy. You need a gardener," honked the goose good-naturedly.

"A gardener?" queried the shepherd dog. "I just need something to wear that will hide me from the deputies surrounding the place."

"Then you need a gardener, yes, a gardener, I'm telling you!" insisted Percival. "Remember now, Hester has a wonderful garden in back of her cottage. Disguise yourself as a bush, and you're home free!"

"But how do I do that? And remember, it has to be something I can take off," said Billy, grinning and enjoying the moment.

"Well, first we raid one of my lilac trees, and then we take one of my long jackets and attach the branches to it and make it resemble a bush. When you get close to Hester's garden, you just slip it on and button it up. And I've got a wide-brim hat that will come in handy too!"

After a couple laborious hours inside the shop, the outfit was completed. Billy gave Percival a warm hug and thanked him for his generosity and friendship.

"Till we meet again," called the gander in a loud whisper, as the dog rushed down the ramp with the camouflage clothes firmly under his arm. "And Billy—save Winston! You're the only one who can!"

CHAPTER FORTY-TWO

THE ARMED CAMP

Twice Billy Bones hid along the fence row as patrols passed up and down the path leading to Land's End. When he got within a half mile, he saw the campfires that had been lit to keep away any intruders. He finally decided it would be wiser if he left the path and crossed Farmer Jason Crow's cornfield and then circled around to the south side of the encampment.

Hester Groundhog's garden stretched behind her cottage for several hundred feet. Below that was the crow's rail fence that separated the two properties. Only one bonfire was burning on the southwest corner, and only two deputies were patrolling along the fence. Fortunately, the deputies were both Peccary Brothers. When Billy discovered who they were, he crouched patiently beyond the fence and waited for one of their countless arguments.

"Will they never learn!" he chuckled to himself, as the two pigs began quarreling over a biscuit that one of them had accidently left in his pocket. Making as little noise as possible, Billy crawled between the two lower rails and slipped into the garden.

Billy quickly ducked behind a large bush close to the garden's edge, donned his camouflaged clothes, and started moving forward from plant to plant. Several times Milton Brown Bear or Walter Lone Wolf sauntered around to the back of Hester Groundhog's tree. Apparently they wanted to check on the pigs or inspect the terrain for themselves. Once Walter even halted a few feet from where Billy was hiding and sniffed the air. It seemed to the shepherd dog that the cagey wolf was trying to make an important decision. When he finally departed, Billy heard him whistling softly to himself.

Shortly after dawn when the shapes in the garden were becoming all too clear, Billy Bones heard the three vultures fly in from the west. Festus and Floyd were shouting to each other and keeping Felix between them on a long leash. They landed just west of the encampment and started roping in their transformed brother with loud jeers and caws. As Lucinda Vulture had predicted, everyone in the encampment except Victor Running Deer raced over to investigate. Even Phineas T. Fox, who had arrived the night before, got caught up in the circus atmosphere that the birds were providing.

Billy threw off his disguise and placed it under the large tarp that was still behind Hester's tree. He found himself shaking uncontrollably as he sneaked around to the front of the cottage. As he had requested, the bottom Dutch door was slightly ajar, and Victor was standing between the hubbub of the vultures' diversion and the groundhog's doorway. The deer made no move to turn but only cocked his head ever so slightly toward Hester's little dwelling.

"Well I guess this is good-bye, old friend," the dog whispered, as he glanced over at the deer's unmoving back.

At that instant out of the corner of his eye, Billy thought he saw the figure of a young human standing just east of Winston Wise Owl's tree. He shook his head and looked again, but this time there was nothing there except the sun's early rays passing through the misty border of The Enchantment.

Not allowing himself to tarry any longer, Billy Bones steeled himself, dropped quietly down on his haunches, and slid undetected into the safety of the snug little cottage.

CHAPTER FORTY-THREE

THE SUMMER SOLSTICE

Shortly before sunrise on June 21, Winston Wise Owl was awakened by an uncommonly shrill commotion coming from beyond the sheriff's encampment. Quickly the old bird slipped on his robe, descended the stairs, and peered out the library window. Beyond the yard and the two campfires that burned on either side of the path, Festus and Floyd Vulture were trying to rope in their brother, Felix. Because of the owl's house arrest, this was the first time he had seen one of the transformed creatures.

"By The Great Spirit, Lucinda wants Felix freed into the outside world! I wonder if she still blames me?" Winston muttered to himself, as he watched Sheriff Walter Lone Wolf trying to move his deputies back to their posts.

At the same time Festus and Floyd were subduing their brother, Winston's sharp eyes caught an even more bizarre incident taking place in front of Hester Groundhog's cottage. Victor Running Deer had placed himself between the disturbance beyond the yard and the groundhog's Dutch doors. All of a sudden Billy Bones appeared from behind Hester's tree. He had removed all his clothes and assumed the appearance of the dog Winston had introduced into The Enchantment exactly one year ago. Winston also noticed that the bottom door had been left slightly ajar. Cautiously the dog crawled over to the door and stole inside. Without turning around, the young buck walked nonchalantly toward the loud distraction caused by Lucinda's sons and helped the beleaguered wolf gain control of his deputies.

"What's going on?" Winston asked himself out loud. "Surely Victor knows what Billy is doing. What are they up to anyway? They must know they can't do anything by themselves!"

Winston pondered the significance of the strange scenario as he retraced his steps back to his bedroom. He knew the sheriff was coming for him later that morning. Even though he would be stripped of his clothes, he wanted to be presentably dressed when he entered the yard for the last time.

"I thought Billy was trapped inside Omar's cave! What's he doing here?" he asked himself again as he donned his striped trousers, bow tie, and tails. "What could Billy and Victor possibly do against the sheriff and all his deputies? I hope they don't do anything foolish and injure themselves on my account. If I could only fly away! Ah, but Brother Fabian's taken care of that possibility."

Shortly after sunrise Winston observed the arrival of Brother Fabian Lynx with some interest, since the expulsion ceremony had been set for nine o'clock, and the solstice wasn't calculated to happen until late morning. The lynx immediately went in search of the sheriff. After a short conversation, the wolf climbed the winding staircase to Winston's door.

"Brother Fabian's requested your presence in the yard earlier than expected, in case the rift opens before nine. He's also ordered me and Victor to guard you until the end of the ceremony," the wolf explained.

Winston was intrigued that Victor wanted to be the other deputy guarding him. The owl was aware that the young buck had been on sentry duty for the last two days and concluded that the deer might want to be relieved. "It must have something to do with the mysterious goings-on in front of Hester's tree house," he mused.

From his library window Winston observed Thaddeus P. Turtle huffing and puffing up the path long before anyone else. By law the prisoner had the right to see his meetinghouse counselor alone before being subjected to banishment.

When Thaddeus finally reached Land's End, Sheriff Lone Wolf quickly escorted him up to Winston's library.

As soon as the turtle entered the room, the owl greeted him and pulled him to one side. "It's good to see you, Thaddeus. I'm sorry you had to walk all the way out here. I know it's a difficult hike for you."

"Ah, never mind, my good friend. For you…." All at once, Thaddeus choked on his words in spite of himself. "I…I still can't believe what's going on! It's…it's like a nightmare! I just never believed that Brother Fabian would actually go through with it!"

"Is anyone doing anything, or are they all hiding in their houses?" asked Winston, somewhat sardonically.

"I'm afraid it's the latter, Winston. The young males are

all out patrolling the streets or guarding your tree because of the state of emergency. And no one else has dared come forward. Especially after we lost Billy Bones," explained the terrapin.

"Are you sure that Billy's still lost? I could have sworn this morning that I…."

"The last I heard, he was somewhere inside Omar's cave in the Hill Country. Phineas T. Fox assigned Bison Bob and Lester Coyote to guard the entrance. As far as I know, they're still at their post," interrupted Thaddeus, showing his concern.

"Then who…?"

Before Winston could finish his inquiry, Victor came discreetly into the room. "I'm sorry to bother you, sir, but Phineas T. Fox has requested your presence in the yard. Mayor Prairie Dog and his City Councilors have arrived." The deer then turned to Thaddeus. "I'm sorry, sir, but I have to ask you to leave. I have to tie Mr. Wise Owl's hands and give him some final instructions."

The old reptile glared over at the young deer and addressed him in harsh broken tones. "Mr. Running Deer, I…I can't believe you're doing this! I thought you had so much promise when I first met you. Now…now, look at you! You should be ashamed!" With those stern remarks echoing in the air, the crestfallen turtle left the room and climbed slowly down to the yard.

Taking advantage of his moment alone with the deer, Winston whispered, "What's going on, Victor? This morning I saw Billy Bones entering Hester's cottage, but

Thaddeus doesn't seem to know anything about it. You knew he was there. I could tell. What's he up to, Victor?" The deer continued tying the owl's hands but did not answer. "Victor, you must tell me. I don't want either of you hurt on my account!"

Finally the deer looked up with an odd expression of uncertainty. "I'm sorry, Mr. Wise Owl, but I don't know myself. All I can tell you is that when pandemonium breaks out, you're to come with me! Whatever you do, don't resist! We'll be moving very quickly!"

When Victor finished tying the owl's hands, Sheriff Lone Wolf entered the great room and addressed Winston courteously. "Sorry sir, but it's ti me to go!"

As the sheriff ducked quickly out the door, Winston held back momentarily. "I'm sorry for the way Thaddeus spoke to you, Victor. He didn't know…"

"It's all right, sir; I actually deserve it," admitted the deer humbly. "Billy's the brave one, not I!"

CHAPTER FORTY-FOUR

THE GOLDEN RIFT

For two hours the owl, the law enforcement offi-cers, and all the dignitaries invited to attend waited for the ceremony to begin. Some of them utilized Winston's and Hester's outdoor benches; others sat along the sides of the path or in the yard between the two huge trees. The sheriff and Victor allowed Winston to sit on the bottom rung of his staircase while they watched over him.

Only the two vultures and their older brother waited east of the trees near the mist. Phineas T. Fox had grudg-ingly granted Lucinda her wish: Festus and Floyd would be allowed to release Felix Vulture as soon as the opening occurred.

Around nine o'clock in the morning, Phineas T. Fox asked all present to stand in the yard between the two trees. As prearranged, Sheriff Lone Wolf and Victor Running Deer led Winston Wise Owl to a small platform east of the yard, within ten feet of the mist. After that the obedient fox introduced Brother Fabian and invited him to stand on another platform just south of the owl and the two guards.

"Mayor Elmer Prairie Dog, distinguished members of the City Council, and other guests, it is my solemn duty to turn this ceremony over to Brother Fabian Lynx, our chairman, who will read the charge. Brother Fabian."

As usual, the lynx wore his long white robe. The owl observed that he was indeed a handsome cat. But this time, because of the morning hour, his back was at an odd angle to the sun. Therefore his white teeth did not have the same sparkle, and the shadow on his face gave him a sinister look rather than one of considerable charm.

The lynx read, "Winston Wise Owl, you are charged with inciting a rebellion against the state and taking property belonging to the state. These offenses are considered by *The Great Book of Rules* to be among the most abominable crimes and are punishable by banishment through the great rift at the start of the summer solstice. Mr. Wise Owl, the time has arrived. Will you step forward, please?"

Before continuing, Brother Fabian Lynx drew another written document out of his belt that had been copied from *The Great Book of Rules*. "The particular articles on this parchment list the proper procedure for banishment from The Enchantment. Article One: The subject in question shall be stripped of all clothing" Brother Fabian looked over and nodded his head at Phineas, who had positioned himself in front of the owl. "Mr. Fox, you may proceed."

At the signal, the fox reached over and ripped the tie off Winston's neck.

"Wait!" shouted Sheriff Lone Wolf, blocking any further attempts with his upraised arm. "Victor, untie Mr. Wise Owl's hands and help me remove his coat."

"But Walter, it says his clothes should be ripped off!" whined Phineas, suddenly intimidated by the larger wolf.

"Phineas, you lay another hand on Mr. Wise Owl, and I will rip your teeth right out of your head!" growled the sheriff, showing his own white teeth.

"But I am the Head of Law Enforcement around here!" continued the fox, trying to maintain his dignity.

"I said stand aside, Phineas! We will strip Mr. Wise Owl of his clothing, but we will not rip them off his body! Have I made myself clear?" growled Sheriff Walter Lone Wolf, placing himself directly between the fox and the condemned owl.

Phineas cleared his throat and glanced over at Brother Fabian Lynx. Winston was quite certain that the fox was looking for help, but the disgusted cat only shook his head and looked away.

Having achieved his objective, Sheriff Lone Wolf turned back to Winston and continued politely, "Now sir, if we may have your trousers…" After picking up the owl's tie, the sheriff proceeded to give it to Victor, who already held the other articles of clothing belonging to the owl. He then motioned for the deer to place them over by the owl's tree.

Since his Head of Law Enforcement seemed to be losing control, Brother Fabian quickly continued with the next article. "Article Two: After the rift opens, the prisoner's hands must be untied. Article Three: The prisoner must then walk through the opening. If he refuses to do so, he must be forced to go by the officers guarding him." The lynx then closed the parchment. "We must now wait until the solstice arrives. At that time, we'll finish the ceremony.

If our calculations are correct, this should take place sometime in the next two hours."

Winston felt surprisingly free and unencumbered as he looked out over the crowd. He thought he would be embarrassed once his clothing was removed, but the good sheriff had allowed him to keep some sense of dignity. He knew very well why the condemned prisoner's clothes were removed and why his hands were untied. They would be a hindrance to him in the outside world. In his case, however, he knew that he would not last very long, since his wings had been clipped. Without the full use of his wings and his gift of reason from the old memories, survival on the ground in the old world would be impossible for any length of time.

From nine until ten o'clock, most onlookers were allowed to wait in the shade. Winston and his two guards, Sheriff Walter Lone Wolf and Victor Running Deer, and Brother Fabian Lynx had to stand in the direct sunlight. The owl noted that Victor's youth and Walter's physical prowess held them in good stead. As for Brother Fabian, he seemed to be only too pleased to keep his front-row seat. Winston, unfortunately, was not bearing up as well. The heat of the morning sun was affecting his equilibrium, and he was starting to feel dizzy. In his distress he remembered Billy Bones and glanced over in the direction of Hester's cottage. Once again her bottom Dutch door had been opened just a crack—far enough to allow someone on the other side to observe the events of the morning.

At ten minutes after ten, the yearly rift occurred between the two tall trees like a giant hand ripping the mist apart from top to bottom and opening a window into the other world. In comparison with The Enchantment, the scene beyond with its much smaller plants and trees seemed somewhat colorless and drab. The assemblage of animals uttered a collective gasp as they witnessed the rare glimpse into the outer world.

Winston struggled to keep his composure when Brother Fabian Lynx ordered the ceremony to commence. He began by calling on the two vultures. "Festus, Floyd, let your brother go!" The two brothers jumped to their feet, slipped the rope off their brother's neck, and allowed him to step awkwardly into the duller world. Because Felix had already gone through the change after the tragic burning, nothing unforeseen happened to him as he tried his great black wings and flew off toward the morning sun.

"And now for Winston Wise Owl," Fabian shouted in an even louder voice. "Untie his hands and make him walk towards the opening!"

Victor suddenly put a hand on Winston's shoulder. "Something's wrong here!" the deer cried, looking around for the shepherd dog. "Something's supposed to happen! This is not right!"

As if on cue, pandemonium suddenly broke loose. A great stag and a herd of younger deer leaped into the clearing just east of the magic portal. To further complicate matters, a pack of wild dogs sprang up out of the tall grass surrounding the clearing. Without hesitation the herd turned, heading straight for the opening in the rift with the dogs yapping closely at their heels. Inside The Enchantment, it was pure bedlam as the mayor, the councilors, and the many deputies ducked and ran for cover.

Winston was shocked when Victor Running Deer quickly grabbed his right arm and started guiding him to the safety of his own tree. He was even more surprised when he realized that Sheriff Lone Wolf had also broken ranks and was holding his other arm.

Out of the corner of his eye Winston looked back just long enough to see a streak of tan rush toward the lynx and into the faces of the oncoming deer. Brother Fabian appeared to be dumbstruck by the sudden interruption of his ceremony and hesitated a moment too long. Without warning Billy Bones tackled him and knocked him within

a few feet of the opening of the rift. When the two animals hit the ground, the lynx tried to fight back, but it was too late. Amid the flying hooves and the barking of dogs, Billy grabbed Fabian's white robe and rolled with him head over heels into the outside world.

Winston Wise Owl, Victor Running Deer, and Sheriff Lone Wolf stayed close to their huge tree and watched in wonder as strange yellow lights enveloped both Billy and Brother Fabian just outside of The Enchantment, shrinking them back to the animals they once were. The lynx was the first to stand on all fours but was trapped by his own robe. By the time he clawed his way out, the dog had adjusted to his new condition and was able to intercept the cat. Time and again, the lynx lunged in the direction of The Enchantment, but each time the dog blocked his progress and forced him back with a ferocity that the inhabitants of the Prairie and the two remaining vultures had never seen.

Back inside The Enchantment after the onslaught of the deer and dogs, Winston noticed three other animals coming from behind the groundhog's cottage and heading for the vicinity of the rift. The old owl instantly recognized the two in back. They were Billy's little companions, Nosey Coon and Needles Porcupine. They were trying desperately to catch a third animal that Winston soon realized was the transformed Georgie Beaver.

Just before the rift closed for another year, the beaver dove through the opening and joined the dog. The raccoon and the porcupine stopped short of the dividing line between the worlds and watched their two friends disappear. The last thing Winston saw was the dog chasing the lynx over the hill and the little beaver, still wearing his leash, following happily behind.

As Winston watched the huge gap disappear completely like the healing of an ancient wound, he felt a gap opening up in his heart. He understood immediately the immense sacrifice the shepherd dog had made for him. Only the memory of the dog's great love for Billy Stuart seemed to relieve some of the pain that was overwhelming him. He wished he could see what was transpiring in that other world but realized it was not for him to know. Finally he let out a great sigh as he turned his attention toward the many deer and dogs that had stumbled unknowingly into his world and were lying about in separate heaps just west of the two great trees. He knew they would soon need his help.

CHAPTER FORTY-FIVE

THE HOMECOMING

Every Friday morning Billy Stuart's grandfather, Will, sat at the old roll top desk that he had inherited from his grandfather and paid his weekly bills. On this particular Friday, Billy had chosen to stay indoors with him. He had smuggled a little kitten in from the barn and was playing with him a few feet from the older man's desk. The young boy had attached a large button to a string and was dragging it back and forth while the cat tried to pounce on it or smack at it with her paws.

"I think I'll call her Buttons, Grandpa," said Billy, grinning. "Look at her! I think she believes it's a bug or something!"

"I told you, Billy, if we're going to have that thing in the house, we need to get her checked out by the vet. Goodness knows what she's brought in here!" explained the grandfather patiently. "I still say you should let me get you another dog. That cat belongs in the barn!"

At the mention of the dog, a look of pain crossed the young boy's face. He stopped wriggling the string and turned back to the older man. "But we can't, Grandpa! You know that!"

"You still think Bones will find his way home, eh?" inquired the older man, putting down his pen. Slowly he got up from his desk and settled down on the floor next to his grandson.

"It's been a year now, Billy. You've got to face the fact that Bones is probably not coming home. Maybe he had so much fun chasing that deer that he just decided to run off and live on his own!"

"But Grandpa, Bones wouldn't do that. Somebody must've picked him up! I'll bet he's still tryin' to get back to us. I just know it, Grandpa!"

Will reached over and affectionately mussed the boy's hair. "Hey! How about a peanut butter and jelly sandwich? I'm buyin'. Besides, it's getting close to lunch time, and I'm starved."

"OK," Billy responded softly, as he resumed drawing the string back and forth across the floor. Billy knew that Will did not like keeping the untamed kitten in the house, but he was glad that his grandfather had finally stopped making an issue out of it. As Will finally managed to get back on his feet, Billy noticed the stiffness in his grandfather's legs.

"I've got to stop sitting on the floor like that," the old man muttered to himself, as he hobbled off into the kitchen.

Before long, Billy heard his grandfather open the back door and jubilantly exclaim, "Well, I'll be hornswoggled! Would you look at that! Billy, you'd better come here! You won't believe this!"

Billy Stuart could tell by his grandfather's tone that something remarkable had just occurred. He immediately dropped the cat's string and hurried into the kitchen.

"Billy, look who's here! And it seems he's brought a friend with him."

"Bones!" the boy cried, rushing to the door and throwing his arms around his long-lost friend. As for the shepherd dog, he returned the affection with squirms of joy and much licking of the boy's hands and face. "I told you, Grandpa! I told you he'd come back!"

"Well, I'll be hornswoggled!" Will repeated, as he bent down and scratched the dog behind his ears. "And look out on the porch, Billy! If I'm not mistaken, he's got a blasted beaver with him!"

"And he's wearin' a leash, Grandpa. You think he belongs to someone?"

"Well I don't know. He seems tame enough. I'll have to check around!" said the older man, still astounded by the sudden change in the boy's fortune.

"If no one claims him, can we keep him?" asked the young boy, glancing over at the unusual beaver. "He doesn't seem to be afraid of us!"

"Well I don't know about that. It's pretty hard to keep a wild animal for a pet. We'll probably have to turn him loose down by the pond."

For the next couple of weeks Billy Stuart and his grandfather tried to find the owner of the little beaver, but no one in the neighborhood seemed to know anything about him. As it happened, the chubby little rodent preferred to spend his nights down by the pond. However, every morning he would be at the back porch waiting for Billy and Bones to come out of the house.

Will finally decided that he and Billy should check with the local Wildlife Zoo. "I'm sure humans must have raised him. He's just too tame. Besides, I know Jake Williams, and I don't want him thinkin' I'd keep an animal that belonged to him."

"No, we didn't lose a beaver," said Jake, shaking his head. "But you know, we did find a lynx that had been missin' for two years. In fact, we picked him up out your way. Old John Gunderson cornered him in his chicken coop. The big cat had been killin' a number of his prize hens. He gave us a heck of a fight though! We thought we'd never get him locked up in the back of our old pickup truck." Jake hesitated for a moment and then continued. "I'll tell you what. If you ever want to get rid of that beaver, just let us know. We could use another one in the new section we just put up about Animals of North America."

"Oh no, I don't think my grandson would want to do that!" Will laughed, glancing down at Billy. "His dog Bones brought that thing home with him, and I'm afraid they're pretty attached to each other!"

"Sounds like you spoil the boy," observed the owner, shooting a dubious look at Billy.

"Ah, but he's a good kid, Jake, and he's had his share of tragedy. I'm just glad to see him happy again," declared Will, putting a hand on the boy's shoulder and turning to go.

In the days that followed, William Stuart III and his dog Bones spent many happy hours exploring around the beaver pond and following the animal trails that led up into the foothills. Often the beaver would tag along with them or go back down to the pond for a swim. On certain mornings when the dog and the beaver were left alone and the mist rising off the old pond was especially thick, Billy would come home and find the two animals lying down by the two ancient trees that stood on either side of the old wagon trail. Strangely they would be waiting just beyond the tall grass, as if something very special was about to happen.

THE END OF BOOK TWO
IN THE SHADOW OF THE LYNX

ABOUT THE BOOK

In the Shadow of the Lynx is the second book with the general title *Billy Bones.* The next books in the series, *Return to the Golden Mist* and *The Ghost of Castle Rock,* continue the story. The books are outgrowths of bedtime stories that I told to my younger brother David and my daughter Laura when they were children. The hero of the stories is a shepherd dog, Bones, based on a dog that I played with on my grandfather's farm in Humbolt, South Dakota, when I was a boy.

The genesis for the fantasies really began when I stumbled across a number of abandoned trunks, plows, and other articles while hiking in Montana as a young man. I imagined that these deteriorating antiques embodied the hopes and dreams of settlers migrating west to the Oregon Territory. This memory gave birth to the idea that the power of the emotion carried within these cherished treasures caused a great rift, a bridge to another world, in which the creatures caught up in its magic were also profoundly changed.

ABOUT THE AUTHOR

Ron Oaks was born in Aberdeen, South Dakota. He earned a degree in speech and drama from Yankton College in Yankton, South Dakota; a degree in voice from the Peabody Conservatory in Baltimore, Maryland; and a master's degree in drama from Catholic University in Washington, D. C. Since then he has written a musical comedy, a religious opera, a number of reviews, plays, and poems and Book One, *Beyond the Tall Grass,* of the fantasy series under the general title of *Billy Bones.*

Ron has directed or performed professionally in numerous operas, musicals, and plays from New York to Miami. He was the artistic director of the Garrison Playhouse in Baltimore County, Maryland, for 10 years and taught drama at Glenelg High School in Howard County, Maryland, for 16 years. More recently, Ron stage-directed seven operas for the Municipal Opera Company of Baltimore, Maryland, and numerous shows for the Woodbrook Players in Baltimore, Maryland. Ron was the bass-soloist with the Brown Memorial Presbyterian Church in Towson for many years and teaches voice in the Maryland and Washington, D.C. areas. Ron lives with his wife Janet in Central Maryland.

ACKNOWLEDGMENTS

I began writing the *Billy Bones* series on June 30, 2003. Since then my manuscripts have gone through many revisions. Over those years I owe a special debt of gratitude to relatives, friends, and students who have patiently given advice and encouragement. I will always be grateful to all of them for their time and consideration.

I want to thank Andrea Glaser and her book club in Olney, Maryland, including Alisa Austin, Mary McQueen, Patty Argyros, Patty Corridon, Alice Wertheimer, Linda Krass, and Colleen Xydis. They not only read one of my earlier manuscripts in 2008 but took the time to meet me afterwards and offer recommendations and suggestions at Andrea's home. I also want to express my appreciation to Jan Chastant, Lynn Ellington, and Maysaa Alobaidi for reading later rewrites of my manuscript and discussing them with me at some length. Then I want to make special mention of Howard Garrett who helped me with the front cover, and Sandy Rothberg who graciously agreed to take my photo.

I owe a special thankyou to Louise Carlson and Anne Ostroff who edited and proofread my book and encouraged me to continue writing. I will be forever grateful for their expertise and professionalism.

Finally, I want to thank my wife and daughter. My wife Jan spent many hours reading chapters in my book after I initially wrote them and advised me on their content and flow. My daughter Laura not only reread the manuscripts as I made changes but offered a number of suggestions in the writing, performed content editing and published the books.

THE HILL COUNTRY

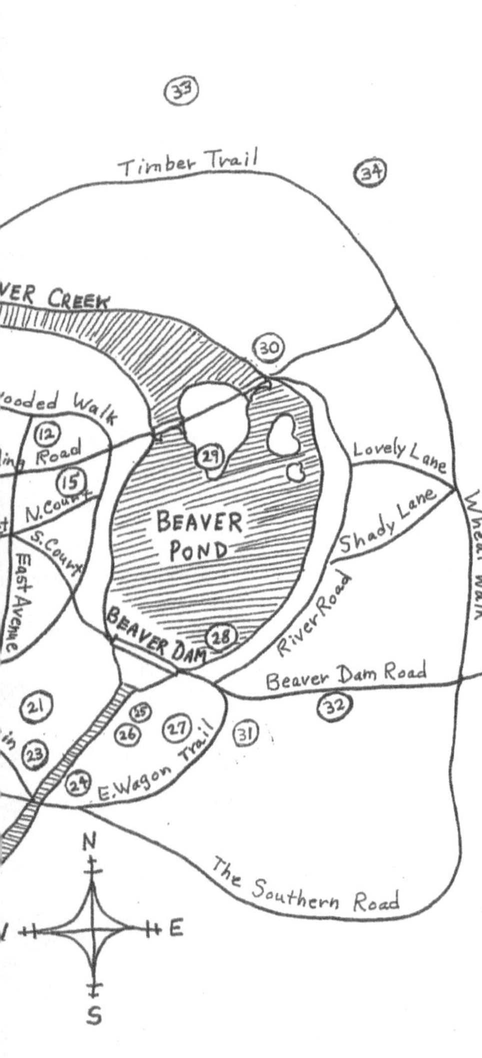

THE PRAIRIE

1. The lodge
2. Arthur Elk's hut
3. Omar Mountain Goat's cave
4. The store
5. Maurice Rabbit's dugout
6. The Vulture Brothers' hut
7. Lucinda Vulture's hut
8. Deputy Eagle's office
9. Calhoun Coyote's chicken farm
10. Sandy Antelope dugout
11. Mary Mc Mink's house
12. The Old Meetinghouse
13. The hotel
14. City Hall
15. Thaddeus Turtle's cottage
16. Elmer Prairie Dog's store
17. Sheriff Lone Wolf's office
18. The boardinghouse
19. The New Meetinghouse
20. The barracks
21. Rodney Wild Deer's lean-to
22. Rodney Deer's hideout
23. Olen Buck's lean-to

24. Victor Running Deer's lean-to
25. Nosey Coon's tree house
26. Needles Porcupine's hollow
27. Billy Bones' cottage
28. Justin Beaver's house
29. George P. Beaver's castle
30. Cornelius Van Mink's house
31. Gloria Meadowlark's farm
32. Percival Gander's shop
33. The Peccary Brother's shed
34. Milton Brown Bear's cave
35. Farmer Jason Crow's farm
36. Winston Wise Owl's tree house
37. Hester Groundhog's tree house

9 781732 349971